DISENCHANTED

KARA PLEASANTS

Quills & Quartos
PUBLISHING

Edited by Marcelle Wong and Lisa Sieck

Cover Design by AMDesign Studios

ISBN 978-1-951033-43-9 (ebook) and 978-1-951033-56-9 (paperback)

For David, who is, to me, even better than Mr Darcy
For Nora and Lina, may you always believe in magic

CONTENTS

A WORD ABOUT MAGIC

There are many types of magic. There's the sort of magic we all know from childhood: the trees that whisper, the dolls that move, the teddy who flies about the room in a tizzy over spilled milk. There's the magic of love at a holiday, that shines in the flickering candles we set out and burns in our hearts as we sing songs from our youth. There's the mystery of the creator in sacred spaces, the unending ever-reaching void of nothing and everything that is the universe which touches all living beings. We all know a little bit about magic.

This story is about a particular kind of magic. It's like our world, but it's also the 1810s during the Regency period in England —specifically in the world of Jane Austen's *Pride & Prejudice*.

What would that world be like—but with magic? That's the question with which I began this story. In this world of *Pride & Prejudice*, most people can perform ordinary magic of the sort that parlour magicians can do in their wildest of dreams. Imagine that even someone not particularly educated in the ways of magic could pick up a spell book from the local bookstore and find a magic spell to make their hair glossy and prevent their clothes from getting rumpled. Imagine you could use magic for trivial little things.

Now, imagine that if you had wealth and privilege, you could do more than simple magic. With the right education and tools at your disposal, you could advance to high levels of wizardry and learn to control perhaps one or two of the elements to a particular degree (depending on your skill, dedication, and concentration). That might allow you to earn the title of 'Wizard' in a society of ordinary magic, like this one. In this magical world, the stakes are slightly higher on the magical front, and those with the inclination and opportunity to use it absolutely use it to their advantage (for good or ill, as you shall see).

PROLOGUE

THE DARKNESS WAS COMPLETE, SMOTHERING THE FIELDS AND THE winding country road in a blanket of mystery. Dark enough that Tom was nearly indistinguishable from the large oak tree under which he sat, snapping his fingers again and again. The stars shone bright above, but there was no moon in the cold autumn night. Another snap, and then a green spark illuminated Tom's face for a flash, his breath a frozen cloud about his face as he exhaled in delight. More snaps—first the green, then pink, then yellow, then orange—his face now a flash of a smile in the dark.

This would do, he thought, to please her. His work on this night was the culmination of a string of good fortune; the crop was coming in richly, and his barn would be full. There was no obstacle remaining to his happiness except winning the affection of one Sally Jenkins, known to have a penchant for magic tricks involving fire. Tom's skills were of a more practical nature—charms to ward off cutworms, a potion to spur calf growth. Sally, with her golden hair and twinkling green eyes, would not be won over by ordinary magic. But this—he snapped again and held the fire at his fingers—

this would impress her. Even some gentlemen with education and training couldn't hold a flame of fire, let alone change its colour.

Another snap and the flame was gone. Tom rose and began to walk home along the familiar road. As his eyes adjusted to the black, he felt the hairs rise on the back of his neck and across his arms. He was not alone in the dark. He turned, first one way and then the other. The dark surrounded, but no shape came into view. He stepped forward again, snapping his fingers and holding out a bright yellow flame—small, but steady above his hand.

"That is quite a feat for a farmer like you," said a voice behind him.

Tom lost the flame as he skidded back and fell to the ground. "Who are you?" he cried as he pushed himself up on his elbows. Before him rose up from the ground a tall figure shrouded in a cloak darker than the surrounding night.

"One who takes a great deal of interest in raw talent like yours. Untapped, unused out here in the middle of nowhere—and quite unnoticed by anyone else." The voice spoke again, and Tom could just see the figure reach out a hand.

"Unnoticed?" Tom croaked. Suddenly his hand moved involuntarily towards the dark figure's outstretched one. He felt a sharp twinge in his fingers that spread, warm, from the tips through his arm, flashing into his heart and through his veins. He felt himself suspended in the air as he burst into flames of many colours, the fire shooting from his fingers and his feet and the tips of his hair. He cried out, but his body did not burn.

The cloaked figure collected the rainbow of fire with methodical precision, winding into a ball as one turns yarn. It took some minutes, and with the passage of time the figure's movements became more energetic. Tom, unable to struggle or stop the procedure, fell into silence and listened to the voice say "Yes, yes—it's more than we thought there would be—just what was needed."

After what felt like an eternity, the fire left Tom's body and was held high above by the dark figure, whose face was still shrouded by the cloak. It took the flaming ball of fire and swallowed it whole in one swift motion. Without another word, it was gone.

Tom collapsed to the ground, panting. He felt his limbs and

clothes and boots—astonished to find himself intact and unsinged. Not even a whiff of smoke hung about him. He rose, legs shaking, and picked up his hat from where it had fallen to the ground earlier. Taking one step forward, he felt unsteady, but with each step his feet grew surer and he broke into a run down the dark road towards his humble cottage. He didn't think of trying to use his magical fire to light his way as he ran, he didn't think except to get home and out of the dark.

IN WHICH A CERTAIN GENTLEMAN TAKES A HOUSE IN HERTFORDSHIRE

HERTFORDSHIRE WAS NOT KNOWN FOR ITS MAGIC. AT LEAST, NOT the kind of magic that was considered modern, effective, or quality. There were two or three schools that boasted of teaching advanced methodology in wizarding and the magical arts, but anyone who was anybody knew that was a fancy way of saying that the local farmers' sons would learn to grow magically enhanced pumpkins, and the farmers' daughters learned to keep their hair up in styles that would hold fast throughout an evening's festivities.

Even amongst the more genteel population of the county, magical abilities seemed to evade their families. There was an apothecary rather talented at bringing down high fevers and delivering healthy babies (for which he was greatly revered), and a solicitor who never seemed to lose a case. All of the gentlemen's daughters with any slight ability knew a few methods of charming, in order to better snatch rich husbands.

Such behaviour was widely encouraged by the mothers of the county, and none more so than one Mrs Bennet. It was rumoured that she held the secret to a particularly effective love potion—for how else could she, the daughter of a country solicitor, have secured

Mr Bennet all those years ago? Love potions were never permanent, and her potion was purported to last three months at least. However, the validity of this rumour had been called into question more and more frequently over the past few years due to the fact that Mrs Bennet had five eligible daughters, none of them yet married.

The Bennet sisters were revered in Hertfordshire not only for their unrivalled beauty, but because some of them did hold claim to a relatively modest magical ability. Miss Jane Bennet, the eldest and most beautiful, was also the most magically talented. Everyone lamented that her father had never allowed her to study in town. Her abilities, particularly in the realm of healing and the spreading of happiness, put the local apothecary to shame.

The youngest Miss Bennets, Miss Kitty and Miss Lydia, had grown so capable in the art of charm, flirtation, and (in Lydia's case) seduction, that the mothers of young men in Meryton were kept busy trying to discover counter-charms and shields so as to prevent anyone from being 'taken in.' The middle daughter, Miss Mary Bennet, had not displayed much talent of her own, but was so knowledgeable about spells, potions, and the history of magic that it made up for her lack of personal ability.

The second daughter remained a mystery to the inhabitants of Hertfordshire. Miss Elizabeth Bennet did not seem, or even claim, to possess any magical ability at all. On the one hand, this was surprising because she most closely resembled her father, who had been an extraordinarily gifted wizard in his day. But Mr Bennet had not practised magic to anyone's knowledge for the last twenty-five years at least. There was much speculation as to the reason for his loss of ability, and his favourite daughter's lack thereof. Some whispered that it had been stolen from him by a dark wizard. Others preferred the idea that he had lost it because of the love potion given to him by his wife.

Mr Bennet never gave any hints one way or the other. In fact, he and Miss Elizabeth seemed to prefer poking fun at their family's and neighbours' attempts at all things magical and supernatural, and so the gossips of Meryton came to the conclusion that whatever magical ability either possessed was squelched due to excessive scepticism.

This information, along with a plethora of history mixed with gossip, was readily available to anyone and everyone who happened to venture through the county—and Mr Darcy made sure to discover as much of it as possible when he learned of his friend Bingley's intention to let a house in Hertfordshire. An exceptionally talented wizard himself, he prided himself as much on his knowledge of magic as its practice. It took only one reconnaissance mission the week before their intended departure to Netherfield to determine that he did not like the look of the area, and he told Bingley as much.

Bingley was not put off. "You do not like anywhere, Darcy, except Pemberley. And I cannot very well move Pemberley to Hertfordshire," Bingley grumbled over his tea. They sat in a large sitting room at his home in town, enjoying an assortment of teas, pastries, and muffins.

"Could you, Mr Darcy? Move Pemberley, that is?" Caroline enquired.

Darcy repressed a disdainful smile, as Bingley's dark-haired youngest sister fancied herself better at wizardry than she actually was. "Even if I could, I would not move it to such a place as Hertfordshire."

Caroline seemed disappointed and sniffed. "I suppose there is not enough magic to move a broomstick in such a place. Must we go there, Charles?"

"I am afraid we must. I really cannot do without you, Caroline, keeping things in order." Bingley flashed a ready smile, which Caroline returned, but directed more in Darcy's direction.

"I suppose I do keep a good table. You do agree, do you not, Mr Darcy?"

"Superb, Miss Bingley." Darcy took another muffin to emphasise his point. "I do not know what I shall do at Netherfield. There will not be much opportunity for research."

"I am sure you may study the locals. After all, folk magic continues to thrive. Perhaps they employ methods that have been passed down through the centuries." Charles Bingley was also a wizard, and while not as well-respected as his wealthier and more intellectual friend, had done a great deal of successful research in the field of botany. He also had a reputation for being an eternal optimist.

Caroline nearly snorted. "If you mean the study of pig feed and fortune-telling—and how to catch a rich husband—then I am sure Mr Darcy will not want for study!"

Bingley scoffed, "Really, Caroline, one does not have to remove to the country to find that sort of thing. Husband catchers lie in wait around every corner here in London. Darcy and I employ the finest charm-repellent spells a university education has to offer, and I am sure Darcy has his perfected to implacability."

"Is that true, Mr Darcy?" Caroline added, rather too hopeful.

"I pride myself on defensive spells more than any others," Darcy replied, straightening up and glancing toward the pink tea-pot, steam still rising lazily from its spout. "Your tea, in fact, reminded me greatly of a potion we once drank during my school-days that was used for, er"—he paused, seeing the deep flush which had spread across her face—"there is nothing that could penetrate my wall of defences. I have made absolute sure of that."

Caroline recovered quickly. "Of course, how stupid of me. Charles, be sure to follow your friend's example, and not be taken in. I will not have you settle for some country bumpkin in Hert-fordshire."

Bingley laughed, his eyes sparkling. "I have no intention of being taken in by anybody—"

Darcy coughed at this.

"—but I would not wish for Darcy's complete armoured shield. With such implacability, one is not likely to let anything through, enchanted or not. Perhaps I am open to love."

Darcy bristled. "And I am not?"

"I am only speaking of myself, Darcy, no need to be tense," Bingley said. "Have another muffin."

Caroline rolled her eyes. "Please, do be serious. And do not open yourself to love of any kind in the country. It simply is not done. Mr Darcy, am I right in thinking that if one is open to that sort of thing, one is also more susceptible to charms of—that sort?"

Bingley laughed again, but Darcy muttered, "She is not completely wrong, Bingley."

"There!" Caroline flushed in triumph. "So you must be on your guard!"

Laughing all the more, Bingley replied, "I will depend on you then, Caroline, and my friend Darcy to save me from this impending unhappy and imprudent marriage. I am sure nothing in Hertfordshire—of all places!—could make Darcy take leave of his senses, much less fall under enchantment!"

Darcy smiled and bowed in affirmation, but Bingley knew that the discussion was not at an end.

～

Some distance away, the ladies of Longbourn were sitting down to tea. Kitty and Lydia were poking at various coloured satchels of tea-leaves vigorously, while their mother reposed on a settee and fanned her flushed face.

"We should try the White Rose tea, I have heard it gives you the most delicious warm sensation," said Kitty.

Lydia pouted. "Oh no, this Jasmine tea spouts butterflies and I do love a good show."

"But we tried it yesterday and I want something new." Kitty looked to her mother for support.

Mrs Bennet fanned herself. "Let us have the Jasmine, for I am overheated as it is, I have such news! Where is your father? Oh—wait a moment!" She sat up and motioned for Kitty and Lydia to bring over the tea-tray. "Jane! Oh Jane! I have just the tea here for you to learn to steep for when Mr Bingley comes!"

Mr Bennet, entering the room at that moment, had to move aside as Lydia rushed past him with a green satchel for Jane, who sat with Elizabeth by the window.

"This tea, Jane," Lydia said, out of breath, "will make any man fall in love with you for the whole of the month!"

Mr Bennet and Elizabeth rolled their eyes. "It does nothing of the sort, Lydia." Elizabeth snatched the bag from her hands, taking a sniff before handing it to Jane.

"And why would I have need of such a thing?" Jane smiled gently as her mother leapt out of her chair.

"You heard from Mrs Long just as I did! Of course you have a great need of it—but Mr Bennet!" She strode over to his armchair, where he had settled down to read his paper. "Have you heard the news, Mr Bennet? Netherfield Park is to be let at last!"

Mr Bennet sighed, not deigning to look up.

"What a thing for our girls! What an enormous prospect! I have had it just this morning that Mr Bingley is worth five thousand pounds a year—and! And, and, that is not all! He is a most talented wizard and could want for absolutely nothing! Imagine, our Jane would be just perfectly matched, perfectly matched and save us all!"

Mr Bennet looked up for a moment. "A wizard, you say?"

"A very fine wizard, he specialises in—in—what was it, girls?" Mrs Bennet turned to Kitty and Lydia.

"Husbandry?" Kitty guessed.

"Dragons!" cried Lydia.

"Good Lord, it is botany," said Mary, with an assuredness of tone that ended the debate.

"Botany, is it?" Elizabeth looked out the window towards the thick woods that stretched between their home and Netherfield Park. "That almost sounds too perfect for a healer like you, Jane. You would have the best of all the herbs in the world!"

"Indeed she would, indeed!" Mrs Bennet trilled, then turned to her husband. "You must call upon him, my dear, as soon as he is arrived."

Jane laughed and hit her sister good-naturedly. "You have encouraged our mother, Lizzy—I manage quite well enough on my own with our garden."

"But Mr Bingley will be all too happy to discover that he is not the only wizard in the county, no indeed. He will not have met a wizard of your quality before," Mrs Bennet said, returning to her own seat and nodding as she took up her fan again.

"Mr Bingley will have met many such accomplished wizards amongst his own circle; he need not come to Hertfordshire to meet me, a man of no talent and no accomplishment."

"You are too modest, Papa," Elizabeth exclaimed.

"You must visit him direct when he comes, Mr Bennet, I will

not be dissuaded. Think of our daughters—think of your poor wife, and how we must be turned out of this house as soon as you are gone. You must know that I am thinking of his marrying one of them."

"It is more than I engage for, I assure you," Mr Bennet declared. "I might, perhaps, write him a letter assuring him of my hearty consent to his marrying whichever of the girls he chooses; though I must throw in a good word for my little Lizzy."

"Lizzy has not half the beauty of Jane nor the good nature of Lydia, but you always show her preference! As it is, she cannot perform magic! You can hardly expect a wizard to marry a woman who cannot perform magic!" Mrs Bennet said with some feeling.

"Aside from the occasional beautifying spell, they have none of them much to recommend them," replied he; "they are all silly and ignorant like other girls, but Lizzy makes up for her lack of magic with something more of quickness than her sisters."

"Mr Bennet, how can you abuse your own children in such a way? When it is you who refuses to develop their magical skills!"

"Papa has spent a great deal of time teaching us magical principles, Mama. You know he speaks in jest. Although," Elizabeth said with a sly look towards her father, "I have often requested that we could learn more if you would permit us to expand—"

"Out of the question." Mr Bennet straightened his paper with a brisk flap. "I put up with enough magical nonsense as it is." As if to prove his point, the tea which Lydia had begun to steep some time earlier began spouting an extraordinary number of butterflies, which fluttered in a small whirlwind above their heads.

While Kitty and Lydia rushed about collecting butterflies, Mrs Bennet wailed, "You take delight in vexing me. You have no compassion for my poor nerves."

"You mistake me, my dear. I have a high respect for your nerves. They are my old friends. I have heard you mention them with consideration these last twenty years at least."

~

It was later that evening when Darcy again took up the subject of

Hertfordshire with Bingley—but this time they were alone. "I know the plan was to take a place out of the way—secluded, uneventful, but—"

"And that," Bingley cried, "is precisely why I chose Netherfield. There could not be a more perfect place to see if something else comes about. As of yet there are only rumours—two victims in different locations reporting a loss of magical powers, one a farmer and the other a scullery maid. You said you wanted to continue your studies and be able to come and go quickly as needed. We need the cover of a country escape to keep up the pretence of normality."

"I concede that it meets those criteria, but I had hoped for subjects of some interest," Darcy grumbled.

Bingley's eyebrows rose. "The threat of the Necromancer's return isn't enough excitement?"

"The Necromancer is dead," Darcy said, "but as to this new threat—there are many possibilities. One of which is that it is nothing at all."

"Then come with me to Netherfield and we shall see. Or go off to Scotland and study the giants if you so choose."

Darcy straightened. "I will follow my own plan—which involves following yours. To Hertfordshire, then."

Bingley smiled.

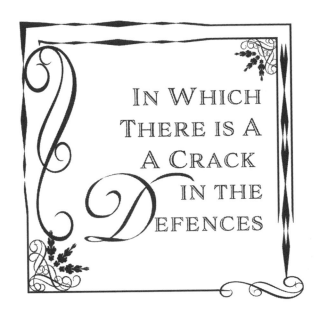

In Which There Is A A Crack In The Defences

"It's magnificent." Bingley stood gaping up at a vine that covered much of the rockwork and the roof of one wing at the back of the great house of Netherfield. Its base was nearly three feet wide, and the green leaves tinged with crimson hissed as he approached.

Darcy regarded the vine with vague interest for a moment, then smiled at his friend. "So this is why you chose Netherfield. Of all places."

"It is not the only reason. Come, Darcy, I haven't seen a finer specimen. Folk magic—old magic—I warrant you are in for more than you bargained with Hertfordshire," Bingley said as he took off his coat and prepared to do battle against the hissing vine.

Bingley had a gift with plants. What had been the scourge of the past three generations of gardeners at Netherfield, he managed to right in one week. He took time to catalogue his findings and send samples back to London and felt that the nearby woods along the edge of the property might hold more interesting flora for his study.

For his part, Darcy was surprised to find that Netherfield Park was more than it initially seemed. His bedchamber displayed the odd habit of vanishing, only to reappear on the other side of the house. While this was not an advanced sort of enchantment, it did provide amusement for Darcy, though not for his valet, Barnaby. Mr Darcy's Vanishing Room was allowed to misbehave for three nights, after which the room was reprimanded and put in its proper place.

Grown accustomed to his own vast and ancient library, Darcy was not impressed by Netherfield's. He did manage to stumble across a few mouldy books from the sixteenth century, and spent several lazy afternoons poring over them. (Whether he gained any knowledge from said books or was merely using them as an excuse to avoid Caroline is left for the reader to decide.) Unfortunately for Darcy, Caroline, like the neighbours, refused to be ignored for long. The former took to skulking about the library whenever it seemed most likely Darcy would appear; the latter arrived in droves before the second week at Netherfield was out.

Darcy and Bingley had arrived at Netherfield with three other members in their party—Bingley's sister and her husband, a Mr and Mrs Hurst, and Caroline (who felt keenly her status as the unmarried sister). The Hursts and Caroline, like all members of the gentry, were trained in the magical arts, but none were as talented as their brother Charles—who was made even more agreeable to the locals by the news that he was worth no less than five thousand pounds a year. Nothing could be more covetous than a man with fortune, education, and real magical abilities—yet neither Bingley's fame nor fortune could match Darcy's ten thousand pounds a year. Naturally, word had gone about that a masterful (and wealthy) wizard had taken Netherfield Park, with skills unmatched in a hundred years.

Darcy modestly gave credit for these rumours to the taming of the vine, but Bingley felt word had spread of Darcy's fame—and of course everybody wanted to meet him. Darcy's guess was not entirely wrong, as evidenced by the fact that their first caller, a Sir William Lucas, arrived with a sick rosebush which had been in the family for years and hadn't quite recovered from last winter's frost. Bingley was only too happy to oblige, and the wilted plant was soon blooming with roses of several additional shades of colour. Sir William was almost speechless with delight.

This first call opened the gates to a deluge of visitors, none of whom were interesting or even slightly talented in the eyes of Darcy and Caroline. On that point, they were in perfect agreement.

"I warned you, Charles," Caroline said with a clenched smile as she waved out the window to their latest departing guest. "Such tiresome company. All they are after is your money! Every gentleman was very careful to drop hints: and you shall meet my lovely daughter at the assembly come Saturday fortnight—did I mention she is lovely? And beautiful? And exceptionally bright? What nonsense!"

"We have not met all the neighbours, Caroline, only the fathers," Bingley said, his expression as stern as he could muster. "I am sure their daughters are lovely. I have yet to meet a girl who was not so."

Caroline and Darcy were not convinced in the slightest, their opinions as to what made daughters 'lovely' quite different from Bingley's.

Late in the afternoon and some weeks after their arrival, when Darcy had begun to hope the days of introductory calls were nearing an end, a Mr Bennet of Longbourn was introduced. The poor footman was hardly given enough time to open the library door and squeak out a name before the gentleman himself strolled in and sat in the most comfortable chair in the room without so much as an invitation.

"I say," cried Bingley, who had risen with haste to welcome his guest.

"Yes, how do you do. Bennet is the name—I hope you do not mind my lack of formality. It is too tiresome; I do without it as much as possible." The gentleman was short and thin, with wiry white hair that stood out at odd ends. He wore a red waistcoat, and immediately took out his pipe.

"Please," Bingley said, drawing up a chair next to him. "I can do with an honest man over formalities any time of the day. And I do very well, thank you."

"Bennet?" Darcy spoke from where he stood at the window.

"Thomas Bennet, author of 'The Fragility and Temperamental Nature of Magical Abilities'?"

Mr Bennet looked startled. "The very same. Why, I wrote that essay so long ago I can scarcely remember it. And you are?"

"Darcy."

"Darcy…" Mr Bennet tapped his forehead. "*Defensive Magic and its Many Uses* Darcy?"

"No," Darcy said as he came forward to pull up his own chair. "That was my father."

"Yes, of course," Mr Bennet replied, coming back to himself. "It was written well before you would have been able to read. Good principles, rather idealistic. I think you will find them difficult to maintain when under actual duress." Mr Bennet seemed not to notice Darcy's blackening look. "But I hope you have read it in any case—you will need all your defences to brave the wilds of Hertfordshire, however tame and insignificant it is purported to be!" Mr Bennet vacated his chair with only the slightest stiffness in his knees and proceeded to inspect the library's selections.

Darcy's shoulders straightened. "I assure you, I have taken great care to study my father's work." He stood to return to the window.

"What my friend here says is true, then," interjected Bingley, "and the population is ready and waiting with charms and potions enough to marry us twelve times over? Mr Bennet, I cannot believe it!"

"Oh, you may well believe it," Mr Bennet said, keeping his eyes on the books so as to hide the twinkle in them.

Darcy raised a brow. "You would encourage us to believe the truth of such rumours?"

Mr Bennet turned slowly. "All true, I am sure. Although there is one involving my wife and a particularly strong love potion—never believe it for a moment, whatever she may say."

Both young men protested that neither had heard of any such rumour, but Mr Bennet laughed as he saw himself to the door.

"I will not trespass any longer on your kind hospitality, Mr Bingley, Mr Darcy, and bid you good day. Mrs Bennet will not believe me when I inform her of my call."

As suddenly as he had arrived, Mr Bennet was gone. The two

friends sat in a few moments of silence, before Bingley turned to Darcy. "Mr Bennet, author of countless well-respected articles and essays, all displaying some of the greatest insight into Magical Theory in a century, who has not practised a jot of it since coming to Hertfordshire some five and twenty years ago?"

"The very same," Darcy replied with a scowl. "I had imagined him an eccentric, but not quite so—"

"Informal? Or was it that he disagreed with the Principles of Defence? I have always said that—"

"Really, Bingley, must we go into this now?"

"Oh, no." Bingley looked abashed. After a pause, he said, "I did not detect any magic about him at all. Did you?"

"None whatsoever."

"Well, there is a study for you. I have never heard of anyone losing their magic who did not retain some small trace of it."

"Have you not?" Darcy replied, as he watched Mr Bennet's carriage roll swiftly down the lane.

∾

The county's first assembly was an evening dreaded by all but the unflappable Bingley. There was no question that they would attend, for what else was one to do when in the country? It was no great surprise to Caroline when the room proved too small for the large company gathered. To Bingley, however, this could be the assembly's only fault. Upon first entering the room, he found the dancing exuberant, the colours lively, the women pretty. A man determined to like everything and everyone was not likely to be disappointed—and Hertfordshire was eager to please.

Unfortunately, the saying is also true in reverse: a man determined to disapprove is unlikely to find anything of beauty or culture, in spite of the population's best efforts. Darcy was not a man easily humoured. His findings proved quite different than his friend's—the women not at all pretty, the colours vapid, the dancing unmentionable. The air was heavy with the smell of perfumes and wig powder, and the entire room seemed to be swimming with primitive magic. Everything from hair fasteners to beauty enhance-

17

ments to dancing improvement charms—Darcy detected wafts of it all. He was soon stricken by a splitting headache.

With a valiant resolve, Darcy straightened and determined to be agreeable—if not civil—for some of the evening. The introductions were somewhat of a blur, there were so many of them. Later he did recollect the family of Mr Bennet—his wife and their endless line of daughters.

"Kitty and Lydia are so fond of dancing," Mrs Bennet was saying. "As I am sure you are, Mr Bingley! And you, Mr Darcy"— she laughed at her own boldness, while Darcy felt his resolve to be agreeable fading—"are you fond of dancing?"

She was a rather short and plump woman, speaking too loudly so as to be heard over the din. The question did not seem to be addressed to any one person, so Bingley and Darcy answered simultaneously.

"Yes," said one with enthusiasm.

"No," said the other with disdain.

Mrs Bennet did not know who to answer first, as she could not remember which had answered in the affirmative. This proved to be of no consequence, for the esteemed and sought-after Bingley turned to her eldest daughter (whose name Darcy had not heard) and asked her to dance. Darcy was mildly disgusted and retreated as soon as possible, the phrases 'not fond of dancing,' 'ten thousand a year,' and 'actual wizard' following him across the room.

It was not Darcy's intention to offend everyone in the room— but certainly nothing in his actions indicated otherwise. With the exception of a few brief words exchanged with a Mrs Long that consisted of 'no thank you,' 'never,' and 'absolutely not,' he spoke to no one outside of the Bingleys and Hursts. Instead, his energy was spent pacing from one side of the room to the other, until at last he came to a corner and felt that he could breathe easy. Darcy was puzzled. Earlier, he had walked the length of the room several times over and had not found anywhere (including this corner) free of the dizzying emotions and magics being carelessly thrown about. Now, it was as if a veil had been lifted. Darcy was grateful, took a few deep breaths, and stayed in the corner.

It was not long before his mind, now free from its oppressive throbbing, set to work on an explanation for this corner where magic seemed to dissolve. He re-examined the area subtly, discovering the space to be about three feet wide, but had only just come to the conclusion that it was all a figment of his strained imagination when Bingley came bounding up, breathless and rather excited.

"There you are, Darcy, I have not had time to pause for a moment! Is it not a splendid party?"

"Oh yes, quite. Listen, Bingley, do you notice anything different about this corner?"

Bingley took a moment to look over both shoulders. "Do you mean the draft of fresh air coming from that window? It is rather refreshing."

Darcy pondered the window. "Of course, that explains it—and to think, for a moment I thought I had found a—"

"What was that, Darcy? I was not following." Bingley's gaze had turned to a young woman dancing amongst the crowd.

"Oh, it was of no consequence." Darcy followed his friend's line of sight. "Is that the young woman you were dancing with earlier?"

Bingley turned to him, his eyes bright. "Do you not remember? Yes, that is Miss Bennet—she is the loveliest creature I have ever beheld!"

Darcy's eyebrows rose. "Bingley, I grant you, she is very pretty, but consider that this hall is swarming with—"

"Yes, yes. And she is not using any sort of spell for that!"

Darcy blinked. "Not one? I had heard that her magical abilities were some of the finest in the county, although in all probability that means nothing when you consider—"

"Not one!" Bingley replied cheerfully. "Come, Darcy, I must have you dance. I hate to see you standing about in this stupid manner. You had much better dance."

"I certainly shall not. You know how I detest it, unless I am particularly acquainted with my partner. At such an assembly as this it would be insupportable. There are such a number of ridiculous spells being used on nearly every person! Your sisters are engaged, and there is not another woman in the room whom it would not be a punishment for me to stand up with."

"I would not be as fastidious as you are," cried Bingley, "for a kingdom! Upon my honour, I have never met so many pleasant girls in my life as I have this evening; no, it is not all because of enchantments—the magic is not nearly so bad as you have implied. There is one of Miss Bennet's sisters who is very pretty—without any enchantment—and I daresay, very agreeable. Do let me ask my partner to introduce you."

"Which do you mean?" Turning around, he looked upon a young woman he recognised from earlier in the evening to be Miss Elizabeth Bennet. Their eyes met for a moment until he withdrew his own coldly and said, "She is tolerable, but not handsome enough to tempt me; I am in no humour at present to give consequence to young ladies without any magical ability who are slighted by other men. You had better return to your partner and enjoy her smiles, for you are wasting your time with me."

Bingley followed his advice. Darcy attempted to walk away but was prevented when several things occurred in rapid succession. Firstly, he stumbled over his feet and almost collided into Miss Elizabeth, who had risen from her chair. Secondly, by a horrible stroke of misfortune, he was forced to take hold of her arm to steady himself, or else fall into the punch.

Darcy was mortified. "I do beg your pardon—I cannot begin to ask you to accept my apologies—I had no intention of—"

She silenced him with a look, the slightest of smiles curved onto her lips. "Not at all, Mr Darcy. We all find ourselves clumsy on our feet at times."

Darcy drew himself up. "I can assure you, madam, that I am never clumsy on my feet." He would have felt much more dignified if a lock of hair had not kept falling across his eyes, making it necessary for him to constantly brush it aside.

"Never?" She laughed. "What makes tonight the exception?"

And darting through the crowd, she left him to wonder in astonishment.

In Which Mr Darcy is Puzzled

"Did you like him, Lizzy?"

"Who?"

"Mr Bingley?" Jane blushed at the mere mention of his name.

"Oh! He is very amiable, all that was charming and agreeable. I give you leave to like him, if that is what you mean," Elizabeth said with a sly grin. "You have liked many a stupider person."

"Dear Lizzy!" The two sisters turned down the lane and sat under a great spreading tree, allowing the sunlight to play on their faces.

"You are a great deal too apt to like people in general, you know," Elizabeth teased after a short while. "All the world is good and beautiful in your eyes. I have never heard you speak ill of a human being in my life!"

Jane laughed. "I only ever say what I think, Lizzy."

"Which is what makes you all the more admirable!"

"Did you see the flower he made for me?" Jane turned her head to display a delicate pink rose tucked into her hair. "It seemed to appear out of thin air! And has not wilted since Saturday—I am inclined to think it will not wither for some time. Is it not a lovely gift?"

"Truly beautiful. But is it not rather early for the bestowing of gifts? Mama will be beside herself to discover your acquaintance has progressed so far in such a short time." Elizabeth smiled to see her sister laugh and continued in mock seriousness. "I hope you do not actually think the rose came out of nowhere. Nothing ever comes from nothing, Papa taught us that before we could speak."

"Of course not, Lizzy! I am sure he had it hidden somewhere, but it is enchanting to think of it as coming from the air. It does not lessen my respect for his magical abilities, which have proven to be quite creditable."

"Mr Bingley is now certainly the most esteemed wizard to ever set foot in Hertfordshire, whether he deserves such praise or not! Now, Jane, you know I am only teasing. I am sure he is excellent at what he does. With Mr Darcy, however, I am most disappointed."

"Mr Darcy! You must forgive me, Lizzy, for saying something disagreeable, but I am not inclined to like him. Not after his slight to you." Jane's lovely features were covered with an uncharacteristic frown.

"Being considered 'tolerable' is not the worst insult one could endure, but I had expected much more from one so well-respected in wizarding circles. Although I suppose those are the sorts of circles that would like his sort—arrogant and unpleasant. As to his talent, that remains to be seen. I am inclined to think it rather less than is rumoured," Elizabeth said with an emphatic nod.

Jane stood and brushed the leaves from her dress. "However unpleasant the gentleman may be, that does not discredit his ability! Why, Mr Bingley spoke of him on several occasions with the highest of respect."

"As his friend, it follows that Mr Bingley would hold him in high esteem. For now, I shall believe you, Jane, and attempt not to think so horribly of him. However"—she laughed as they linked arms and walked back towards the house—"I do not think he will ever be in humour to give consequence to young ladies of no magical talent who are slighted by other men. You will not convince me to think so well of him as that!"

Despite his best efforts, Darcy could not forget the events of Saturday evening, puzzled by many things he could not put into words. Had there been a part of that overcrowded room shielded from the multitude of rampant magics? Why had the charms he used and depended upon since childhood—most particularly the one that prevented his feet from tripping—slipped beyond the realm of control, if only for a moment? Was it something inherent to the room? Or was it someone in the room, tampering with other people's magic? He remembered the young woman's half-smile, laughing at him, and his puzzlement increased.

"You are sure Miss Elizabeth cannot perform magic?" Darcy enquired as casually as possible over coffee the next morning.

Bingley laughed. "Are you still rattled over your unfortunate misstep?"

"It was not a misstep. I never misstep."

"Mr Darcy could not possibly have tripped of his own accord. Someone must have done something." Caroline's eyes widened with excitement, but Bingley only shook his head.

"No one's spells, even yours, Darcy, are invincible," Bingley countered. "Miss Elizabeth has no magical ability. I had it from Miss Bennet herself—and I understand the two to be very close. You are feeling remorseful for not having danced with her, as I daresay you should. Why, the entire assembly must despise you now!"

"Hertfordshire's feelings of cordiality towards me, or lack thereof, do not concern me. What concerns me is—"

"The hole in the room where magic seemed to not exist? I have the highest respect for you, Darcy, but such a thing is not possible. It was the draft of fresh air coming in from the window, nothing more. You said so yourself."

Darcy, unaccustomed to being contradicted by anyone, could not help seeing the logic behind his friend's reasoning. What Bingley insisted was true. Such holes had been attempted, but never successful. He resolved to put the whole unfortunate mishap—and Miss Elizabeth—from his mind entirely.

Their next scheduled social event was an evening with the Lucas family, for a small and intimate dinner followed by cards. The 'small' dinner party proved to be much larger than intended due to the fact that a regiment of militia had recently been quartered at Meryton. Sir William Lucas felt obliged to invite all the officers to join them. It was there that Darcy's resolve to forget about the assembly was significantly weakened, for the first person he laid eyes on after entering the room was Miss Elizabeth. She stood some twenty feet away from him talking to her sister, Miss Bennet, and Miss Lucas. Even from a distance, he could see the light catching glints in her hair and eyes. At first he looked only to criticise, but soon found himself drawn to know more of her.

No sooner had he made clear to himself and his friends that she had hardly a good feature in her face, than he began to find it rendered uncommonly intelligent by the beautiful expression of her dark eyes. To this discovery succeeded some others equally mortifying.

Though he found more than one failure of perfect symmetry in her form, he was forced to acknowledge her figure to be light and pleasing; and in spite of his assertion that her manners were not those of the fashionable world, he was caught by their easy playfulness. Of this she was perfectly unaware—to her, he was only the man who made himself agreeable nowhere, and who had not thought her handsome enough to dance with.

He heard a dramatic sigh at his shoulder and turned to see Caroline smiling at him. "Another long evening ahead of us, Mr Darcy, and I see Charles has already taken the best of the company for himself."

Darcy looked over to see his friend deeply engaged in conversation with Miss Bennet. His eyes searched briefly before locating her sister, still talking with Miss Lucas.

"What is it you find so interesting, sir?" Caroline asked, trying to follow his gaze, but he had already turned his attention back to her.

He thought for a moment before replying with a slow smile. "I have been meditating on the very great pleasure which a pair of fine eyes and the face of a pretty woman can bestow."

She gasped in mock astonishment. "Pray tell who the subject of your study is? I find it hard to believe there is any genuine beauty in this room, so much of it puffed up with enchantments."

Darcy assured her that while this was true in some cases, in Miss Elizabeth Bennet's case, it was not.

"Miss Elizabeth Bennet!" Caroline said with only the trace of a sneer. "Pray, when am I to wish you joy?"

"I expected such a response from you. A lady's imagination is very rapid."

"So serious, Mr Darcy! Then I am sure the matter is absolutely settled. You will have a charming mother-in-law, who I am sure will always be at Pemberley with you." Caroline and Darcy both looked towards Mrs Bennet, who was bragging to their hostess Mrs Lucas about the prospect of marrying into five thousand pounds a year. Caroline shuddered slightly. "And your children, I am sure, will be most superbly magically talented—although I forgot! Their mother has no talent at all!"

Darcy bore her abuses with equanimity and even some amusement before he fixed his gaze upon the young lady in question. "I am not certain that is true."

"Oh," Caroline said with a wave of her hand. "It is true. I have taken tea with the ladies of Longbourn, and I can assure you that Miss Elizabeth is no more magical than that armchair over there— meaning no disrespect to the lady, of course. We cannot help what we are."

Darcy returned his eyes to Caroline's rather flushed face. "No," he said, emphasising each word, "we cannot."

~

"Mr Darcy seems to look your way often, Lizzy." Miss Charlotte Lucas smiled. "Can it be that your wedding will follow soon after your sister's?"

Elizabeth could not suppress the urge to roll her eyes at her dearest friend. "I cannot think why he looks in our direction unless it is to criticise. He is very disagreeable."

"He may be disagreeable, but he is certainly your match in

25

education and talent—and he is not poor, which must add to his eligibility considerably."

Charlotte Lucas, at the age of twenty-seven, was unmarried. She was not beautiful in the usual sort of way, but the purple of her gown that evening set off the tone of her skin in a pretty way. She and Elizabeth had been friends for some time in spite of their obvious difference of opinion when it came to matrimonial prospects. Charlotte considered herself to be more practical and attuned with the ways of the world than her more romantic friend.

Elizabeth laughed. "I am certain that Mr Darcy is superior to me in every way. His education is far beyond my reach—"

"Do not discredit your father, Lizzy!" Charlotte said. "He has spent many years teaching you more magical knowledge than any other woman of my acquaintance."

This gave Elizabeth momentary pause. "As to talent, there we could not possibly be equal, for you know as well as any that I cannot perform magic!"

Charlotte smirked, and was about to say something, when the gentleman in question spoke up behind them. "You cannot perform magic?"

Both ladies jumped and turned to see Mr Darcy looking very solemn. "Has it often been your habit to eavesdrop on other people's conversations, Mr Darcy?" Elizabeth said with no little annoyance.

She watched the faintest hint of a blush spread across his cheeks, but perhaps it was only from the warmth of the over-crowded room. "I could not help but overhear your remark. The question has been on my mind for some time, since fame of your family preceded my entrance into the county."

"Fame of my most talented father and sibling, and of a certain love potion possessed by my mother?" Elizabeth and Charlotte laughed, while Mr Darcy's face remained impassive. "I should take offence, Mr Darcy, at the implication of your words. I assume you imply that my family is rumoured to be talented—and everyone wonders why I am not."

Mr Darcy shifted his stance. "It is not my intention to cause offence, nor to be impertinent."

"As a man of study," Charlotte offered, "I am sure you are greatly interested in the run of magic through family lines."

He bowed.

Elizabeth's eyebrow rose. "In that case, I may reply—for the benefit of your study—that I am unable to perform magic. Are you satisfied?"

Mr Darcy bowed again, but instead of walking away as Elizabeth desired him to do, he remained standing next to them. Elizabeth heaved a sigh and could barely conceal the pout of her lip. Conversation was at a standstill and yet Darcy did not move away, so the three watched people milling about the crowded room—until finally Lydia convinced Mary to play them a dance.

As the couples formed a line, Sir William came to stand next to Mr Darcy. "What a splendid amusement this is for young people, Mr Darcy!"

"Sir?"

"Dancing! I consider it to be one of the first refinements of every polished society," Sir William said with a great smile.

"Certainly, sir; and it has the advantage also of being in vogue amongst the less polished societies of the world. Every savage can dance."

Elizabeth was hard pressed not to smile at this, in spite of herself.

"Your friend performs remarkably well," Sir William continued, seeing Mr Bingley join the group with Miss Bennet. "And I daresay you perform just as well! My dear Miss Eliza," he cried, noticing her for the first time. "Why are you not dancing? Mr Darcy, you must allow me to present this young lady to you as a very desirable partner."

Elizabeth's cheeks flushed. "Indeed, sir, I have not the least intention of dancing. You cannot suppose that I moved this way in order to beg for a partner!"

Mr Darcy, unsmiling, requested the honour of her hand; but in vain. Elizabeth was determined.

"You excel so much in the dance, Miss Eliza, that it is cruel to deny me the happiness of seeing you, and though the gentleman dislikes the amusement in general, he can have no objection, I am sure, to oblige us for one half hour."

"Mr Darcy is all politeness," said Elizabeth, smiling.

"He is indeed—but considering the inducement, my dear Miss Eliza, we cannot wonder at his complaisance; for who could object to such a partner?"

Elizabeth looked archly and turned away. Her resistance had not injured her with the gentleman, but it did turn his thoughts back to the assembly, leaving him puzzled for the rest of the evening.

It had been decided between Caroline and Louisa that they must invite Jane Bennet over for dinner. It seemed they had no other recourse, for they had declared her to be a sweet, amiable sort of girl, and their brother had taken that to mean he could think of her any way he liked. It appeared that he liked her very much.

Both Caroline and Louisa admonished Mr Darcy to discover once and for all whether Bingley was under inducement or enchantment. As much as it pained him to do so, Darcy reported that he could find no faults with Jane, other than the fact that she smiled too much. Bingley was triumphant; his sisters, resigned. Some time went into the question of whether or not they should merely invite her for tea—or perhaps a walk about the grounds. In the end, Louisa pointed out that they must have a suitable length of time in order to (subtly) discover all of her connexions. She even went so far as to suggest that, while only a girl from the country, Jane was a gentleman's daughter and perhaps not so ineligible as she appeared. Caroline was not convinced, but she did write the letter of invitation, and made sure to send the gentlemen out to dinner with the officers.

"I know it will be a disappointment to her, dining without the gentlemen present," Caroline said as regretfully as she could. "But I know of no other way of keeping her to ourselves!"

The two sisters almost began to look forward to Jane's coming, as they really had no idea what else to do with themselves in Hertfordshire away from their usual amusements. Still, when it began to pour rain on the day of the intended dinner, Caroline almost hoped that she would not come. All hope was for naught, however, when Jane arrived on horseback, dripping wet, with unfashionable punctuality.

Several minutes—fifteen at least—were spent fussing over the poor girl, and another ten in finding her dry clothes. At last the ladies were able to sit down for dinner, whereupon the Inquisition began. Was Jane very magical?—she did not consider herself to be so. But did others?—others might exaggerate. Did she enjoy the country life?—very much. And ever wish she could be more in town?—well, she could visit her aunt and uncle in town whenever she liked. And where did they live?

"On Gracechurch Street," Jane replied with barely a blush. "My uncle and aunt are well-respected wizards in that area."

Caroline managed a stiff smile, and Louisa whispered, "Is that in Cheapside?" The Inquisition was over. The two sisters had all the information they ever needed to know, and they were satisfied. Jane would not do, despite her personal attractiveness. The connexions were too horrendous.

Dinner came to a hasty close, Jane seeming oblivious to her hostesses' change in manner. They strove to be polite, but now focused their conversation mainly on the weather and latest fashions. They were eager to give Jane instruction, and she was only too happy to receive their advice, however unlikely it was that she would return home and immediately begin making up new gowns.

"Tea-time, I think. Miss Bennet, would you join us?" Caroline announced abruptly, and they led her into the smaller tea room, furnished with stiff green velvet chairs. "Do sit, Miss Bennet, are you comfortable?"

Jane was not, particularly, but she reassured them that she was. Comfort, after all, was relative.

Caroline began making the tea. "In town, of course, I never make my own," she explained. "But here in the country, I thought, well, that I might return to the simple pleasures of life. Making my own tea, picking our own flowers, et cetera. It is quite refreshing, actually. Do you not agree, Louisa?"

Louisa tilted her head in confusion, but blurted, "Of course, dear."

Caroline handed Jane a steaming dainty cup. "Do tell me you like it?"

Jane felt the tea to be quite delicious. "It is just the thing to warm me after the rain this afternoon." She smiled.

Conversation continued as it had before until somewhere around eight o'clock in the evening, when Jane began to cough up green smoke.

Caroline noticed it first. "Miss Bennet? Are you quite well?"

Jane, who was losing colour and coughing up more smoke, found herself unable to answer. She attempted to nod in reassurance but was prevented when, suddenly, she fainted.

OF RIDDLES AND THEORIES

"*DEAR LIZZY*," ELIZABETH READ OVER BREAKFAST TO HER MOTHER and father, "*I apologise for my absence last night and this morning. I have been taken ill, but do not be alarmed. Other than a fever, headache, and cough, there is not much the matter with me. Miss Bingley has been most kind, both she and Mrs Hurst insist I stay in bed until I am well. My cough produces a green smoke—it seems the cook accidentally purchased some cursed tea—and I am unable to remedy it myself with the usual spells. I hope to be well soon and back in your company. Yours, et cetera.*"

Elizabeth looked up in disbelief. "Green smoke?"

"Jane staying at Netherfield!" exclaimed Mrs Bennet. "Is it not exactly how I planned, my dear? I knew that when it rained yesterday the thing was to send her without the carriage. Now she must stay there and will be thrown into Mr Bingley's company, and then they will marry and Jane will see to it that we all prosper after you are gone!"

"I am confounded," Mr Bennet said. "Jane has never been so ill that she could not remedy herself. My dear, you seem to forget that she is a talented healer. She has not taken ill in nearly ten years."

"Green smoke!" Elizabeth cried again. "And she writes that the cook must have purchased cursed tea? Of all the most ridiculous explanations for a curse, I've never heard of such a thing. I must go to her immediately."

"Lizzy, do not be rash." Mrs Bennet sniffed. "Jane has not been cursed by anyone—these things are a regular occurrence with imports. And why would the Bingleys wish to curse our dear Jane when she means so much to the gentleman? No, indeed; you must stay here and let my plan run its course."

"Papa." Elizabeth rose from her chair. "Jane needs me."

He nodded. "Of course, but the carriage is not to be had this morning."

"I will walk, Papa."

"You will walk three miles through that forest after a rain?" Mrs Bennet was rather alarmed.

"Your mother is right. The forest is dangerous, child." Mr Bennet raised his eyebrows warningly.

Elizabeth managed a smile in spite of her concern. "You know very well that the forest holds little danger for me."

∼

The previous evening had not been pleasant for the gentlemen of Netherfield. Dinner with the officers had been tedious at best, aggravating at worst. Where Darcy had hoped to find men dedicated to the county's protection and regulation of dark magic, they seemed to feel themselves assigned to an area of no consequence, where nothing of importance ever happened. Darcy was indignant. He could not abide the shirking of one's duty. Upon their return to the house, and subsequent discovery of Miss Bennet's ailment, an hour's worth of inquisition had gone into the discovery of the source of her illness, the culprit proving to be the evening's tea.

"Oh Charles!" Caroline had cried. "If I had only known—and to think Louisa and I almost took a drink of it ourselves. I do not know where it was bought; the rest must be disposed of immediately!"

Darcy had chosen not to question Caroline further after her brother left the room. He stood silently for some moments, staring into the fireplace while Louisa whimpered, and Caroline clenched her hands.

"If I am not mistaken," he began at length, turning to bore his eyes into Miss Bingley's, "and I rarely am, that tea was enchanted by a counter-love potion gone awry. Poorly executed. How strange that it should find its way into Miss Bennet's cup." With that, he excused himself from the room, and the rest of the evening had been spent locked away in Bingley's study, trying to discover an antidote without success.

Morning brought the apothecary, a Mr Jones, who was equally unable to administer a remedy. Jane's condition remained the same; the apothecary recommended that she not be moved, and that the illness should run its course within the next few days or so. Everyone was distressed, but Caroline and Louisa found comfort in attending to Jane's every need, Bingley found solace in pacing about the gardens, and Darcy decided to go for a walk in the woods adjoining Netherfield's grounds.

Darcy had not slept well—therefore what follows is perhaps more understandable, given the circumstances. He wandered rather aimlessly for some time, keeping an eye on the Park; but there came a point in his ramblings when the trees all began to take a glimmering shade, and Darcy realised that he wasn't quite sure where he was. He chuckled, and righted himself to walk in the proper direction (for wizards can never truly be lost), when he was distracted by a noise in the brambles behind him. Imagine his astonishment when out of the thicket appeared a ruffled Miss Elizabeth Bennet, eyes sparkling, mouth twitched into a teasing smile.

"Miss Elizabeth!" he cried, turning to manage a bow.

"Mr Darcy." She laughed. "Have you not been told that these woods are dangerous to walk in alone?"

Darcy drew himself up rather stiffly. "I can assure you, madam, that I am in no danger."

His answer seemed to please her, for she laughed again, and took a few steps back to sit on a fallen tree. Her hair seemed to have come undone, for she took off her bonnet and hastily twisted it back into place. "I take it, then," she said, with a pin between her teeth, "that you like adventures?"

Darcy turned his head to the side and did not answer.

"Riddles, then, do you like riddles?" She finished with her hair but did not replace her bonnet.

"Riddles?" Darcy repeated, a slight buzz sounding in his ears. He shook it off, distracted by the sunlight playing on her hair. "I should be surprised if you asked me a riddle that I could not answer."

Miss Elizabeth laughed again. "Shall we play a game then? You will answer me three riddles: if you win all, you may go as you please; but if you cannot answer, you must give me anything I ask."

"You need not ask me riddles for that," Darcy replied slowly, puzzled at the sudden warmth in her manner of address. He tried to focus on the young lady before him, but something was nagging at the back of his mind. Something he could not remember—and Darcy hardly ever forgot anything.

"Oh. But where is the fun in that?"

"May I ask what you are doing out here in the woods alone?"

Miss Elizabeth smiled wider and moved her dark hair so that it fell over one shoulder. "Come now, if you answer me this, I will tell you."

Darcy considered that if he played her game, she might answer further questions about her lack of magic. His gaze moved from her shoulders back again to her eyes. He bowed in assent.

"For your first riddle"—she moved ever so slightly closer—"the more you see of me, the less you see. What am I?"

"Darkness," he replied without hesitation.

The lady frowned, and something flickered across her face—an emotion Darcy could not recognise. Then she laughed again, shrugging. "And what, Mr Darcy, do liars do when they die?"

Darcy could not help but chuckle at this, feeling her riddles to be rather uncomplicated. "They lie still."

She huffed, tossing her hair with annoyance. "I assure you, sir, that I am very good at riddles. No one ever guesses all three."

"Are you quite sure of that?"

"Quite sure." She drew him closer with her sparkling eyes. "I am always coming, but never arriving, Mr Darcy."

His breath caught. Their faces were very close, and he could almost catch the scent of her hair, when suddenly, he remembered what he had forgotten. Leaping away from her, he cried, "Tomorrow! For when it arrives, it is today! And now"—he pointed his hand forcefully—"You will reveal your true form!"

Miss Elizabeth—or rather, what had seemed to be Miss Elizabeth—burst into angry tears. She was shrinking, soon the size of a small child, and turning a rather golden colour. Little wings sprouted from her back and she rose up, hovering just above him, crying and turning red, yelling nasty things.

"You wretched duke of limbs, you ill-begotten gollumpus, I curse your name to the zenith powers. I always, always win!" she cried. "I have not lost a game in a hundred years!"

There was a burst of sound, and another small, golden creature appeared next to her, shaking his first. "And did I not warn you," it shouted, "not to try and claim a wizard! Now you have used up all my magic, and we shan't have anything!"

Darcy would have laughed at their fighting had he not felt himself so foolish for having agreed to any sort of game. It shook him, that his defences had proven so slow to react, when he had trained himself so rigorously to recognise magical forms for what they truly were (under any circumstance). The two creatures were beating their wings, growing angrier by the minute, when suddenly there was a flash, and both disappeared in a sparkle of golden pieces raining down onto his head. Darcy sneezed, mortified to hear the resulting sound of laughter behind him.

Turning, he jumped to see Miss Elizabeth Bennet—the true Elizabeth—standing some distance behind him. He was quite sure it was her, for his defences were in perfect working order now. She did not look nearly so pleased to see him as the other Miss Elizabeth had been and, while her petticoat was covered in mud, her bonnet was firmly in its proper place.

"Mr Darcy," she said. "Have you not been told that these woods are dangerous to walk in alone?"

"I have heard something of that sort, yes," he said stiffly, brushing a fine golden dust from his jacket.

"But I see you are not a novice when it comes to pixies," she said, raising a brow. "There are not many people in Hertfordshire

35

who know that they still exist in the wood—and the men who do encounter them are rarely believed."

Darcy cleared his throat. "May I enquire as to your purpose in the forest?"

"I have come to see my sister, Jane. Will you take me to her?"

Darcy, still rather shaken, nodded in reply. Their walk back to the Park was brief, with few words exchanged between them. Miss Elizabeth was shown directly to the breakfast room, where her appearance caused a great deal of surprise.

She was received politely, but not without contempt on the part of Bingley's sisters. Miss Elizabeth appeared relieved to be taken to her sister without the need for further conversation.

Caroline was preparing to say something witty on the subject of Miss Eliza's petticoat when Darcy abruptly turned to her brother. "Bingley, I would speak with you in private." If Bingley was surprised, he did not show it. Instead they removed to his study, where Darcy began pacing about.

"Recite to me the theory we learned on pixies, Bingley," he said, running a hand through his hair.

It took Bingley a few moments of staring at the ceiling before he replied, "Pixies. Always work in male and female pairs, most often brother and sister; highly dangerous, seductive, known to draw men into the woods and confound them with riddles, thereby tricking the victim into doing their bidding for as long as they so choose, possibly forever. One can only defeat the pixies by answering all three riddles correctly, never before, never after."

"You have forgotten an important element."

"The female pixie always appears in the form of one's heart's desire—whatever that may be?"

"Well—" Darcy blushed. "That is correct, in theory—although I am certain, that is—that was not what I was thinking of."

"You are referring to the fact that they are extinct?"

"That they are thought to be extinct, Bingley." Darcy sat across from him, and proceeded to tell him the tale in full, with the exception of the form the female pixie had chosen to take.

Bingley was quite delighted. "Not extinct after all? Do you realise that this means a wealth of study and prestige? What we can learn from these creatures!"

Darcy smiled ruefully. "I would perhaps be more enthusiastic, had I not almost succumbed to their magic."

"I cannot accept your answer—the form must be of significance. Was it a human form? Did it offer no hints as to its true nature?"

Darcy sighed and moved towards the window, looking out at the forest. "Human form, yes, without an initial hint of magic. Desirable, true to life—a masterful work of deception. There might have been a hint of—it took me all of ten minutes to regain my senses. An insupportable failure."

Bingley moved to pat his shoulder. "We all have our weaknesses, Darcy, even you."

"At a time like this, weakness is unacceptable—I cannot support it. I must improve." He looked again towards the woods, nodding. "And there you were right to say I would not want for study. Hertfordshire has proven to be a much greater puzzle than I anticipated."

"Not so backwards after all." Bingley clapped him on the back again. "And those woods—if they contain pixies, they are sure to hold other such deep magics."

"Deep magic…" Darcy paused. "Older magic. I must practise."

"Of course you must—but I'd expect nothing less. Guard yourself against your heart's desire, eh?" Bingley almost laughed thought better of it.

"That is—" Darcy paused again. "I am in no great danger there; I did not, after all, succumb to the pixies' magic."

"But you did accept the game of—"

Darcy silenced him with a meaningful look. "I do believe that you have a letter to write."

"Of course! Although I am certain the letter would be much better coming from you. No one ever seems to understand half of what I write." Bingley was already scribbling something down on a piece of paper.

Darcy shook his head. "I have sent too many over the past few months, and I hope to avoid suspicion." He rose and headed for the door. "Also," he said, turning, "I have a theory about Miss Elizabeth Bennet."

"Another theory?" Bingley did not look up from his letter.

"Yes, although it is similar to the first. The test is being conducted as we speak—for if she emerges from that room and her sister is improved, then my theory is correct."

Bingley shook his head. "Once again, you choose to keep your theories to yourself? You will not enlighten me as to what you believe her capabilities to be?" Given no encouragement one way or the other, Bingley continued, "I think Miss Elizabeth to be a lovely girl—such affection towards her sister is very admirable—but I am not convinced there is anything out of the ordinary about her, as you seem to be. Although, after encountering pixies in the forest, perhaps anything is possible."

"We shall see," came the reply, and Darcy left the room.

The Phenomenon of Counter-Magic

"Darcy, I may need your assistance," Bingley called into the library, where Darcy was attempting to read. "Miss Elizabeth seems to have requested our carriage."

Darcy rose and followed Bingley into the hall where Miss Elizabeth stood, her expression bordering on outrage.

"Mr Bingley," she began slowly, her fists clenched, "I do thank you for your kindness and care for my sister, and I understand that you had nothing to do with her unfortunate illness. But I must respectfully request our immediate removal from Netherfield. Her dangerous symptoms are now at an end. I feel that her needs might be more adequately addressed at home."

"Miss Elizabeth, I understand your concern for your sister, but the apothecary informed us that her recovery would take place over several days. You cannot insist that she be moved before she is recovered," Bingley said.

"Indeed," Darcy added. "Properly fashioned curses are easy

39

enough to remedy once the counter-spell is discovered. However, the nature of this particular spell was poorly done, and I am afraid the side effects difficult to remedy, no matter the skill of those involved. It is impossible that your sister should be recovered so soon. You must be mistaken."

"I am afraid you are mistaken, Mr Darcy, if you think that I am not aware of the nature of curses and their effects—poorly executed or not. I can assure you that Jane is much better—"

"And I must insist that to be impossible," Darcy cried with some emotion, "unless you are privy to magical powers that none others are capable!"

Miss Elizabeth flushed, and raised her voice. "As I have stated emphatically to you before, I am not able to perform magic! My sister's recovery has very little to do with the performing of spells. If you desire for the apothecary to return and examine her, by all means, send for him."

"That will not be necessary, if you will allow me to examine her myself. I was not impressed with Dr Jones's capabilities, magical or not."

As her eyebrows rose, Bingley hastened to interject, "Mr Darcy means nothing untoward, but you may believe that we would be able to ascertain your sister's condition."

"There is no need of that." All three turned to see the eldest Miss Bennet, pale but no longer coughing, attempting to descend from the top of the stair.

"Jane!" cried Miss Elizabeth, seeing her sister almost slip. All three rushed up to meet her and return her to her room. With a gentleman on either side to support her, Miss Bennet was returned to her bed, her sister standing close watch. "I had intended to take you home, but not for you to attempt the stairs yourself!" she admonished.

"I am sure I shall be perfectly well. I cannot abide trespassing on your kind hospitality any longer," Miss Bennet said with a look towards Bingley.

"No, please," he cried. "It is entirely our fault that you are in this position in the first place. Darcy?"

"Your symptoms do seem to have disappeared, Miss Bennet," Darcy said, still holding her hand. "It is quite extraordinary." He turned his gaze to Miss Elizabeth.

"Please, you are much too weak to return home this afternoon!" Bingley said with great concern. "I must insist that you stay until tomorrow. Miss Elizabeth, you both must stay until your sister has made a complete recovery."

She stood reluctantly for some moments. "I see that my sister has been weakened more than I had anticipated." Indeed, Miss Bennet was struggling to remain awake now that she had been returned to her bed. "We may decide upon a time tomorrow, if Jane is sufficiently recovered. I am only concerned—" She hesitated, at a loss for words.

"I can assure you, Miss Elizabeth," Bingley said, "that nothing of the sort will happen again. I have taken every precaution—and Darcy has spent several hours adding to our number of defensive charms. Netherfield is now perhaps the safest home in the county."

Her mouth turned to a slight smile. "I thank you again for your kindness, Mr Bingley."

It was with reluctance that Bingley left the room, sending longing glances towards Miss Bennet's sleeping form, giving cause for another smile from Miss Elizabeth, and a frown from Darcy.

～

Elizabeth stayed with her sister for some hours. Jane slept restlessly at first, but soon fell into a deep slumber. In spite of her certainty of Jane's recovery, Elizabeth now began to regret her earlier insistence upon a departure. She appeared to have been weakened both magically and physically by her ordeal.

As the evening drew on, she hoped that Jane might awaken and give her an excuse not to join the ladies downstairs for dinner, but she did not stir, and Elizabeth found herself obliged to put on a fresh gown—a trunk having been kindly whisked over by the thoughtful Mr Bingley—and make her way to join the ladies in the dining room. As much as she detested the idea of dinner with Caroline and Louisa, Elizabeth was not pleased when she was interrupted in the hall by Mr Darcy.

"Miss Elizabeth," he said, surprising her as she rounded a corner. "If I might speak with you."

She hesitated for a moment, but out of curiosity (and perhaps against her better judgment), she walked into the library. "Will you not be joining your party, Mr Darcy?" she queried.

He did not reply, instead gesturing to her to take a seat.

"Am I here for another inquisition?" She took a seat across from him.

"Only the truth, Miss Elizabeth."

A large and dusty book was open across the table between them. She glanced at the open pages, then looked up, startled. "Of magics that might be transferred from one to another—" she read, and turned an accusatory eye back towards Mr Darcy. "You are studying a deep and powerful magic. The ability to possess and use another's magic is a dark power—one that has been a plague on the wizarding society for hundreds of years."

"Yes, I know."

"I would hope you are not implying that I—"

"I do not know what else to think," he said, leaning closer across the table. "You claim to not use magic, and yet you counter spells. But that is not the only reason for my concern. As you have not been in the company of many accomplished wizards, perhaps there have been none who noticed the absence of magic whenever you are present. I have noticed it."

Elizabeth's eyes flared. "You are suggesting the reason for such an absence is that I take other's magic to use for myself!"

"Do you contradict me?"

She flew to her feet. "One hundred times over!"

"Then how can you explain the power you possess—that I know you possess? Do not think me such a fool. Your magical abilities are blatant to anyone of sense and education."

"I cannot perform magic," Elizabeth said.

"That is not the truth!" cried Mr Darcy, also rising.

"It is not magic!"

Elizabeth walked towards the door while Mr Darcy sat back down. "Then my theory is correct, however improbable it seems."

Elizabeth turned. "Your theory?"

"Counter-magic," he stated, crossing his arms.

Elizabeth inhaled sharply and moved back into her chair. "I would hear your theory, Mr Darcy."

"There is nothing more to it. Little is known of counter-magic, I have no personal experience with it. My knowledge is limited to what has been speculated upon—that some, for inexplicable reasons, are immune to magic. Not just immune to it," he added, seeing her smirk, "but able to counteract the performances of others."

Elizabeth glanced back down at the book between them. "Your suggestion that I was practising dark magic was a ruse to uncover my secret."

"A rather clever one, I might add."

"I have not acceded that you are correct."

"But I am." Mr Darcy's face was now unreadable. "Why have you chosen to keep such talent a secret?"

Elizabeth considered her reply. "Upon the insistence of my father. You must be aware that he no longer practises magic."

"Yet your sisters do."

"He has provided us with an education in the magical arts, but does not want me to become an object of curiosity."

"This protection would also deprive you of the opportunity to explore your capabilities," Mr Darcy said, almost to himself. "Do you not retain any semblance of the spells you disassemble?"

"Not that I am aware."

"Are you aware of the power you possess, Miss Bennet?" Mr Darcy cried, his face suddenly alight. "To be invulnerable to magic! Are there no spells that you are unable to counter?"

"None that I have attempted."

"But that accounts for your inexperience," Mr Darcy insisted, his face returning to its customary solemnity.

Elizabeth raised an eyebrow. "Such as your enchantments? I am well aware of your achievements, and your philosophies." She moved her hand almost imperceptibly, and Mr Darcy's hair fell into his eyes. "I found it amusing that a man such as yourself would have need for such a great number of cumbersome spells. Particularly one for keeping hair out of one's eyes."

Mr Darcy quickly righted the spell, making his hair return to its proper place. "Do you take delight in stripping people of their spells?"

He thought he detected a hint of a smirk on her lips when she replied, "Only when they are unnecessary."

"And you are the proper judge of that?"

Elizabeth's cheeks flushed in anger. "I have no reason to defend my actions to you, sir."

He almost smiled but caught himself. "The most primitive forms of magic, evident even in Hertfordshire, have been used to modify, control, or enhance appearances in all forms. A well-trained wizard learns to see beyond the façade we project for ourselves—but I assume that you are not deceived by it?"

"The façade? No. Such spells are distracting and tiring."

"You have noticed that none of my enchantments are used for the purposes of deception, but rather practicality. Disguise of every sort is my abhorrence."

Elizabeth laughed. "Practicality? Is that what you call it?"

Mr Darcy rose from his chair. "Have no fear of exposure. You may be assured of my secrecy."

"May I?" she replied, rising to meet his gaze. "You are not going to offer me as a subject of study to your colleagues in higher circles?"

Mr Darcy stiffened. "A person is not a subject, but there is much to discuss—your ability would naturally be of interest to any scholar."

She laughed. "You will excuse me, Mr Darcy, when I doubt your assurances of secrecy. I am sure there is much to discuss, but now is not the time."

Darcy looked reluctant but bowed in acquiescence.

∾

Dinner that evening was a singularly quiet affair. Bingley was preoccupied with worry over Jane's health, while his sisters were much subdued, to the point of making honest attempts to be agreeable to their guest. For Jane's sake, Miss Elizabeth appeared to look upon them with a kinder, forgiving eye.

Darcy was left to his own thoughts. He noticed the regularity with which he had begun to turn his eyes towards Miss Elizabeth. Admittedly, he felt triumph in the correctness of his theory, and a fascination with her talent. Who would not? But now he remembered with surprising accuracy the picture presented to him in the forest—although not Elizabeth herself, but rather a form taken by the pixie. He was thinking of her too much. There was no question in his mind that she was not his heart's desire—perhaps the pixie had taken that form because he had so greatly desired to discover the truth of her secret. He could not lead her to hope for something that could never be.

"What are you thinking of, Mr Darcy?" Caroline said, sliding into the chair next to him. Their game of cards was at an end, and the company scattered themselves in various places throughout the room. In spite of his earlier thoughts, he quickly located Miss Elizabeth in a corner, opening a book.

His line of sight was not lost on Caroline, who said, "What is it you read, Miss Eliza Bennet? Mr Darcy and I are greatly desirous of knowing."

Elizabeth looked up with the same expression of amusement to which Darcy was now becoming quite accustomed. "*Defensive Magic and Its Many Uses.*"

"Indeed?" exclaimed Caroline. "That is your father's work, is it not, Mr Darcy?" She turned away from Elizabeth and back towards Darcy. "I have read it myself, of course, and found it to be one of the greatest influences over my own practices."

Darcy was trying to find a way not to reply when Elizabeth spoke up from her corner. "And what principle did you find the most useful, Miss Bingley?"

"Principle?"

"Yes, of the five."

"Why, the spells, of course."

"But Mr Darcy—the author, that is—does not emphasise the use of spells in his theory. His emphasis tends to be on concentration," Elizabeth said, turning the pages of the book.

Darcy was surprised. "You have read the book?"

"Yes, but thought I might refresh my memory, due to the interesting conversation we had earlier. I understand your methods to be based heavily upon this theorem."

"Concentration." Darcy raised his eyebrows. "Indeed. But you disagree."

"How could she disagree?" Caroline cried. "Your father's principles have been the cornerstone for defence over the past twenty years!"

"I did not say that I did not agree, Mr Darcy." Elizabeth closed the book with a snap.

"That does not take away from the fact that you do," he said. "I might enquire as to why."

"The principles are good in theory, but not in practice. How concentrated is one going to be when a dragon is breathing fire down onto your house?"

"And how many dragons have you fought, Miss Elizabeth?" Darcy almost smiled, but she looked somewhat miffed.

"I was not implying that I had fought any, Mr Darcy. That is not the point."

"Mr Darcy has fought against five, Eliza! Five dragons," Caroline added. "How interesting you should choose that as an example."

Darcy felt his neckcloth had grown rather tight. The conversation had taken an unintended turn. "Miss Bingley, I beg you would not—"

"What of pixies, then," Bingley suggested, to Darcy's astonishment.

"Pixies are perhaps a better example, Mr Bingley, I thank you." Elizabeth smiled. "As they take the form of a man's heart's desire. I have never heard of any man, wizard or not, who resisted the offer of a game of riddles, no matter how great their concentration. Have you, Mr Darcy?"

Darcy scowled. "No, I have not." At this, Bingley felt he could not in good conscience expose his friend's earlier mistake and fell into silence, whereas Elizabeth, feeling herself to have won the conversation, turned back to her book and the discussion came to an end.

Unusual Correspondence

THE NEXT MORNING PROVED TO BE A DRIZZLY ONE. ELIZABETH ROSE early with the intention of walking about the grounds, only to be confined to her room upstairs by the rain, unwilling to venture down until absolutely necessary. Jane had awoken once in the night, murmured that she was exceedingly tired, and then fallen back to sleep. Elizabeth resigned herself to another day at Netherfield, unless Jane should awaken and find herself completely recovered.

Caroline and Louisa made their way up to the room sometime around ten to enquire after the patient and invite Elizabeth down for breakfast. In spite of their obvious distaste for Elizabeth, the two sisters did fuss over Jane for some minutes, and ordered a tray brought in with tea and rolls should she awake to find herself hungry. Elizabeth thanked them for their kindness, but not before she had discreetly ascertained the magical contents of the breakfast offered. As she could detect nothing amiss, she was obliged to return downstairs with them and leave Jane to her rest.

The company had just sat down to eat when Elizabeth's mother was announced. Mrs Bennet strode into the room without embarrassment, confident that the attentions she believed Bingley was bestowing on her eldest daughter extended good will towards all members of the Bennet family. She was followed closely by her three youngest daughters. She was adamant in her demand to see Jane, profuse in her thanks for Bingley's hospitality, and pointedly ungracious towards the person of Darcy.

Mrs Bennet was a woman of mean understanding, who consequently prided herself upon her unerring judgment of people's characters. Mrs Bennet felt that she was rarely ever wrong. A man like Bingley, so agreeable and interested in one of her daughters, could not receive too much praise in her eyes. But a man such as Darcy— whose fame preceded him, and who did not live up to Mrs Bennet's idea of 'standards'—could not receive too little.

The three youngest Miss Bennets said very little but professed themselves to be greatly in awe of Netherfield's many splendours. They preferred to stay in the breakfast room, rather than accompany their mother upstairs with Elizabeth. It was with great amusement that Darcy noticed Elizabeth strip them of their charm enhancements before leaving the room—although he was certain she must know full well that such trifling charms could hold no influence over himself or Bingley.

Caroline chose to accompany Elizabeth and Mrs Bennet to the sickroom, rather than remain in the company of three such young women. The visit was short-lived, for Mrs Bennet ascertained that Jane was too weak to be moved and returned to the breakfast room post-haste to say as much to Bingley.

"I can assure you, madam," he replied with the greatest of respect, "that your daughter will not be moved until she is sufficiently recovered."

"Mama, Jane is sleeping. After she awakens, it will be a more appropriate time to assess her state of illness—or lack thereof. We might return this afternoon, if she is better," Elizabeth whispered into her mother's ear.

"This afternoon! You could not possibly return this afternoon, she might take a turn for the worse on the road! In any case, after our return the carriage is needed for the rest of the day," Mrs Bennet replied as she found herself a seat.

"Our carriages are at your disposal, Eliza, if you should ever need them," Caroline offered.

"Your daughter is no longer in any danger, Mrs Bennet," Darcy added. "She might be moved when she has regained her strength."

Mrs Bennet sniffed. "I have been informed by Mr Jones that she would be ill for several days."

"Her circumstance has—changed," Darcy said with a glance at Elizabeth. "I can personally attest to the fact that whatever symptoms were caused by the curse are completely gone."

"I understand you to be a knowledgeable wizard, Mr Darcy," began Mrs Bennet, without any notice of Elizabeth's slight tugging at her sleeve, "but I am sure Mr Jones has a much greater understanding of such things. Hertfordshire is not so very backward as some might think, whatever they say in town. I might venture to say there are some people here more talented than any! Would you not say so, Mr Bingley? My Jane, for instance."

Seeing Bingley at a loss for words, Elizabeth whispered, "Mama, Mr Bingley could hardly ascertain her talent in such a short acquaintance."

"Miss Bennet is gifted," Darcy put in. "But Mrs Bennet, you must not underestimate the knowledge and talent that can be found in London or elsewhere, where there is a greater opportunity for study and education."

"You imply that there is no such opportunity here in Hertfordshire!" Mrs Bennet cried.

"Indeed, Mama, you are mistaken," said Elizabeth, blushing for her mother. "You quite mistook Mr Darcy. He only meant that there was not such a variety of opportunity to be met with in the country as in town, which you must acknowledge to be true."

"I do not mistake the gentleman, do I?"

Everyone assumed Mrs Bennet's question to be rhetorical and deigned not to answer. She continued, "My husband, with whom you are well acquainted, may be known as one of the greatest wizards in the history of our country."

"Mr Bennet's studies are some of the finest published," Darcy replied in earnest agreement.

Bingley added a hasty "Indeed," in the hope of pacifying his guest.

"Has he, perchance, published anything recently?" Caroline enquired. "Within the last twenty years?"

Elizabeth's cheeks flushed in anger, while her mother's flushed in mortification. "I am sure I don't understand you, Miss Bingley," Mrs Bennet replied. The silence stretched out over the course of several moments before she turned towards Mr Bingley with a smile. "What remarkable tapestries. I have always told people that Netherfield possessed the finest quality in the county—Hertford- shire craftsmanship for you! Indeed, if you will note the design patterns shift—"

Conversation continued in this vein for some time, until the youngest Miss Bennet mentioned to Mr Bingley that he had promised a ball—to which he replied that indeed he had, and so on and so forth.

Elizabeth bore her mother's behaviour with as much restraint as possible until they took their leave. It caused her great mortification to discern that she was not the only one of the party to breathe a sigh of relief as their carriage rattled away towards Longbourn. Caroline and Louisa did not linger in the breakfast parlour, soon absenting themselves in order to discuss 'private matters.'

Jane finally awoke from her slumber late in the afternoon, tired but with sufficient energy to come downstairs and rest by the fire with a blanket. Bingley was most attentive, his warm affection apparent to everyone in the room except perhaps Jane, who was too modest, and Darcy, who was writing a letter and trying not to look at Miss Elizabeth. Jane accepted an offer of tea from Caroline with graciousness, and everything seemed for a moment to be as it should be. But of course, it is always during such moments that something out of the ordinary occurs.

"Of all things," Caroline cried. She sat on the divan with Louisa, a pile of letters on her lap, holding one up to the light. "I cannot make out the wording in this at all!"

Darcy and Bingley looked up from their separate activities, their sudden motion causing Elizabeth to look up from her reading.

"Whose letter is that, Caroline?" Bingley asked sharply.

Caroline was prevented from answering when Darcy strode across the room and snatched the letter from her hands just before it incinerated. She gasped to see Darcy's glare, and Louisa let out a small shriek.

"Whose letter was that, Caroline!" Bingley repeated with some feeling.

"I...I had thought it to be a missive from a friend in town!" Caroline stammered, holding a hand to her throat.

Darcy began to pace about the room. "Your sister goes too far, Bingley!"

Bingley gaped at his sister. "It was one of Darcy's letters! Caroline!"

Caroline was turning red. "I did not know it was his, I thought—"

"You thought?" Darcy snapped.

Jane was pale from worry that anyone should be distressed. "I am sure it was all a mistake!"

"A letter addressed to me—enchanted, of course, so that no one but I could read it—and also enchanted to self-destruct!" Darcy moved to the door. "This is a matter which cannot be overlooked. I will return as soon as possible, Bingley. In the meantime, be so kind as to ensure that missives addressed to me do not find their way into the hands of the wrong person. You understand the importance of this."

Darcy closed the door with the hint of a slam, leaving the room in stunned silence until Caroline burst into tears.

∼

Jane and Elizabeth returned to Longbourn the following morning. Bingley sent them off with warmth and some reluctance, while Caroline could hardly contain her delight at saying goodbye. Darcy seemed to have disappeared, and Bingley offered a farewell on his behalf.

Elizabeth said, "You will forgive me when I say that I am not at all sorry we returned home as soon as we did." She and Jane sat together in Longbourn's sitting room, the only other person in the room being their father (who was pretending not to eavesdrop).

"I am happy to be home and not ill," Jane agreed.

"I know you miss Mr Bingley's chivalrous company, although you will not admit it."

"You know I will not, Lizzy!"

"If not for my belief in the sincerity of his goodness—and affection for you!—I would advise you not to think on him at all, if only for the sake of his sister. A more ridiculous woman I have never met. Poisoning you with cursed tea and accidentally opening other people's personal missives!" Elizabeth let out a short, incredulous laugh. "Poor Mr Darcy, with his very important business."

"You doubt the seriousness of his business, Elizabeth?" Mr Bennet enquired, giving up the pretence.

"Mr Darcy is an extremely serious man, Papa. I am sure his business is equally important," Elizabeth said with a solemn expression such like Darcy's that Jane laughed aloud.

"You do not like him," Mr Bennet stated. "I cannot blame you. He does not present himself affably."

"He is much too self-satisfied. Although…"

"Although?" Mr Bennet's eyebrows rose.

Elizabeth turned to her father with a look of consternation. "He knows that I can perform disenchantment. You see, I was able to disenchant the cursed tea that Jane was given, and it did not take him long to confront me with his suspicions."

"He discovered your secret," Mr Bennet said, leaning back in his chair.

"Does that worry you, Papa?" Jane asked with an anxious glance at her sister. "We have not met many wizards of his calibre. I am sure it was not a mistake on her part."

Mr Bennet sighed. "No, Jane. it does not worry me. Not yet."

"Wizards of his calibre? Forgive me if I am not as convinced as you, Jane, that he is as talented as purported to be." Elizabeth laughed, but checked herself when she saw the serious gaze of both

Mr Bennet and Jane. "I confess to not having seen much of anything in Mr Darcy to intimidate me. But, Papa, when might I—"

Her question was cut short by the entrance of Mrs Bennet, followed by Mary, Kitty, and Lydia.

"We have such news!" cried Kitty, helping their mother into a chair.

Mrs Bennet was out of breath and quite distressed. "Horrendous news!"

"Of the very worst kind," Lydia said.

"There has been another attack," Mary said flatly.

Mr Bennet and his two eldest daughters looked at each other in alarm. "Was anyone killed?" cried Jane.

"Or dismantled?" Elizabeth leaned forward.

Lydia shook her head fiercely. "La, no! It was all a design to trap the Thieving Necromancer into capture!"

"You and your ridiculous names, Lydia," Elizabeth scoffed.

Kitty moved to sit next to Elizabeth. "But that is what he is called, Lizzy!"

"No one knows who or what it is, let alone whether or not it is a he or she," Elizabeth replied. "What is it you were saying about a trap?"

"You are such a bore, Lizzy. We shan't tell you anything if you will be so dull." Lydia crossed her arms.

But Kitty could not contain herself. "I do not understand all of the particulars—there is only so much they will reveal to the papers, or so Uncle Philips says—but it was originally to be carried out by a militia in some northern city that I cannot remember—"

"York," Mary said. "The Wizarding Court had laid out a trap for the Thief in the city of York. It was rather sophisticated—a young woman was rumoured to be able to conjure hailstorms. They spread about the rumour, and planned to have her travel to York and wait for the Thief to come."

Kitty was eager to add to the conversation. "But apparently—"

"Apparently the Thief ambushed the girl en route and there was a terrific row with sparks and lightning and all sorts of smoke!" Lydia finished, causing Kitty to pout, but Lydia never did care if Kitty was sulking or not. "Now no one knows where the

Thief might be, and he will be ever more alert to potential capture."

There was a moment of silence until Mrs Bennet spoke from her chair where she had been sitting in silence since the beginning of the conversation. Her face was pale, and her voice quavered as she turned to Mr Bennet. "Do you think there is any chance of something happening to us? These attacks all over the country—and with the trouble in Europe, I cannot help but fear for our very lives!"

"Tush, Mrs Bennet," her husband said, chuckling. "The Thieving Necromancer in Hertfordshire? And what do you suppose he would find here to add to his collection? Beauty charms and love potions that do not work? However highly you might think of our little county, it is quite inconsequential in the eyes of such a sorcerer."

Mrs Bennet did not look at all reassured. "Suppose he came in our sleep, and nothing could be done to prevent it! We could not defend ourselves!"

"I am sorry, my dear," Mr Bennet said as he shifted in his chair. "Circumstances prevent me from assuring you of any magical protection on my part—I would defend your lives to the death if necessary—but you are very aware of my limitations." He glanced at Elizabeth. "That being so, you may be happy to learn that another gentleman will be residing for a time at Longbourn as my guest. Perhaps now you will be more welcoming at the thought of him—although I have no notion of the strength of his abilities."

All six women immediately demanded to know who the gentleman was and what his business could possibly be with them.

"It is my cousin, a Mr Collins—the rector of a respectable parish in Kent who, when I am dead, may turn you all out of this house as soon as he pleases." Mr Bennet could not help laughing at his wife's immediate protestations of disdain.

"I ask for reassurances of our protection in such treacherous times and you bring up that odious man!"

"If you would read his letter, my dear, you might think differently," he said.

Several minutes were spent in perusal of the gentleman's correspondence. Kitty and Lydia found it to be (perhaps) the dullest letter written in the existence of man. It was next to impossible that their cousin should come in a scarlet coat, and it was now some weeks since they had received pleasure from the society of a man in any other colour. Mary thought its style to be quite elegant, Jane hoped he might have a safe journey, and Elizabeth guessed from its tone that Mr Collins was something of an oddity.

Mrs Bennet found herself begrudgingly grateful. In fact, the letter seemed to have done away much of her ill-will. "If he is disposed to make amends to my daughters, I shall not be the person to discourage him," she proclaimed.

Mr Bennet chuckled, but only remained in the room a few minutes longer. Elizabeth noted how he had turned the conversation from the recent attack to something less alarming—and thought his demeanour more troubled than he would allow his wife to see. She resolved to speak with him on it in the morning.

Mr Wickham's Tale

THE MORNING WAS CHILLY, AN AUTUMN MIST SPREADING ACROSS the ground. Elizabeth often walked in the forest surrounding Long-bourn when few others had yet arisen, and the light barely showed through the trees. She did not expect to encounter anyone; she hoped to be left to herself. But that morning proved different than most for shortly into her walk, on the outer skirts of the property, Elizabeth was startled by movement in the trees not ten feet in front of her.

"Who's there?" she called out, somewhat alarmed.

"Nay, answer me. Stand and unfold yourself," came the reply.

Elizabeth was astonished. "Mr Darcy?"

"That is not the proper answer," he said, stepping into the open. He wore a long dark coat, his customarily pristine appearance ruffled. He brushed the hair out of his eyes.

"I do not understand you." Elizabeth sniffed. "And I do not understand what you are doing here."

Mr Darcy looked bemused. "You do not?"

"No."

"Then perhaps it is best I keep it to myself. It is unnecessary for you to understand everything."

"I should have thought you would not stray so far into the woods, after your previous encounter here." Elizabeth arched a brow, regaining some of her composure. She was not afraid of Mr Darcy.

"I should have thought you would know such a trick cannot work on a wizard twice." He paused. "The proper answer is 'Long live the King'."

"The proper answer to what?"

"To my earlier demand."

"That I unfold myself, like a sheet of paper?"

"I prefer to think of it as a banner of allegiance. In any case, you would say 'Long live the King,' and I would reply by saying your name. And you would reply by—"

"Mr Darcy"—Elizabeth shook her head impatiently—"I do not see where this turns."

"You have not seen the play?"

"It is a play?"

Mr Darcy brought himself up stiffly. "I see. Your father might know, perhaps you should ask him."

"Most people are not so presumptuous as to dictate the manner of my addresses. I was walking alone in the forest by my home, having every right to ask who trespassed."

"You scold me for walking alone in the wood when you yourself make it a common enough practice. Do you think that because you are impervious to spells, nothing could befall you?" His tone was cold, even as the sun began to turn the frost into drops of dew on the grass around them.

"Not in these woods, Mr Darcy," Elizabeth said, glancing about her with great warmth of feeling. "It is quite safe for me here, when I am alone."

"These woods are joined to the woods of Netherfield Park. I do beg your pardon for having strayed into Longbourn's. I had not realised."

Elizabeth's eyes flashed. "A wizard is never lost; or do you think me such a simpleton as to not know?"

"I do not think so."

"Then you will admit you have some purpose to have strayed thus far."

Mr Darcy bristled. "Whatever my purposes, if I have not yet revealed them, do not hope for me to begin revealing them presently."

"I see."

"I suspect that you do not."

Elizabeth chose not to reply. With a curtsey, she took her leave of the gentleman, and turned towards the direction of home.

❧

Upon her arrival back at Longbourn, Elizabeth discovered the house was in an uproar. Two guests were now sitting in the parlour—one expected, one unexpected—both having arrived much earlier than was proper to ever consider calling. Of the household, only Mary was ready enough to descend to greet them.

"It is our cousin, Mr Collins, and Mr Bingley, Lizzy," she said, her eyes wide. "Will you come with me? I do not want to sit with them alone."

At Elizabeth's assurance, both sisters entered the parlour followed closely by Mr Bennet, who was still removing his nightcap.

"Well, Mr Collins," he said with a curt laugh as both men rose. "I know why you are here, but cannot fathom the reason for your coming at such an unearthly hour—let alone Mr Bingley!"

"Mr Bennet." Mr Bingley bowed quickly. "I have come to ask your permission to—"

"I do beg your forgiveness, Mr Bennet, for my speedy arrival," Mr Collins said, much to the shock of everyone in the room. "I have made it my habit to avoid magics of all sorts, you see, due to the fact that my most esteemed patroness, a Lady Catherine de Bourgh, completely discourages all such practices. But given that you yourself are—or rather were—a wizard of some repute, and I heard tell of some no small skill amongst your beauteous daughters, I took it upon myself to secure the most magical of conveyances and arrived with such speed that my head is nearly spinning and I really must—could not have possibly imagined the success with which my endeavour at speed was accomplished."

The room remained in shocked silence until Mary whispered to her father, "Was it by magic carpet, or perhaps winged horses?"

Without waiting for an introduction, Mr Collins turned to address her directly. "It was by enchanted post, and I would not have believed the efficacy with which—"

Mr Bennet interrupted forcefully. "You will of course convey to me a full review of the magical transport by post after Mr Bingley has explained his own unaccountable presence here this morning." All eyes shifted to the forgotten Mr Bingley, who gave a nervous cough.

"Yes, well, that is…I came—and I do apologise for the early hour—I came to request your permission to add protective charms around your property, in light of the recent attack near York."

Mr Bennet looked surprised and bid everyone sit. "Of course, I will not stop you, Mr Bingley. But what causes Longbourn to be the recipient of such attention?"

Mr Bingley blushed, stammering, "It is a service I wish to offer all the houses in the neighbourhood. Having already administered the spells for Netherfield's tenants yesterday—why, yours was the first house on my mind. If I might begin as soon as possible, the day is short, and there are—other houses in the neighbourhood."

"An attack at York?" Mr Collins exclaimed. "Are we in danger here?"

"It seems that there is, in all truth, a wizard of ill repute who has taken to stealing other people's magic. The papers are calling him the Thief. He has not, so far as we have heard, attacked a full-fledged wizard as of yet—his targets seem to be those with little magical training—but this recent incident was swifter and more unexpected than the officials could have anticipated." Mr Bingley turned an expectant gaze to Mr Bennet.

"I am flattered, Mr Bingley, that you should choose to honour us as the first house after your own estate to receive such attention. Although I suspect," he said with a twinkle in his eye as Jane appeared at the doorway, "that this decision was not done without some sort of motive."

"None at all, I assure you," Mr Bingley stammered all the more.

It was at this moment that the rest of the household appeared in the parlour. Mrs Bennet was profoundly sorry that she had not been present to greet Mr Bingley herself, and hoped he would stay for breakfast tea. To her great consternation, he could not be persuaded to do so. After a few wistful glances in Jane's direction, and several apologies for the early hour, he took leave in order to go about his business.

"Well!" Mrs Bennet exclaimed, sitting into her chair with a sigh. "I was so certain that he had come to propose!"

"Mama!" Jane protested.

"Do not be so modest, my dear, Mr Bingley will surely—"

"Mama!" Elizabeth cried. "Have you been introduced to our cousin?"

Mrs Bennet looked startled, then turned to see Mr Collins standing by the window. "Oh Mr Collins! I did not see you there!"

The gentleman, who had been looking uncomfortable, smiled readily. Whatever misgivings he had entertained during his moments of neglect by Mrs Bennet were soon put to rest. Indeed, he monopolised the family's attention in its entirety for the next five hours. They all breakfasted; afterwards, Mr Collins was shown the house, the garden, and all the surrounding land save the forest (which he was told specifically to avoid at all costs). Even still, this amount of time was not nearly enough for Mr Collins to expound upon the suitableness of the estate, the munificence of his patroness, Lady Catherine de Bourgh, and the amiability of Mr and Mrs Bennet's five daughters in full. At long last, Mrs Bennet was required to interrupt him in order to ready herself for dinner. The rest of the family took this as a hint that they might do as they liked, and Mr Collins was left to his own devices.

❧

Mr Collins was not a sensible man, nor talented in any particular respect. A fortunate chance had recommended him to Lady

Catherine de Bourgh when the living of Hunsford was vacant, and the respect he felt for her high rank and his veneration for her as his patroness, mingling with a very good opinion of himself, of his authority as a clergyman, and his rights as a rector made him altogether a mixture of pride and obsequiousness, self-importance, and humility. He had also come to Longbourn with the intention of taking a wife from one of its daughters—a prospect which Mrs Bennet was anxious to secure.

It was evident to her that Jane was the obvious initial choice of Mr Collins; she was, after all, the first in beauty and talent. But it did not take long for Mrs Bennet to mention that she thought her eldest might soon became engaged. Mr Collins had only to change from Jane to Elizabeth, despite the fact that she was not magically talented—that was not of utmost importance to him in a wife, and Elizabeth, equally next to Jane in birth and beauty, succeeded her of course.

Mr Collins had not been long in the house—no more than three days—before Mr Bennet began to grow exceedingly tired of him. When his daughters resolved to walk out to their little village of Meryton, Mr Bennet was quick to request that Mr Collins accompany them. This suited the gentleman far better than it suited the ladies, since they universally abhorred Mr Collins's company; the two youngest girls were quick to run ahead and leave the weight of the conversation to the three older sisters. Still, Mr Collins was now assuredly and pointedly doting upon Elizabeth, who was required to take the brunt of his droning with no little forbearance.

It was exciting for all of the ladies, then, that upon their arrival in Meryton, another gentleman caught their attention entirely. The man in question was young, of a most gentleman-like appearance, walking with an officer (a Mr Denny of their prior acquaintance) on the other side of the way. Everyone was struck with his air and wondered who he was. It was fortunate for all that, by chance, he should prove to be a friend of Mr Denny's—who introduced them there on the street—and had just accepted a commission with the corps. Even Elizabeth, who often looked upon others with a critical eye, was drawn to his handsome features and pleasing, engaging manners. It was with astonishment that she noticed he—a Mr

Wickham—was not adorned with the frivolous spells and enchantments worn by so many of his rank in order to improve appearance or give an air of goodness. His manners and looks were his own, and they pleased her. The company was engaged for some minutes in conversation, when round the corner appeared Mr Bingley and Mr Darcy.

On distinguishing the ladies of the group, the two gentlemen came directly towards them, and began the usual civilities. Mr Bingley was the principal spokesman, and Jane the principal object. He was then, he said, on his way to Longbourn to enquire after her. Mr Darcy corroborated with a bow, and was beginning to determine not to fix his eyes on Elizabeth, when they were suddenly arrested by the sight of the stranger, and Elizabeth, happening to see the countenance of both as they looked at each other, was all astonishment at the effect of the meeting. Both changed colour, one looked white, the other red. Mr Wickham, after a few moments, touched his hat—a salutation which Mr Darcy just deigned to return. What could be the meaning of it? It was impossible to imagine; it was impossible not to long to know.

To her great surprise, Elizabeth's curiosity with regard to Mr Wickham was satisfied sooner than anticipated. They met again that same evening at the home of her aunt and uncle Philips, who were hosting a dinner party in Meryton. Mr Wickham approached the subject himself. He began by inquiring about Netherfield, and Mr Bingley—and then asked in a hesitant manner how long Mr Darcy had been staying there. He wondered if she had noticed the cold manner of their greeting, and if Elizabeth was much acquainted with the gentleman. Elizabeth assured Mr Wickham that she was as well acquainted with Mr Darcy as she ever wished to be. She, along with the rest of Hertfordshire, found him to be proud, and very disagreeable.

Mr Wickham sat thoughtfully for a moment. "I cannot say that I am sorry, although perhaps for his father's sake I might be. But I am surprised at his reception. Mr Darcy's reputation as a wizard of high quality most often precedes him."

"Mr Darcy is renowned for his abilities—although I must say, I have seen scant evidence to justify the rumours."

"Mr Darcy has been able to keep up that pretence—and his father did, in fact, deserve all of the credit that is due him."

"Mr Wickham," Elizabeth said, leaning forward. "Do not think me impertinent, but what is the nature of your connexion to that family?"

"My connexion is now no longer existent, but I was once a great favourite of the late Mr Darcy—his pupil, in fact, although but the son of his steward."

"A pupil of his father's! But then you must have great talent of your own! It is strange that—"

"No." He sighed. "What powers I possessed as a child seemed to seep away as I grew older. I have my suspicions as to the reason —but none that I would dare voice aloud. Even still, what I did retain was remarkably useful, and I should have had a career. But that was taken from me, prevented by—" He paused. "Miss Elizabeth, I fear I speak too much."

"No, Mr Wickham, have no fear of me. You need not speak if you do not wish it."

He looked over his shoulder into the crowded room and then, assured that no one was listening, began to speak in a voice just above a whisper. "George Darcy was the founder of a group known as the Wizarding Court. The society has been kept a secret for some years, although recently, word of its existence has spread. Perhaps even you—"

"Yes," Elizabeth said, her eyes wide. "I had heard mention of it, in connexion to the recent attacks."

"Of course, for its purpose is the protection of our country against evils. I was to be given a position in this society—it was the greatest desire of my heart—but George Darcy died before it could come to fruition, and his son has barred me from entry to the Court, in spite of the expressed wishes of his father."

Elizabeth sat in stunned silence for some moments. "I can hardly speak. I had suspected Mr Darcy of—I know not what, but not of this. How can you choose to live under such circumstances? Why not expose him?"

"You forget that the Wizarding Court does not exist officially, and the members have complete control over its government. They are independent, and now that Darcy has persuaded them to be set against me—no doubt because of my inferior rank and magical abilities—there is not a chance in the world that I might pursue such a career. I think—I know that Mr Darcy's dislike of me must have been founded upon jealousy. And yet, my respect for his father is such that—"

At the sight of her face, Mr Wickham smiled. "You must not look so downcast on my account. Can you not see that the work I will do here with the militia in some way fits with my ultimate wishes? That I can serve and protect my country well?"

"I could not bear it as you do, Mr Wickham," Elizabeth cried warmly. "It is a testimony to your character!"

Soon, their conversation was interrupted. Elizabeth was not the only lady present who admired Mr Wickham, and Lydia came over to persuade him to dance.

Elizabeth, her mind full of the evening's revelations, related them to Jane as soon as possible the next day.

Jane, in her goodness, would not allow either party to be in the wrong. "There must be some misunderstanding," she said. "No man of common humanity, no man who had any value for his character, could be capable of it. Can his most intimate friends be so excessively deceived in him? Oh, no!"

"I can much more easily believe Mr Bingley's being imposed upon than that Mr Wickham should invent such a history of himself as he gave me; names, facts, everything mentioned without ceremony. If it be not so, let Mr Darcy contradict it. Besides, there was truth in his looks."

"You say there was truth, but could it be possible?"

Elizabeth laughed. "Jane! For you to even suggest that I am under some kind of bewitchment! No, and therein lies the truth: Mr Wickham did not use enchantments to persuade me, for there was no need of them."

Jane was silent in contemplation. "It is difficult indeed—it is distressing. One does not know what to think."

"I beg your pardon. One knows exactly what to think."

FIRE WATER, WIND, AND EARTH

As October came to a close and the air became chilly, the gossip surrounding the ball to be hosted at Netherfield grew increasingly steady. Indeed, it overtook almost every other subject. There were those who were convinced Mr Bingley would be inviting his illustrious friends from higher wizarding circles to attend (although this was, of course, preposterous). Others were concerned that he might welcome non-human guests, and whether or not they would be obligated to dance with them (whomever they were). To Mrs Bennet, however, magical subjects were nothing to the compliment the ball meant to her Jane, and the hope that soon after they might be preparing for another kind of celebration at Netherfield.

Jane bore all of this with equanimity, some might even say indifference. But Elizabeth saw in her eyes a joy that had not been there before, a certain softness whenever his name was mentioned. She did not like the talk or the prodding of her mother, but now she did not protest when Elizabeth teased her. For her part, Elizabeth loved the company and liveliness that came along with a ball, but this one would hold particular pleasure for her—the first being the prospect of seeing Jane even more happy, and the second, dancing with Mr Wickham. Her enjoyment would have been guaranteed, were it not for three things: the irksome and now pointed attentions of Mr Collins, her father's poor spirits, and the presence of Mr Darcy.

There was nothing to be done about Mr Collins. Her mother was determined he should be thrown in Elizabeth's company, and she could do nothing but bear his presence for as long as possible. As to her father, his company had been elusive. On three occasions, Elizabeth had broached the subject of the attacks, only to be laughed away by Mr Bennet. The attacks, he said, had nothing to do with them, or anyone of such inconsequential status in the magical realm. Elizabeth was not satisfied but could do nothing more. She attempted to put the subject out of her mind until her aunt and uncle came during the winter and could provide her with more information. It was fortunate for everyone that no new attacks had occurred since the end of September, and so a sense of security had returned to the neighbourhood.

The problem of Mr Darcy, however, grew with each passing week. They had not spoken since their confrontation in the forest, but Elizabeth saw him often on her walks. He was there at least three times a week, pacing the length of a field on the outskirts of Netherfield, close to where they had met before. He never again strayed onto Longbourn's grounds, and she did not think he saw her walking through the trees. She wondered what he did, and why he was so often there. At times, she could sense a tingling about the wood, a magical rippling through the air. She could not place its direction, nor its purpose, and could not help thinking it had something to do with his presence in the field.

If it were not for the frequent company of the officers at Longbourn, Elizabeth would have felt herself to be too downcast. As it was, the young men provided lively conversation and a distraction from their everyday concerns. Elizabeth could almost forget weightier issues, her only cause for worry what she should wear to the Netherfield ball and how to contain the overly flirtatious nature of her two youngest sisters.

As is often the case, these weightier concerns refused to be ignored for long. The issue of Mr Darcy was brought forth again one afternoon when the officers were taking tea at Longbourn. Mr Wickham was in attendance, and by an unfortunate stroke of luck, forced to spend nearly half an hour in Mr Collins's company. It was also unfortunate for Mr Collins, for neither gentleman was fond of the other (something to do with each feeling the other spent too much time in a certain lady's company), but being Mr Collins, he could not prevent himself from explaining to Mr Wickham with intimate detail the magnificence of his patroness, Lady Catherine de Bourgh.

Mr Wickham came away from the conversation greatly amused. While his opinion of Mr Collins had not been improved, he had taken the time to listen and ask a few questions of his own. Elizabeth noted their conversation with curiosity and made a point to speak of it at the first opportunity afforded.

"You have taken a great interest in Mr Collins's patroness and her fireplace at Rosings, Mr Wickham?" she asked with a twinkle in her eye.

Mr Wickham turned his head to the side thoughtfully. "Yes, indeed. I have been connected with that family before. Well, not actually connected, only through the Darcys. Hearing news of Lady Catherine is almost like hearing news of that family."

Elizabeth had not expected such an answer. "I do not understand you, Mr Wickham! In what way could Mr Darcy be connected with Lady Catherine de Bourgh?"

Mr Wickham looked at her with mock seriousness. "She is his aunt, Miss Elizabeth. It has been speculated that he shall marry her daughter, Anne de Bourgh, thereby joining their two great estates."

"'Tis an interesting coincidence." Elizabeth laughed. "One I think Mr Collins unaware of, or he would have been much more anxious to become acquainted with Mr Darcy!"

"You laugh, Miss Elizabeth, but perhaps you should not. Mr Darcy's connexion to that family is a significant one on several levels. I suppose you have heard of the Necromancer?"

Elizabeth's eyes widened, and her laughter ceased at once. "But he is dead, Mr Wickham, defeated long ago. The recent attacks—"

"The recent attacks have been strangely reminiscent of the Necromancer's tactics, who was famed for stealing wizards' magic.

This Thief—or Thieving Necromancer—has not been as destructive...there have been no deaths, and the victims are hardly persons of repute. Yes, the connexion of the two names is deliberate on the part of the newspapers, for there has been speculation that this Thief may be the same individual."

Elizabeth shook her head. "It cannot be possible."

"Many things are possible, for many things have been attempted in the past." Mr Wickham took a deep breath. "What is not commonly known is that the Necromancer's true identity was discovered, but kept secret in order to protect the family—his family. The Necromancer was none other than Lady Catherine's husband, Lewis de Bourgh."

"Mr Darcy's uncle!" Elizabeth cried.

Mr Wickham placed a hand on her arm. "I beg you would not be so alarmed! I had no intention of causing such distress."

Elizabeth's face was flushed. "Oh, no, indeed. The Necromancer was only the most powerful dark wizard of his generation!"

"And defeated by a member of the Wizarding Court known as the Jester, also a fact that is not commonly known. You see the delicate position in which this places Darcy, and his aunt, and the entire court. It is understandable that the Necromancer's identity should be hushed up, for the sake of those connected."

"I can see that Mr Darcy would not desire such a connexion to be well known!"

"He is very careful how he lives since that incident—which happened when we were very young—and more recently, the suspicious nature of his father's death. Mr Darcy is very guarded, especially with regards to his sister."

"Miss Darcy! I have heard mention of her, perhaps, from Miss Bingley. She will be sorely disappointed to discover his betrothal to Lady Catherine's daughter. Is she very like him?"

"The sister?"

"Yes."

"Very like. It is a shame, for she was once a pleasing child. But she has grown very proud—accomplished, of course—but too much like her brother. The secrets surrounding that family, and the pride with which they keep them—I could not even begin to describe, Miss Elizabeth. I have frightened you enough for one evening."

Try as she might, Elizabeth could pry no further information from Mr Wickham. He was determined not to remain so solemn and expressed concern for Elizabeth's nerves.

Unfortunately, her spirits had been shattered for the evening. After exchanging a few more pleasantries, she found she could not bear to remain in the company of others for much longer.

~

"How long have you known of the connexion between Mr Collins's patroness and the Necromancer?" Elizabeth stood with her back against the library door, her father looking up from his desk in alarm.

"Sit," he said with a motion of his hand, "and please rephrase the question."

It was late in the evening, the rest of the house preparing for bed. Elizabeth moved to a chair across from him, leaning her elbows against piles of paper and books to look into his eyes. "You did know of it. And yet you are not concerned for our safety? How could you not tell me!"

"I did not think it to be of any importance. The Necromancer has been dead these three and twenty years! His widow was cleared of any blame for his actions—indeed, believed to be totally ignorant of them—as was the entire family, immediate and extended."

"But the rumours of the recent—"

"The Necromancer is dead, Lizzy. There is not a chance of his having returned. That is merely the sort of rubbish used to sell the papers."

Elizabeth leaned back in her chair. "And what of Mr Darcy's connexion to it? He is Lady Catherine's nephew."

Mr Bennet's eyebrows rose. "You think so meanly of the man as to suspect him of involvement with a dark wizard at the age of six or seven!"

"I have reason for concern—"

"Whatever Mr Darcy's sins, involvement in that case was not one of them. Might I enquire as to the source of your information?"

Elizabeth related much of what Mr Wickham had told her.

Mr Bennet listened in silence, thoughtfully lighting his pipe. "Mr Wickham's tale does not suggest to me an evil tendency in Mr Darcy's character, but rather a conceited one. Do not stretch his misdeeds to such lengths, child."

Elizabeth sighed. "You are more concerned than you will admit, Papa. I have attempted to speak with you before. You do not seem yourself. Will you not confide in me?"

He took a few puffs of his pipe, watching as the smoke floated hazily above his head. "I confide what is necessary, Lizzy. No more, no less."

"I am not a child!" Her eyes flared. "You expect to keep me here and to do nothing, when you know that soon—"

"Soon you will go to London to be with your aunt and uncle, joining in their ideas of saving the world? Is that your plan? As if there are not enough people attempting to do so. Why do you think the militia have been quartered at Meryton? Men are being positioned across the country to protect our citizens and our homes."

Elizabeth snorted. "The militia have certainly proven to be most effective against attacks in the North!"

"Well," Mr Bennet countered, "there have not been any attacks since the last outside York." His tone turned more serious. "If there is ever a time when I fear you, or any of your sisters, or your mother, to be in true danger, I will not hesitate to confide in you. Do you doubt me so much?"

She took his hand to reassure him, although they both knew she was disappointed. "I understand, Papa."

"You will try to understand, in any case." He chuckled. "I am sorry for the smoke."

She answered with a kiss on his cheek and, leaving him alone, climbed the stairs to prepare for bed.

～

That night, Elizabeth slept fitfully. It was in the dark hours after midnight when she finally arose to stand by the window, her shawl wrapped snug about her shoulders. She stood for some time, tracing pictures in the frost that collected on the cold glass and staring resolutely out into the darkness of the forest.

The flash startled her. She thought it to be lightning at first, until it repeated itself three more times, changing colours from white, to yellow, to red. With horror, she realised the flashes were growing brighter and flew to her father's bedchamber, flinging open the door. Mr Bennet was not to be found.

She hastened to his study and found him staring out of the window, overlooking the forest. "Papa," she cried, breathless. "What can it mean?"

He turned when she moved to stand at the window next to him. He did not seem surprised to see her, and not alarmed in the least by the spectacular show of lights coming from the forest.

"The flashes? Do they frighten you?"

Elizabeth threw him a withering look. "Is it an attack?"

"No, indeed. An attack would not be in that sort of colour array."

"They are coming from the direction of the forest, but I have a suspicion," she said, realisation dawning across her face, "that they actually come from the fields just beyond—on Netherfield's estate."

Mr Bennet chuckled. "You walk there often, I think."

"Not in the fields—but Mr Darcy does."

"It is Mr Darcy. He has been practising there for some nights. Would you like to walk with me to observe him?"

Elizabeth looked startled. "Practising?"

"You did not think Mr Darcy so capable a wizard that he would not need to practise?"

"I did not think him a capable wizard at all."

Mr Bennet moved towards the door. "You will need a warmer coat, Lizzy, and shoes," he said, donning his nightcap. "We will not take a light so as to remain undetected. Under ordinary circumstances, Mr Darcy might be aware of our presence—but since you will be with me, we might observe him undetected."

Elizabeth crept up to her room, wrapping herself in a long cloak and pulling her shawl over her head. Her father waited for her in the garden, where they set off into the darkness towards the flashes of light. As they drew nearer, Mr Bennet slowed, at last halting some twenty yards from where Mr Darcy stood. They remained concealed in the thickness of the forest, but Elizabeth could almost see the concentration of Mr Darcy's face as he held something bright in his hands. The light converged and moved as if he held a rebellious ball of blue fire.

Suddenly the fire burst forth in streams of hot blue light, illuminating the entire forest and reaching some one hundred feet in the air before Mr Darcy pulled it back into his hand and the light disappeared altogether. In the darkness, it took several minutes before Elizabeth's eyes could trace his shape, pacing in a circle about the field as she so often saw him do in the mornings.

Mr Bennet shivered next to her, as if from the cold. She saw something white beneath Darcy's feet spreading over the entire field. Elizabeth was mystified at first, until a cloud formed above Mr Darcy's head and white snowflakes rained down upon him. He worked with the snow and ice for nearly twenty minutes before it too seemed to melt back into his person, the field as it had been before. This enchantment gave way to another, with rocks and stones and the bending of trees, and then yet another, involving the swirling and howling of the wind.

Elizabeth was amazed, and afraid. She had been taught the principles and theories of magic by her father since infancy. The mastery of the four elements—fire, water, wind, and earth—was the greatest accomplishment a wizard could ever hope for. Most became masters of one, perhaps two. But to master all four…it was necessary for the enchanter to wield a great deal of power.

Mr Bennet startled her out of her thoughts when he moved to stand behind her. Elizabeth's gaze returned to the field, now dark and silent as if nothing had ever happened. Mr Darcy stood motionless in the field, barely distinguishable from the black of the night.

"Who's there?" he called, his voice reverberating through the trees. It was not a question, but rather an enchanted command. Elizabeth knew that if not for her ability to disenchant the spell as it reverberated towards them, her father would have been compelled to reveal himself, and her, in the process.

As it was, Mr Darcy received no answer. He stood watching the forest for another ten minutes, and then he was gone.

Mr Bennet let out a sigh. "We should return, Lizzy," he said. The sky was slowly beginning to transform from inky purple to grey.

They walked back to Longbourn in silence, where the household remained asleep. Neither father nor daughter returned to their beds, but instead sat across from each other in the library. It was some time before either spoke. Mr Bennet lit a fire, and Elizabeth busied herself with making some tea.

At last, Mr Bennet said, "He has been there almost every night for some three weeks."

"You knew of this!" Elizabeth cried in shock, almost spilling her tea.

Mr Bennet nodded, waving his hand dismissively. "Of course I knew. I knew Mr Darcy walked the fields and made pretty pictures with lights. I did not know the extent of his experimentation—or skill—until tonight. I could not approach so close without the protection you provided."

"Protection? Because I am not magical?"

"And because you are impervious to it, yes."

"Papa—the elements."

"Yes." Mr Bennet sighed again. "Do not take it too far, Lizzy—but I confess I fear it. His father was a marvellous wizard, excellent in offence, a master with fire and water. Not so good in defence, but we all have our downfalls. Oddly enough his defence papers were the only ones ever published—"

"Papa, we are concerned with the son, not the father. You fear him? Then you suspect him, as I—"

"I do not suspect him of anything, other than his powerful capabilities. Remember, his performance under ideal circumstances—under no duress, near a magical forest, without any hindrances—is by no means the same way he might perform under stress." Mr Bennet sipped his tea. "I fear him, because of the power he possesses, and because of what he might be. Time will tell, Lizzy. You must not assume too much."

Elizabeth stared into the fire. She did not agree, but she would not argue at this point. Finishing her tea, she slipped back to her room for a few hours of restless sleep.

The next morning, she rose only a little later than usual, and set out for the forest. She waited in the field for an hour, but Mr Darcy did not come. Every morning for the next week she waited—and still he did not come.

In Which There Is Dancing

TWO MEN STOOD ON A HILL OVERLOOKING DARK, MISTY FIELDS. THE night was still; the air cold. Both figures were of about the same height, one leaning heavily on his left leg and the other holding his arm against his chest.

With a glance at his companion's leg, he said, "I am sorry, I should have been more help."

"Do not think on it," was the curt reply.

"I am older, and should take responsibility."

"As you often do when you remember not to lose your head, Fortinbras."

He laughed. "Do you persist in keeping to that name?"

The other raised his eyebrows. "Have you forgotten so quickly who was here not long ago? And that nothing has been achieved, except now both of us will be useless for some time."

"If you insist on calling me by that name, I shall call you by yours," the one called Fortinbras replied, laughing again.

"I beg you would not."

"The policy remains that members must always be named—not name themselves. Alas, since it is my fault we are in this predicament, I will refrain from tormenting you. Pendragon it is, although officially you remain the—"

The rest of Fortinbras' speech was prevented by a sharp thrust to the diaphragm. "It is fortunate that whoever invented that policy remained anonymous," Pendragon growled. He tested the weight on his right foot with a gasp. "That will not do."

"Useless indeed," Fortinbras scoffed, rubbing his side with his good arm. "Why haven't we found a healer to add to our midst, eh?"

"Difficult to find," Pendragon replied, gritting his teeth as he carefully lowered himself to the ground. "There is not much time remaining, and much more to discuss."

"To discuss? Our next meeting should clarify how we might go forward from this point—"

"Do you think I wish to speak of nothing else with you?"

Fortinbras chuckled as he sat down next to him. "Are you seeking advice?"

"No." He paused. "Yes. Tree is giving a ball."

"And this alarms you because…you cannot tolerate dancing? At least now you may have an excuse not to."

Pendragon sighed. "It is not the ball; rather, the ball is the exact sort of nonsense that I had hoped to avoid. I am beginning to think it was a mistake."

"What was a mistake?"

"Being where we are."

"Since I do not know where you are, I cannot very well give you sound advice," Fortinbras replied.

"Tree is much too besotted with the locals," Pendragon said. Shifting his injured leg, he constructed a log through enchantment and propped his leg up against it.

"Clever, my Pendragon, I should have thought of that sooner," Fortinbras said. In an instant, his arm was secured in a sling. "To return to the task at hand, when have you ever known Tree not to be besotted?"

"Never, but he had been improving. He understands the risks. Attachments cannot be risked, at any cost. It is difficult enough with—" Here, he paused. For a moment, both were lost in their own recollections. "Imagine how it would be with a wife."

"There are those among our number who are married."

"Precisely my point."

Fortinbras sighed. "I take it that Tree is in love with one of the locals, not several."

"At least the ball is good for something—I will be able to assess his true feelings."

"Of course, you are above such things as enchanting him to extract the answer."

Pendragon straightened. "You should not even suggest it, Fortinbras," he said with some annoyance, but they understood each other well and neither took offence, remaining in amicable silence for some time.

"Dawn is nearing. Time is wasted, and yet you make no move to return. There is something else gnawing on your mind," Fortinbras said.

"Wickham is there."

Fortinbras started. "And you have not moved to a new location?"

"There is no danger from him, other than perhaps poisoning the opinions of the townspeople—and I care little of what they think. In truth, that is not what I was thinking of."

Fortinbras looked expectant.

"No, no—" Pendragon shook his head. "It is of no consequence. That is, I will think more on it; discover more—discover her trustworthiness, and then I will tell you."

"Her?"

"I did not mention anyone!"

"You mentioned someone!" Fortinbras said. "So concerned over Tree, when you yourself—"

"Do not be ridiculous!" Pendragon stood, hobbling as he tested his injured leg. "It is nothing of that sort. It could not be. I was seen practising—by someone."

"You are alarming me," Fortinbras said.

Pendragon walked slowly into the mist, towards the bright streaks of sunrise. He winced as he turned, his hand on the wound.

"We will speak of it at the next appointed time."

"I am sorry, again, for your injury. It was stupid of me," Fort-inbras cried, just before they were enveloped by mist and vanished.

⁓

In spite of great hopes for the reverse, the morning of Mr Bingley's ball was cast in gloom. There had been another attack, this time near London. Many people felt it had been done purposefully to ruin their good cheer for the evening.

Mrs Bennet felt the loss of her spirits acutely. "There will be no dancing or singing this evening. Who would want to dance after such a fright!"

"I shall dance in any case, Mama!" Lydia declared. "I do not care how frightened anyone else is."

"And so shall I," Kitty echoed, although with a slight waver in her voice.

"The officers will all be there, I am certain they would protect us in any case." Lydia laughed. "I should think it would be marvel-lous to see them do battle!"

"I should imagine not," Elizabeth said, narrowing her eyes as she watched Lydia. "But I agree that Netherfield is perhaps a safer place than many. You need not fear, Mama, the last thing the Thief wants is to enter a place where he might be caught."

Mrs Bennet propped herself up from her reclined position on the couch. "Perhaps you are right." She sighed. "I had so wished tonight to be a compliment to my Jane!"

"Everything is a compliment to Jane," Elizabeth said, her face softening into a smile, and no one would accept Jane's humble protests to the contrary.

By evening, the gloom of the morning was almost forgotten with all of the pinching and pulling and tying that goes into dressing for a ball. Kitty and Lydia adorned themselves with a large number of creative enchantments—all of which Elizabeth dismantled amidst much protesting. If any depressed spirits remained as they finally rode in the carriage, they were banished at the sight of Netherfield lit up with a thousand lights, and Bingley's smiling face to greet them.

Netherfield seemed to shimmer in the glow of laughter and music. Mrs Bennet could not have been more gratified when their host could hardly keep his eyes away from the vision of Jane's loveliness. Here everything was as it should be, and troubles vanished as if by magic. Caroline greeted Elizabeth most cordially, with almost no condescension, and Mr Collins was preoccupied with complimenting Mr and Mrs Hurst on the delightful display for the evening. Elizabeth at first wondered whether Mr Bingley had wrapped the place in some sort of happiness spell—but she could detect none.

She looked for Mr Darcy with apprehension and breathed a sigh of relief when she did not find him. She wondered at his absence, but knowing he felt so much above his company, did not allow it to surprise her. She had counted on Mr Wickham's presence, however —and was very disappointed when she could not locate him. She had dressed with great care that evening, and prepared in the highest spirits for the conquest of all that remained unsubdued of his heart, trusting that it was not more than might be won in the course of the evening. She wondered if his absence had been caused by Mr Darcy. While this theory proved not completely true, Mr Wickham's absence from the evening's festivities was confirmed by his friend, Mr Denny.

"Mr Wickham has been called away to town on business," Mr Denny said with a knowing look. "I do not imagine his business would have called him away just now, if he had not wished to avoid a certain gentleman."

Such reports distressed Elizabeth for a time; but she was not a creature formed for ill-humour, and after relating all of her trouble to Charlotte Lucas, whom she had not seen for a week, felt herself able to laugh again.

"There is my cousin, Mr Collins," she said mischievously. "I have been so unfortunate as to be claimed by him for the first two dances."

Charlotte turned to see him speaking again with Mr Bingley. "He interrupts Jane's conversation," she observed with a slight smile, and Elizabeth laughed.

"I am sure he is unconscious of it!"

"To return to the other matter—" Charlotte said.

"You would return me to my ill humour, Charlotte!" Elizabeth protested. "You must understand my grievances—it is a comfort, at least, that Mr Darcy is not here to triumph over them."

"Have you spoken to him of Mr Wickham?"

"No, indeed, why should I?"

Charlotte pursed her lips and would have continued speaking, but Elizabeth was called away to dance the first set with her cousin. These two dances brought a renewal of her distress; they were dances of mortification. Mr Collins was not a good dancer. He was awkward, more often apologising than attending to the music, and moving in the wrong direction. The moment of her release from him was ecstasy. Elizabeth danced with another officer and was gratified to be able to talk of Mr Wickham, discovering that he was universally liked.

"You spoke too soon, Lizzy," Charlotte whispered when Elizabeth returned.

"Of what?"

"Of Mr Darcy. He is not absent, he is just over there," Charlotte said, pointing.

Elizabeth turned in dismay to discover that Mr Darcy was indeed standing by the wall close to them. Their eyes met for a moment before Elizabeth turned back to Charlotte in the hopes of resuming their conversation, but it was not to be.

Mr Darcy closed the distance between them and bowed. Elizabeth thought his grave expression better suited for a funeral than a ball. "Would you do me the honour of dancing the next with me, Miss Elizabeth?"

Elizabeth was so astonished that she could think of nothing to do but accept. As he walked away, she was left to fret over her own want of presence of mind; Charlotte tried to console her.

"I daresay you will find him very agreeable."

"Heaven forbid! That would be the greatest misfortune of all! To find a man agreeable whom one is determined to hate! Do not wish me such an evil."

The musicians struck up again and the two women saw Mr

Darcy approaching to claim his dance. Charlotte warned Elizabeth not to throw away her chances with a man of such consequence for one such as Mr Wickham.

Elizabeth pretended not to hear. She had no intention of striking up any sort of conversation, she could not think of where to begin. They danced in oppressive silence for some minutes, until she noticed something peculiar.

"Mr Darcy, are you quite well?"

He looked over at her, his eyes bright, and nearly stumbled at the turn. "I am well, Miss Elizabeth."

She looked at him crossly. "You are limping, Mr Darcy."

"It is nothing."

Elizabeth frowned, turning her mind towards the ever-present magic about him in an attempt to make its various aspects distinguishable while keeping in step with the movements.

"Indeed, Mr Darcy, have you been injured? Are you under some sort of enchantment? There is a magic about you that is unfamiliar to me."

He nearly stumbled again, although with more grace than her first partner had. "I can assure you that it is nothing."

"I can assure you that it is not!" Elizabeth said when the opportunity afforded itself.

"I have been practising. I made a…blunder and injured my leg." They stepped forward, joining hands briefly.

"You consider what you have been doing in the fields to be practising?" she said in a low voice that others could not hear.

"What else could it be? I am a determined scholar," he said with the ghost of a smile.

"You practise to further your study?" she said with scepticism.

"Naturally."

"I do not believe you."

His eyes flashed. "You accuse me of not telling the truth?"

"I know that you are not telling the truth. There are enchantments about you associated with concealment—whether performed by yourself, or someone else—and I would hope you would not allow yourself to be held under another's enchantment."

Mr Darcy actually did smile at this. "I am not at liberty to speak of the circumstances surrounding my injury."

Elizabeth seethed in silence until Mr Darcy addressed her again. "Are there other enchantments that you detect?"

Elizabeth's curiosity was pricked at this. "All the sorts you usually employ for wear. I have noticed you do not use the one for your hair—but the one for your balance seems to be triple-fold."

He brushed a hand through his hair. "I have not been myself today."

"There is something," she said softly, deep in concentration as they moved closer together. "I do not recognise what it is for, although…is it for paralysation? And something else, entirely unpleasant—"

"Pain?" Mr Darcy said abruptly as they moved away.

"Yes." She looked into his eyes, startled. They seemed bright not from enjoyment, but almost as if from fever.

His face remained impassive. He seemed desirous of changing the subject and asked whether or not she and her sisters often walked to Meryton. She answered in the affirmative and, unable to resist the temptation, added, "When you met us there the other day, we had just been forming a new acquaintance."

Mr Darcy's expression darkened at this. "Mr Wickham is blessed with such happy manners as may ensure his making friends —although whether he may be equally capable of retaining them is less certain."

"He has been unfortunate enough to have lost your friendship, Mr Darcy," she replied curtly, her cheeks flushed. "Is there no hope of his regaining it?"

"None."

"Your resentment, once created, is then insurmountable. It must follow that you are very careful of allowing your resentment to be created?"

"I am," said he, with a firm voice.

"And never allow yourself to be blinded by prejudice?"

"I hope not." He paused. "It is imperative that I do not."

Elizabeth, feeling herself become more frustrated by the minute, was anxious for the dance to be finished. "I can make no sense of your actions."

Mr Darcy's normal impassiveness was replaced with a look of genuine surprise. "What actions do you speak of?"

"I hear such different accounts of you, as puzzle me exceedingly."

"And do you believe everything you hear, Miss Bennet?"

She bristled at this. "I am not so foolish as to believe anything without sufficient proof—and you must understand that I am not fooled by silly enchantments and tricks which give the image of truth, but are in fact the opposite. It is astonishing that you would suggest such a thing, when I know you are attempting to conceal something from me by means of enchantment."

As the musicians rang out their last chords, she started to withhold her hand, but Mr Darcy did not release it. "The most talented of liars have no need of enchantments—they lie without the aid of any magic, and are therefore the most dangerous."

They stood awkwardly, both tense with anger. Mr Darcy at last offered her his arm, and they walked away from the newly formed dance line.

"Have you spoken to your father—did you remember?" Mr Darcy asked, in almost a whisper.

Elizabeth was confused by his question. "I do not think…"

"You did not remember."

Elizabeth searched her mind, trying to bring forth details from one of their earlier encounters. "I cannot recall anything of importance, Mr Darcy," she said at length.

"I see," Mr Darcy said stiffly. He bowed, leaving her feeling unaccountably disappointed.

THE OTHER COURT

"THAT WAS DISASTROUS." CAROLINE SIGHED, LOWERING HERSELF onto a chair with as much elegance as she could muster.

"Caroline," Bingley said groggily, lifting his head up from where it rested on the desk. "Must we talk of this now?"

"Can you think of a better opportunity?"

"I had a marvellous time this evening," he said with some clarity, ignoring the inelegant snort issued in reply.

"Mr Darcy will agree with me, will you not"—she nodded in his direction—"when I say that perhaps the only other person who enjoyed the ball as much as you did was Mrs Bennet. The behaviour of their family this evening—I cannot even begin!"

"The pretentiousness of their cousin!" Louisa nodded.

"The behaviour of the younger sisters! That unfortunate officer —what a stroke of luck that you should catch the charm, Mr Darcy, before it wrought serious damage!"

Darcy, who sat in a corner by the fire, did not reply.

"Such charms are common enough in the drawing rooms of London," Bingley sputtered. "It was ridiculous that an officer, who has received ample training, should find himself in such a position in the first place."

"I almost pitied poor Miss Mary Bennet," Louisa said with a sniff. "She sang so very ill. But to have been interrupted by her father!"

Caroline laughed. "I am sorry for Jane—but Charles, I am afraid—"

"That is enough, Caroline. Enough for one evening," Bingley said, rising from his seat.

Caroline sighed again as he stalked out of the room. "You do see our way of it, Mr Darcy?"

Darcy sat motionless for some time, before leaning forward. "I will follow him shortly after his departure." He sighed. "I will speak to him upon this subject; have no doubt of that."

Caroline and Louisa smiled at each other in relief. "We will go with you," Caroline said. "And put this dreadful place behind us— no matter how sweet Miss Bennet's smiles, they are no great consolation!"

~

The days following the Netherfield ball did not improve for Elizabeth; if anything, they worsened. Mr Collins presented his proposal of marriage to her and was promptly rejected. This was a great disappointment not only to him, but also to Mrs Bennet. She had set her hopes upon Elizabeth's joyful acceptance of Mr Collins's hand —thereby ensuring the security of herself, her sisters, and her mother for the rest of their lives. Her agitation was expressed most pointedly towards Elizabeth, who had never been a favourite to begin with. Elizabeth was supported in her decision by her father, which did assure her she acted rightly, but did not lessen the difficulty of her mother's slights and aggravations.

Elizabeth was given an opportunity to improve her tired spirits when reunited with Mr Wickham for a short time. They laughed together, and he was given the opportunity to apologise for his absence from the Netherfield ball.

"You understand," he said with a concerned smile. "I found, as the time drew near, that I had better not meet Darcy. To be in the same room, the same party with him for so many hours together, might be more than I could bear, and that scenes might arise unpleasant to more than myself."

"I do admire your forbearance," Elizabeth said. "But you must understand that your absence only added to my list of grievances."

"You refer to the shadows cast by the attack on the day before?"

"That and other events, yes." Elizabeth smiled ruefully when she thought of the humiliation caused by her family.

Mr Wickham sighed. "As to my forbearance, I can only credit it to love for the father, rather than any concern for his son."

Their conversation continued, but Elizabeth, for reasons she could not explain to herself, did not tell him of her encounters with Darcy in the forest, or of their dance. She could not bring herself to speak of it.

Shortly thereafter, news came that Caroline, along with the entire party at Netherfield, had followed their brother to town. They intended to remain there for the winter, with no intention of returning to Hertfordshire. The loss of both Mr Collins and Mr Bingley was almost too much for Mrs Bennet to bear, but most insulting of all was the astonishingly swift engagement of Mr Collins to none other than Charlotte Lucas.

The engagement brought great distress to Elizabeth, for very different reasons than her mother. She could not comprehend that Charlotte, one she had believed to think like her in most respects, would give herself to a man whom it was impossible to respect. Charlotte, for her part, required from Elizabeth an understanding that she was unwilling to give. Elizabeth congratulated her, but their friendship could no longer exist as it had before. Jane and Elizabeth spoke of it at length, the loss of one friendship drawing the two sisters closer together; but try as she might, Jane could not convince Elizabeth to believe that Charlotte would be happy in her choice.

For her part, Elizabeth urged Jane not to despair over Mr Bingley's departure—his regard had been clear, and Elizabeth was certain that it was only a matter of time before the young wizard returned. Jane was not so optimistic, inclined to doubt his affection. As time went by and he did not come, even Elizabeth's optimism was depressed. She remained in no doubt that Mr Bingley had loved her sister—but now felt that his feelings were too easily persuaded by the opinions of his sister, and that of his friend.

As much as possible, Elizabeth avoided thinking of Mr Darcy. For some days after the ball, she had struggled to remember what he had asked her about—to no avail. Since any remembrance of him now brought anger on behalf of Jane, she resolved to no longer think of him at all.

Her spirits, and those of the entire family, were lifted by the Christmas visit of Mrs Bennet's brother and his wife, Mr and Mrs Gardiner. Mr Gardiner was a sensible, gentleman-like man, greatly superior to his sister by nature as well as education. Mrs Gardiner, who was several years younger than Mrs Bennet and Mrs Philips, was an amiable, intelligent, elegant woman, and a great favourite with all her Longbourn nieces.

The majority of the family's troubles had already been related by letter to Mrs Gardiner through her two oldest nieces, with whom she was particularly close. It was with great interest that they listened in person to the strange goings-on in Hertfordshire, in particular the revelation of Mr Darcy's frequent practising—and Mr Wickham's information in relation to him.

"Mr Darcy is well-respected amongst the highest circles, as you well know," Mr Gardiner said. "But I had not heard of this black mark on his character. I was also unaware of the strength of his magical abilities." He sat by the fire in Mr Bennet's study, along with his wife, brother-in-law, Elizabeth, and Jane, while the rest of the household slept soundly. "It is a disappointment to me. I have been working towards a connexion between ourselves and the Wizarding Court for some time. It has been difficult—difficult to even discover whom to contact. I had known that the Court was comprised of only the gentry, but I had not thought the selection of its members to be controlled so arbitrarily."

"Mr Darcy is, after all, his father's son. Mr Wickham mentioned that George Darcy was the founder of said Court," Elizabeth said.

"It is careless of Mr Wickham to bandy about the names of its members," Mr Bennet said, smoke trailing above him as he smoked his pipe in the corner of the room. "No matter how justified his grievances."

Jane said, "I am certain Mr Wickham intends no harm."

"No, no one suspects him of that," Mrs Gardiner hastened to add. "He has been done an injustice—one that we would willingly remedy were he now free to work where he pleases. But the Wizarding Court is no laughing matter. Who do you think these recent attacks have been directed towards? Ordinary wizards are no match for this new Necromancer—and indeed, such a Thief is not searching for the ordinary talent, but the extraordinary."

"Or so they say," Mr Bennet mumbled, before clearing his throat. "Am I to understand that by 'ourselves,' Edward, you mean the society you have been forming?"

Elizabeth and Jane turned their faces to their uncle in eager interest. He beamed. "Yes. In fact, the group has been established with moderate success in London already. We call ourselves the Merchant's Court—inferior, perhaps, to the legacy of greater wizards, but a Court nonetheless."

"Inferior!" Elizabeth scoffed.

Mrs Gardiner smiled. "Your uncle speaks in jest, Lizzy. We may not be of noble birth, but the talents of our members are considerable. But we had hoped to work in conjunction with the Wizarding Court, as well as the government."

"As if there are not already enough people risking their lives for nothing!" Mr Bennet said, tossing his pipe aside with a clatter.

Mr Gardiner did not seem surprised. "As we have discussed, Thomas, we do not presume to interfere with what has already been established, but to help where there is a need. None of our work involves high danger at present. Our goals are to prevent and protect against magical crimes at the lower levels of society, as well as provide education and training to those who could not otherwise afford it. We are not capable of capturing a wizard such as the Thief —but we are capable of aiding those who can. Although now that we hear of such rumours..." He shrugged his shoulders in resignation.

The five of them continued to talk late into the night. Reluctantly, Mr Bennet agreed to allow Jane to remove with the

Gardiners to London for a time. The purpose of her visit was twofold: under the Gardiners' tutelage she would improve her skills (not, under any circumstances, involving herself in work that might place her in danger). The other purpose was of a more personal nature: she hoped to discover once and for all whether Mr Bingley still cared for her.

Elizabeth was impatient to join her sister in supporting the Merchant's Court, but her father was against it. Her skill was not an ordinary kind of magic, if it could be called that at all, and both he and the Gardiners were in agreement that for the time being, Elizabeth must bide her time and remain home.

The Gardiners remained at Longbourn only a week. Before their return to London, Mrs Gardiner—rendered suspicious by Elizabeth's warm commendation of him—was afforded the opportunity to observe Elizabeth with Mr Wickham. Without supposing them, from what she saw, to be very seriously in love, their preference for each other was plain enough to make her a little uneasy; and she resolved to speak to Elizabeth on the subject before she left Hertfordshire, and represent to her the imprudence of encouraging such an attachment.

"Mr Wickham is amiable—charming—but not of your station," Mrs Gardiner said. "I think you should be more guarded in your open delight of his attention, my dear."

Elizabeth laughed. "Is this because he is the son of a steward? Or perhaps because he does not employ many magics about his person, like so many other young men are wont to do?"

"Be serious, Lizzy. I do not mean that you must marry a man like Mr Collins to benefit your family, but a man like Mr Wickham is no—"

"I understand you." Elizabeth sighed, almost surprising herself by what she said next. "You may set your concerns aside. I find that he is the most agreeable man I have ever met. I will remember to be wise and ensure that he does not fall in love with me unless I could return the affection."

It was perhaps fortunate that Mrs Gardiner gave the hint, for it was not long afterwards that Mr Wickham's apparent partiality subsided, and he instead attached himself to a Miss Mary King—a young woman of reasonable magical talent who had recently come into possession of ten thousand pounds. Elizabeth was disappointed, but not crushed. She discovered that, while partial to him, she had never been in love. Her acceptance of his desire for financial independence with the help of a fortuitous match was perhaps more forgiving than she had felt towards her friend, Charlotte Lucas—although it would be many months before this inconsistency of feeling and judgment would be fully known to her.

The days at Longbourn grew long and dreary as winter awaited the spring. Affairs returned as they were before Bingley had come into Hertfordshire, and no new rumours of attacks or battles at the hands of the Thief were whispered about the countryside. Charlotte, before her marriage, had extended an invitation for Elizabeth to join her in March at her new home in Kent.

Elizabeth at first had no intention of accepting it, but found that as time went on—in part because of Jane's absence—she missed Charlotte's company acutely. She was curious to meet Lady Catherine de Bourgh, the wife of the long-dead Necromancer and aunt of Mr Darcy.

To Kent it was decided she would go, along with Sir William and Maria. Mr Bennet did not seem overly fond of the scheme, but Elizabeth attributed this to a reluctance to part with her company, rather than any danger that might await her at Rosings.

"Remember, Lizzy," he said in parting, "while Mr Darcy knows of your secret, I would beg you not to reveal it to any other person."

"I will not, Papa. I will be careful and must learn to be discreet as I go about in broader company; you can be assured of my caution. I should like to give you a full report of the goings-on at Rosings and the most illustrious Lady Catherine de Bourgh. If she is half as ridiculous as Mr Collins, you know I shall not want for amusement."

Elizabeth sighed. She looked at her father in earnest. "In truth, I do not know what to expect when I see Charlotte. We did not part on the friendly terms to which I was accustomed. How will she receive me? I have been so lonely, Papa. With Jane gone, I feel the loss of Charlotte's friendship keenly. I think…I know you oppose my desire for independence—but surely venturing forth to the confines of Kent and a parson's cottage will not be so much adventure? I admit to being curious about the widow of a Necromancer—but as she does not condone the use of magic, I see little reason for me to even discuss my lack of gifts in that area. There won't be any spells for me to dismantle!"

"You are right, I suppose," he said as she walked to the door. "Still, if anyone should ask whether or not your father performs magic—say that he does not."

Elizabeth nodded in assent, and Mr Bennet bestowed a rare kiss on her forehead.

~

After his departure from Hertfordshire, Darcy threw himself into work. What was most difficult was maintaining the appearance of the frivolous, leisurely life of a gentleman, when almost every other day he was off to some new location for one project or another, formalising a method, or travelling across the country and back again.

He did not often think of her. Miss Elizabeth Bennet had been nothing more than an infatuation—less with her actual person than with her exceptional gift. He and Bingley rarely spoke of their time in Hertfordshire now. When once they broached the subject, Darcy expressed his disapproval of the Bennets and pointed out that Miss Bennet had never seemed to return Bingley's affections—a verbalisation of what Bingley had feared in the first place. It was fortunate that the Bennets did not frequent town.

Therefore it came as a surprise when Caroline informed Darcy of Jane's visit in January. She had concealed it from Bingley and hoped Darcy would agree that she had taken the right course. Darcy could do nothing but agree. Bingley was almost out of danger—the sight of Miss Bennet's lovely smiles would only make him wish for what might have been and cause him to lose sight of the path set before him.

Yet there were moments, most often while he practised, when Darcy could not seem to forget the way she had looked at him and the manner of their parting. Might it have been different if she had shown more interest in him than believing whatever Wickham had told her? Had he been too hasty in his dismissal of her? Had she even indicated that she believed Wickham? Was there a possibility of her being in any danger—a possibility of someone acquiring her gift? These were the questions which Darcy pondered most often when he was alone, as he wielded the bright blue fire in his hands.

He would remind himself of the position and circumstance of her family, and the impossibility of any connexion between them. It was better to never have begun, than to begin something that could never be...was it not? Such thoughts began to affect his concentration. Those who knew him attributed it to his injury, but in truth, his injury was nearly healed.

He would forget her. Even as the days and weeks slipped by, he thought of her less and less often. She had been nothing to him. Nothing at all.

Travelling at High Speeds

Elizabeth's earlier misgivings were laid to rest by the warm welcome she received from Charlotte upon their arrival at Hunsford parsonage. Marriage had not improved the manners of her husband, but Elizabeth had not expected as much.

Indeed, Mr Collins was more than civil, taking several minutes at least to enquire after her family. After this, he eagerly took them into the house where he impressed upon his guests the modest loveliness of the furniture and sturdy superiority of the parsonage walls.

Mr Collins did seem to direct his commentary towards Elizabeth, as if to make her regret what she had lost in refusing him. But though everything seemed neat and comfortable, she was not able to gratify him with any sigh of repentance, and rather looked with wonder that her friend could have so cheerful an air with such a companion.

Charlotte, while at times unable to hide a blush at some remark or another made by her husband, for the most part wisely did not hear Mr Collins's absurdities.

Their tour included a walk about the garden, where Mr Collins was often encouraged to work by his wife, and a view through an opening in the trees of Rosings itself. Mr Collins would have taken them round to see his two meadows, but as Elizabeth's and Maria's shoes were not fit for the remains of a white frost, they turned back to the house. Alone with Charlotte, when Mr Collins could be forgot, there was a great air of comfort throughout; and by Charlotte's evident enjoyment of it, Elizabeth supposed he must be often forgotten.

"I would offer you tea, Lizzy," Charlotte said with a rosy smile. "But as you could not appreciate it, I must make some in the ordinary way."

"Do not trouble yourself, Charlotte." Elizabeth smiled in return as she surveyed the room.

"Oh, it is no trouble; I must make up some for my husband in any case."

"Mr Collins will not drink your enchanted tea?" Elizabeth raised a brow.

"No, indeed, and Maria, you must listen carefully now too, for Mr Collins will have nothing of magic performed in his presence," Charlotte said as she busied herself with the kettle.

"He was not so in Hertfordshire," Elizabeth said in puzzlement as she moved to sit across from Charlotte.

"He is not when in company, but it is a principle he has adopted for the sake of his patroness."

Elizabeth laughed. "But of course, she does not approve of magic!"

"It is quite true. Lady Catherine de Bourgh insists that magic is never used in her home. I do not know the particulars, but I understand her husband died in an accident several years ago involving magic. His death has left her averse to enchantment of any kind."

"Even the building and grounds of an estate like Rosings are not kept up by use of magical aid?" Elizabeth said.

"None. I think there are few great houses in all of England like it," Charlotte replied, handing her a cup of ordinary tea.

"It will not be as tasty as mine." Maria giggled.

"I am quite fascinated by the idea of no enchantments," Elizabeth mused, hardly minding her cup. "It is rather extraordinary. With a nephew so deeply involved—and her husband!" Elizabeth paused to sip her tea and collect her thoughts.

"Lady Catherine considers herself anything but ordinary, Lizzy," Charlotte said with a smile. "She is a most attentive neighbour."

Shortly thereafter Mr Collins and Sir William returned to the house to take tea with the ladies. The remainder of the afternoon and evening was spent in leisurely conversation and the retelling of all Hertfordshire's news. Briefly, the subject touched upon the absence of attacks since the day before Mr Bingley's ball—but here Mr Collins turned the conversation, reminding everyone in the most serious of tones that Lady Catherine was not to be distressed by any talk of such sort. They might discuss it in moderation while in his house, but under no circumstances were they to allude to magic of any kind to his patroness, unless she brought it up particularly herself.

That evening, Elizabeth was grateful for the solitude of her room. Noticing that the blue curtains were pulled across a small window, she moved to open them. Elizabeth stood for some moments at first looking over the gardens, then surveying her small room. Rosings was barely visible through the trees, darkened by the long shadows. Elizabeth wondered what she would find within the Park and miles of green forest. She had grown accustomed to the magics alive within the woods at Longbourn—but she was now uncertain whether magic had been permitted to thrive in Rosings Park at all.

Her room was neat and comfortable, as was everything in the house. In spite of the fact that Mr Collins had reiterated his patroness's involvement in almost every detail of the parsonage, Elizabeth gave the credit for the pleasantness of the room to her friend—who else would have placed the fresh-cut flowers on the night stand, or the two small books so conveniently within reach? Elizabeth let out a sigh, drawing the curtains closed, and felt that she had been right in coming.

The following afternoon, Elizabeth ventured out for a walk in the meadows, circling round to the fences that surrounded Rosings' grounds. However tempted, she did not venture beyond the paling, and so was disappointed that she could not detect anything—magical or otherwise—about the place. She was just returning to the parsonage lane when a phaeton came round the bend at an exhilarating speed. She jumped to avoid a collision, but the vehicle halted with purposeful magic in front of Hunsford parsonage. Two women sat in the phaeton, straightening their bonnets. The younger of the two looked up and was alarmed to see Elizabeth standing against the hedgerows with her mouth agape.

She motioned to her companion, who looked up immediately. "Are you quite all right?" the older woman called out.

Elizabeth closed her mouth and stepped forward, her legs trembling. "Fine, thank you, if a bit terrified. I do not recall ever having seen a phaeton move so fast."

The older woman, her dress denoting a lower station than that of the younger woman, shifted uncomfortably. "You saw us driving quickly?"

"I—" Elizabeth paused. She realised that the phaeton had been under enchantment from the beginning, perhaps to conceal its actual speed, but she had no way of conveying her understanding without revealing too much.

The younger woman, who was slight and pale, turned to her companion and whispered something. Turning back to Elizabeth, she attempted a smile. "You will be so kind as to not mention this incident to Mr Collins, or any other person."

Elizabeth was taken aback by her haughty manner of address and turned her head to the side questioningly.

"You are his cousin, or his sister-in-law, are you not?" The young woman continued, "You must be his cousin, for you do not look at all like Mrs Collins. Will you not oblige me, then, in this one request? Mrs Jenkinson must have…miscalculated. Under ordinary circumstances, you would never have seen us moving at such a pace. We have not much time," she added with some urgency, glancing at the parsonage windows.

"I am not obliged to grant any requests when they are demanded in such a manner," Elizabeth replied with some laughter, attempting to conceal her vexation and curiosity. The young woman pinched her lips together, while the other clucked disapprovingly.

As the sound of Mr Collins's hurried footsteps approached, Elizabeth gave them a sly smile just before he reached the gate. "I will oblige you on this instance since I am, at least this time, unharmed."

The young woman's shoulders relaxed, and she turned her full attention to the parson. Breathless and flustered, Mr Collins was profoundly confused as to how Elizabeth had come to meet Miss de Bourgh, the young woman to whom the phaeton apparently belonged. Although she wished to return to the house, Elizabeth could not now avoid remaining for a proper introduction.

When Charlotte came out to join them, Elizabeth was certain they would remove indoors to get out of the wind, but Miss de Bourgh was not so courteous. They stood longer while Mr Collins gave his many respects to Miss de Bourgh and to her mother; his gratefulness could hardly be described in words when he learned that Miss de Bourgh had come to extend an invitation for the whole party to dine with them the next day.

Her message having been relayed, Miss de Bourgh uttered a clipped farewell and the phaeton lurched off with enormous speed. Elizabeth noted with amusement that Mr Collins continued to wave long after the vehicle was out of sight, realising that there had been nothing wrong with Mrs Jenkinson's spell at all, only that their concealment spells could have no effect on her.

Mr Collins's triumph as a consequence of this invitation was complete. The power of displaying the grandeur of his patroness to his wondering visitors, and of letting them see her civility towards himself and his wife, was exactly what he had wished for; that an opportunity of doing it should be given so soon, was such an instance of Lady Catherine's condescension as he knew not how to admire enough.

"What thought you of Miss Anne de Bourgh," Charlotte whispered as they walked into the house, Mr Collins in deep conversation with Sir William.

"Yes, Lizzy!" Maria said. "Oh, that I had gone out with you!"

"I liked her appearance—" Elizabeth said. "She looked sickly and cross. Yes, she will do for him very well. She will make him a very proper wife."

"Lizzy!" Charlotte caught her breath so as not to laugh. "Who do you speak of?"

"Why, Mr Darcy, of course!" Elizabeth cried, at which all three women could not prevent themselves from laughing. "Although I did think her abominably rude to keep you out of doors in such wind, Charlotte."

With a knowing glance, Charlotte hushed the women as her husband approached, but Elizabeth had a question to ask of Mr Collins.

"Does Miss de Bourgh ride out often?"

"I have known them to ride out as often as twice a week, Cousin Elizabeth," Mr Collins replied.

"It was a very fine phaeton—"

"Very fine, indeed!" echoed both Mr Collins and Sir William.

"—but with such a vehicle, do they not often ride at speeds which might be detrimental to Miss de Bourgh's health?" Elizabeth finished, raising her brow.

"Dearest cousin," cried Mr Collins. "Your concern is admirable, quite in its proper place! But I have never known them to travel at anything but the most respectable—indeed, very slow!—pace. Lady Catherine has said that the fresh air is beneficial to her daughter's lungs."

Elizabeth smiled, not noticing the puzzled look which Charlotte threw in her direction.

~

The next day proved bright and sunny—Mr Collins could not have chosen a more perfect day himself to dine at Rosings Park.

"Do not make yourself uneasy, dear cousin, about your apparel, or your lack of magical talent," he said as they readied to leave.

Elizabeth was amused. "Neither is ever a cause for unease, Mr Collins."

"I must remind you that Lady Catherine is an extremely magical person herself, but it is of the utmost importance that magic or enchantment never be mentioned in her presence."

Elizabeth tried not to laugh, assuring him with as much serious-ness as possible that it would be no obstacle for her.

"I have no small amount of knowledge in such areas myself," Mr Collins explained. "And Charlotte, of course, is also quite talented. Since you, Cousin Elizabeth, have not been blessed with such a gift, you have no cause for alarm. But, Maria, do remove any extraneous spells which you might have adorned for beauty's sake —Lady Catherine cannot abide magic of any sort."

Elizabeth's first full view of the house was what she had expected. It was a fine building, built in the modern style; Mr Collins made sure to point out the many windows which adorned it. She thought it fit any relative of Mr Darcy's perfectly—the sort of place she imagined him to feel most comfortable. Intrigued by Mr Collins's insistence that the estate was not run with magic, she directed her concentration to the detection of any sort of spell—and could discover none. While she had not doubted Charlotte's word, this remained something remarkable. Even Hertfordshire, in all its meagre talent, was saturated with enchantments of every kind. Eliz-abeth often found the number of spells being used by others exhausting to her sensibilities and had trained herself rigorously to ignore the constant bombardment to her senses. Here, it would be unnecessary to construct the barrier she usually employed to create a breathing space between herself and pulsing enchantments.

"I understand that you do not perform magic," Lady Catherine said to Elizabeth, causing the others to turn to her in shock. The question was a continuation of many such impertinent inquiries that Eliza-beth had been asked throughout the evening, but one that she had not expected due to Mr Collins's warnings.

"No," she replied.

"That is very strange, but not at all unfortunate." Lady Catherine nodded at her daughter Anne, who was sitting close to the fire with Mrs Jenkinson hovering close by. "My daughter and I are not bereft of talent ourselves, but we choose not to take advantage of it."

Elizabeth hesitated only a moment. "Miss de Bourgh never employs magic?"

Miss de Bourgh started, glancing at Elizabeth. Lady Catherine noted her daughter's expression and spoke on her behalf. "None of us employ magic, did I not tell you?" She paused. "Do any of the rest of your family perform?"

Elizabeth almost did not attend, busy thinking of this new revelation, but managed to reply, "Three of my sisters; my mother makes attempts. We are not considered to be greatly talented."

Sir William looked as though he wished to speak on what he considered to be the Bennets' great talent but was too much in awe of his hostess to do so.

Lady Catherine nodded. "Your parents rightly did not encourage such behaviours—they are quite dangerous."

Elizabeth forced a smile. "With the exception of my sister, whose particular talent falls along the lines of healing. I suspect there is little danger there."

Lady Catherine seemed unaccustomed to being contradicted, but that did not deter her from furthering her questions. "Your father does not perform magic."

"No."

"Yours is a complete lack of talent?"

"Yes."

"Of great interest, I am sure, to those who study such things," Lady Catherine replied. "But do not take it as a misfortune, particularly in this house, where it is not mentioned."

Elizabeth smiled again at this but made no reply, and so the conversation turned in another direction.

Fortinbras and Pendragon sat in a darkened library, illuminated only by the flickering of the fireplace.

"You are brooding," Fortinbras said, flicking a yellow burst of light in Pendragon's direction.

"Do not be so tiresome, Fortinbras." Pendragon sighed, not even bothering to remove the ball of light from where it now hovered above his head.

"What could she have written that put you in such a fright? We must go, there is no getting out of it—two weeks from now, and not a long stay. You will be able to move back and forth easily enough. And I shall too, if circumstances call for it."

Pendragon straightened from his lounging position in the chair, rubbing his neck thoughtfully. He looked up at Fortinbras with some trepidation. "What if I said that we should go now—early? Could you bear it?"

Fortinbras leaned back in mock horror. "You cannot mean voluntarily extending our stay! What are you about?"

"That is my own affair."

"Has it anything to do with—"

"No."

"We never spoke of it again, and you promised that you would reveal the identity of your 'true love,'" Fortinbras said with a laugh, ducking to avoid the ball of fire that Pendragon shot back at him.

"It came to an impasse."

"This young lady is not the same you met over in—"

"I will discuss it with you after further investigation," Pendragon said sternly, leaning back into his chair.

Fortinbras let out a deep sigh. "Must you brood? I cannot abide your sulking about."

Pendragon's reply was another ball of fire, this time blue. Fortinbras did not duck in time, and his beard was singed.

❧

"I understood from Lady Catherine that you were not expected for another week." Elizabeth smiled at the young man sitting before her, barely sparing a glance for the other man who stood in formidable silence on the other side of the room.

"Yes, indeed, but out of necessity there has been a change of plans. Our aunt must be visited, and we had a need to escape the wiles of town." The young man laughed, answering her smile with a grin of his own. "And now it is my turn to ask you a question."

"It is only fair, since you made an attempt to answer mine, however ambivalently. But I am accustomed to that; I am acquainted with your cousin, after all," Elizabeth said with another glance at Mr Darcy.

The young man, a Colonel Fitzwilliam, laughed again, turning to his cousin. "You must come sit with us, Darcy, rather than stand glaring like a fool."

Mr Darcy raised his eyebrows and moved to take a seat, still keeping a good distance between himself and the others.

"I understand from numerous sources that you do not perform magic, Miss Bennet," Colonel Fitzwilliam said, shaking his head. "Is this true?"

"Quite true," Elizabeth said cheerfully.

"How unfortunate!"

"I suppose that depends upon one's point of view. Having never practised magic, I cannot give an opinion one way or the other," Elizabeth said, trying not to look at Mr Darcy.

"I do understand from my cousin that Hertfordshire is not acclaimed for its magics—perhaps your opinion would change were you to observe it in a different setting?" Colonel Fitzwilliam continued.

"Such as a more educated populace?" she said, causing the colonel to blush. "Mr Darcy underestimates Hertfordshire's capabilities. Your curiosity is well understood, Colonel, but do you mean to make me regret what I can never possess?" Elizabeth said.

Colonel Fitzwilliam's hasty apology was cut short by Mr Darcy. "Hertfordshire is of course filled with raw talents, the forest near your home also containing deep magic not often found in other regions. But I must insist, as I have before, that your perception of magic might change when you are exposed to higher forms."

"Higher forms?" Elizabeth smirked. "Such as your talents, Mr Darcy?"

He looked like he might speak but instead remained silent, the colonel more than happy to pick up the conversation.

"Darcy is unquestionably always pursuing higher forms of magic!" He laughed. "But I fear that this topic of conversation is unpleasant to you, Miss Bennet, and one in which you cannot so easily participate."

Elizabeth's secretive smile was not lost upon Mr Darcy. "Perhaps you are right, Colonel; my knowledge naturally cannot be as complete as I might wish it. We should speak of something ordinary and dull. The weather, perhaps?"

The arrival of Lady Catherine's nephews one week early had been cause for great astonishment amongst the neighbourhood. That they should call upon the parsonage so soon after their arrival—Charlotte could only account for it as a compliment to Elizabeth. For her part, Elizabeth was pleased with the change in company, but laughed at her friend's assertion that Mr Darcy meant to pay a compliment to her.

Their visit was brief, leaving Elizabeth with a favourable impression of Colonel Fitzwilliam, and confirming all of her previous impressions of Mr Darcy's disagreeableness.

That same evening, Elizabeth was detained by Charlotte and Maria, who kept her until late into the night with their confidences. The hour nearing midnight, Elizabeth at last stumbled to her room in fatigue, nearly spilling her candle onto a book that lay across the bed. She paused and lifted the book gingerly after having set the candle on the bedside table. She did not recall having left a book there, and this one seemed peculiar. Her hands tingled as she opened the pages, and with a shock Elizabeth realised that it had been placed in her room by magic—the residue of the enchanter immediately recognisable to her.

At this, she almost put the book away, but curiosity overcame her other feelings. Reading no further than the first few lines, she closed the book with a snap, blew out the candle, and slipped under the covers. Sleep did not come easily that night, Elizabeth's mind filled with too many questions unanswered.

Speaking with him was now of the utmost importance—and she had a suspicion that she knew where to find him the next morning.

PRACTISING

HAVING LIVED AT HUNSFORD FOR OVER A WEEK, HER COMPANIONS
had grown accustomed to Elizabeth's long morning rambles. She
generally liked to walk early enough to return before breakfast. This
meant rising earlier in Kent than she was accustomed to at Longbourn, for the Collinses were not so concerned with the fashionable-
ness of the hour as Mrs Bennet; they breakfasted at nine.

On her first two walks, Elizabeth nearly despaired of finding
any sort of wilderness in the Park; everything was orderly and well
trimmed. But on the third morning, by taking a different route, she
stumbled across a patch of birch trees cluttered to form a grove.

Elizabeth was charmed, noting that here remained the thinnest
vibrations of magic—faint, but discernible. There was no possible
way of knowing why any magic was there at all when everywhere
else was so seemingly sterilised. Perhaps a band of wandering elves
had danced there in the moonlight (elves being known for their
potency of enchantments). It was possible that some magic would
remain years after a mere passing through. Elizabeth confessed to
Jane in her letter that she found it odd to miss the presence of magic
so, when she herself could make no use of it.

It was to this grove that Elizabeth went on the morning following her discovery of the book. The area would have naturally drawn anyone with magical tendencies to it; she had a suspicion that if Mr Darcy had spent any time at Rosings previously, he would know of it.

Expecting to catch a hint of his presence as she drew closer, Elizabeth was surprised to detect none. He stood with his back to her, looking out towards the house. At the sound of her foot snapping a twig, he turned to face her.

"Who's there?" he called.

"Nay, answer me. Stand and unfold yourself!" Elizabeth called back with only some hesitation.

Mr Darcy grinned. "And what would my proper response be?" he asked with a laugh.

Elizabeth raised her chin. "You tell me, Mr Darcy."

"Long live the King," he said, his face returning to its customary impassivity—although his eyes still sparkled.

"Mr Darcy?"

"He."

"You come most carefully upon your hour."

He laughed again. "That is far enough, Miss Bennet. You read the play? I was not certain if you would be able to."

"You placed the book in my room by enchantment, but as it was a real object and not a construction, I was able to handle it. I did not read through the entire thing," she added. "Only the first few lines. I have read Hamlet before but did not recognise its opening."

They stood awkwardly for a moment, before Elizabeth shifted her feet. "I do not understand why it was of such great importance."

"You would not, because I have not yet told you," Mr Darcy replied, leaning his arm against a birch trunk.

Elizabeth's brows rose. "Well?"

"It is a code."

"Is that all?" Elizabeth tapped her foot.

"Yes."

"To what purpose would we greet each other in code?"

"In case we should need to conceal our true identities," he replied.

"Would you answer to the name Bernardo, then?"

"No, I would answer to something else—Pendragon, for example."

"That is your code name?"

"One of them."

Elizabeth sighed. "I never understand what you are about, Mr Darcy."

"You will think of a name for yourself?" he continued with some eagerness.

"I am too old for childish games," Elizabeth replied shortly. "Why would you wish me to speak of this with my father?"

"That is something you will have to ask him—in person, and not by post." Mr Darcy straightened. "I trust you will not reveal this information to anyone else."

"People are always making unreasonable demands of me, with no explanation for them!"

"I should think the reason would be obvious."

"It is not."

Mr Darcy ran a hand through his hair with impatience. "I do not wish you to speak of it with anyone—the exception being your father—for fear of its being discovered by a person of questionable intentions."

"Why should anyone concern themselves with your code, Mr Darcy?"

His mouth curved into a slow smile. "Invent a name for yourself, Miss Bennet, and you shall receive more answers."

"I should return to the house," Elizabeth said. "I hope you will have a pleasant rest of the morning." In light of her dismissal, she expected to walk alone, but Mr Darcy fell into step next to her.

"What think you of Rosings?" he said after some time had passed.

"It is very…civilised." Elizabeth said, surprised by further conversation.

"I find it empty without magic," he said, gazing up at the trees overhead.

"You seem to be devoid of magic yourself this morning," Elizabeth countered.

He looked at her keenly. "You noticed?"

"Rather, I did not notice anything. I am not capable of assessing whether or not one is magical—only that they are using magic. Your aunt, for example. Mr Collins has informed me that she is highly magical, but I cannot detect a trace of anything magical about her."

His eyebrows rose in interest. "Fascinating. And that is why you sought out the birch grove—for the same reasons I did."

"There is something there, something pleasant." Elizabeth glanced back at the trees, missing Mr Darcy's soft smile. "I have not explored all of the Park. There might be other areas not so tightly controlled."

"My aunt does not forbid our use of magic in her presence, although she detests it," he said. "It has become a habit to forgo enchantments here. It provides some relief."

Elizabeth glanced at Mr Darcy in puzzlement. He was looking ahead, towards the parsonage, and did not notice her gaze. She did not understand his desire to confide in her in one moment, while previously so reluctant to reveal anything.

"You will not use any magic while you are at Rosings?" she said sceptically.

"No, yes—when necessary, of course," he stammered. He glanced apprehensively at the parsonage windows, seeming desirous of walking back towards Rosings. Elizabeth, feeling not the slightest regret at the idea of separating, indicated that she might walk the rest of the way alone. Relief passing over his features, Mr Darcy bid her a courteous farewell.

~

"You were walking with Mr Darcy?" Charlotte asked when she came in for breakfast.

Elizabeth laughed. "Unfortunately we met in the Park! It must be very disagreeable to him to converse with one so beneath him, but I believe my lack of talent continues to intrigue him as a matter of study."

"Perhaps *you* intrigue him as a matter of study, not your lack of talent," Charlotte said slyly, but Elizabeth only laughed again.

It was not long before another invitation to dine at Rosings was issued to the Collinses and company. With the addition of Colonel Fitzwilliam to their party, Elizabeth found the evening lively and significantly more enjoyable than they had been before.

"What does Miss Bennet desire?" The colonel laughed. "Shall we play at cards, or music?"

"Miss Bennet, I believe, prefers reading to cards, Fitzwilliam," Mr Darcy said with gravity.

"Do you propose we read, Mr Darcy?" she said.

"Darcy reads enough as it is," Colonel Fitzwilliam said. "Unless your heart is set on it, I would much rather hear you play."

"That is one talent, at least, of which I am capable!" Elizabeth said, her eyes twinkling. "But you might learn to regret your request after hearing me play."

The two gentlemen both protested gallantly that they should not, but Elizabeth managed to put them off until after coffee had been served, when Colonel Fitzwilliam again reminded her of her promise to play. He turned the pages for her; Lady Catherine and the rest listened for close to half a song before turning their attention to other things. The colonel and Elizabeth were left to themselves for a length of time until Mr Darcy, who had been detained by his aunt, moved his way back to them. With his usual deliberation, he stood directly across from Elizabeth, so as to receive the best view of her countenance.

Elizabeth saw what he was doing, and at the first convenient pause, turned to him with an arch smile. "You mean to frighten me, Mr Darcy, by coming in all this state to hear me? But I will not be alarmed though your sister does play so well. There is a stubbornness about me that never can bear to be frightened at the will of others. My courage always rises with every attempt to intimidate me."

"I shall not say that you are mistaken," he replied, "because you could not really believe me to entertain any design of alarming you, and I have had the pleasure of your acquaintance long enough to know that you find great enjoyment in occasionally professing opinions which in fact are not your own."

Elizabeth laughed heartily at this picture of herself. "Mr Darcy would have you not believe a word I say, Colonel Fitzwilliam. I had thought to pass myself off with some degree of credit. It is very ungenerous of you, Mr Darcy, and impolitic too, for it may cause me to retaliate!"

"I am not afraid of you," he said, smiling.

With some disappointment, Elizabeth remembered that at this moment, he used no enchantments that she might disrupt.

"Pray let me hear what you have to accuse him of," cried Colonel Fitzwilliam. "I should like to know how he behaves among strangers."

Elizabeth turned to him. "Hertfordshire is perhaps a more dreadful example, Colonel, as it is not known for its magics. For your cousin to find himself in such a location, and in such company! I first saw him at a ball, where he danced only four dances! I am sorry to pain you—but so it was. He danced only four dances, though gentlemen were scarce; and to my knowledge, more than one young lady was sitting down in want of a partner. Mr Darcy, you cannot deny the fact. How tiresome our company must have been to you!"

"I had not at that time the honour of knowing any lady in the assembly beyond my own party."

"True; and nobody can ever be introduced in a ballroom. Well, Colonel Fitzwilliam, what do I play next? My fingers wait your orders."

"Perhaps," Mr Darcy continued as Elizabeth sorted sheet music, "I should have judged better to seek introductions. But I am ill-qualified to recommend myself to strangers."

"Indeed?" Elizabeth turned to address Colonel Fitzwilliam. "Mr Darcy, wizard extraordinaire, whose father is published and well-respected, and who is said to soon come out with his own ground-breaking research? Ill-qualified in the company of lesser wizards in Hertfordshire?"

"For some the tone and expression of a conversation is easily caught—and they are able to appear interested in the concerns of a complete stranger within two minutes. I have not that talent," Mr Darcy said.

"Perhaps if you applied your practising disciplines as diligently to conversing as you do to your magic, the problem would then be solved!" Elizabeth laughed, resisting the urge to roll her eyes. "If I were to employ even a significant amount of discipline to my own practising"—she indicated the piano, but thought instead of her own abilities—"my skills would be significantly improved."

Mr Darcy smiled. "You are perfectly right. You have employed your time much better. No one admitted to the privilege of hearing you, can think anything wanting. We neither of us perform to strangers."

Catching his eye, Elizabeth wondered if he had understood her true meaning. Shrugging her shoulders, she turned back to the music before her. "There is a page missing, Colonel Fitzwilliam," she said, laughing again. "I am certainly not capable of inventing an appropriate finish!"

"Will this suffice?" With a flourish, another sheet of music appeared before her eyes.

Mr Darcy looked surprised, gazing at Elizabeth curiously, but she only laughed, and did nothing to disturb the enchantment. "I am not certain that Mozart will appreciate his piece being finished with the last page of a Bach fugue, Colonel!"

Colonel Fitzwilliam let out a hearty laugh at his mistake, while Mr Darcy moved to stand behind them. "If I may," he said, replacing the colonel's enchantment with the correct last page.

Elizabeth smirked, but began playing. Mr Darcy removed to his former position at the piano, but when she came to the last page, it suddenly began to flicker and soon faded out of sight.

"How strange, Darcy!" Colonel Fitzwilliam exclaimed. "Your enchantment wore through rather quickly!"

Mr Darcy's eyes narrowed, but Elizabeth did not meet his gaze and instead turned to the colonel in amusement. "I suppose your trick would have lasted longer?"

The colonel glanced at Elizabeth's sparkling eyes. "My enchantments could outmatch anyone's, even Darcy's."

Mr Darcy looked disgruntled. "A match then, it is," he declared, much to Elizabeth's astonishment. "A ball of fire. That is difficult to maintain."

"Red fire; you are altogether too masterful with blue," the colonel countered. Elizabeth, highly amused, watched as Colonel Fitzwilliam rose from his chair to stand across from Mr Darcy. Simultaneously, both men conjured between their hands a blazing spark that grew to be half a foot wide in circumference, now and then shooting sparks out to the sides.

It was not possible for the rest of the party to remain ignorant of what the two men were doing. Lady Catherine stood in indignation, but neither of her nephews seemed to notice, both deep in concentration. Colonel Fitzwilliam let out a laugh of delight as Mr Darcy's flame flickered; a strange look passed across Mr Darcy's face, his brows drawing together but otherwise displaying no discernible emotion. Steadily, his flame weakened until it fizzled into nothingness, just before Colonel Fitzwilliam's disappeared with a bang.

Colonel Fitzwilliam collapsed into a nearby chair. "Darcy, that must be the first time—"

"Fitzwilliam!" Lady Catherine's voice thundered as she approached. "It is unseemly of you to disrupt your cousin's spell!"

"I can assure you that I did no such thing." Colonel Fitzwilliam's face flushed.

Lady Catherine's eyes narrowed. "Did you feel your spell to be tampered with by Fitzwilliam?" she said to Mr Darcy.

Without even a blink in Elizabeth's direction, who had paled upon realising her mistake, Mr Darcy replied, "Not at all."

Lady Catherine's eyes wandered over them for another moment before she admonished them to never employ such tricks in her home again—most particularly in the presence of company. It was for these very reasons that she despised magic in general.

~

"That was not fair of you, Miss Bennet," Mr Darcy said two mornings later, when their paths crossed again in the Park.

"I will not quarrel with you over fairness," Elizabeth said as they walked. "But I will say that it was a foolish step on my part. As you know, my father does not wish me to reveal my ability. It was fortunate that my demonstration went unnoticed. I thank you for your silence." She almost blushed to think of the humility he had displayed by insisting that he had lost the competition honestly. She had not thought him capable of it; indeed, humility seemed uncharacteristic.

"You delight in making fun at my expense," he said with a smile, but Elizabeth avoided his gaze. "I am certain, however, that had I been adequately warned, I could have withstood your disenchantments."

Elizabeth turned to look at him with a laugh. "Here we must quarrel. I have respect for your power, Mr Darcy, but as I told you before, I have not yet encountered a spell that I could not break."

"And as I have told you," he said, raising his brows, "that accounts for your lack of experience."

"Mr Darcy." She halted, placing a hand on her hip. "Your methods make it entirely too simple to break your spells. You follow your father's method of defence to the letter, and it is easily overcome."

"We shall see," he said. "Can you break this, then?" A brightly coloured bird appeared and began looping about their heads.

"I am almost sorry to dispose of it!" Elizabeth said in some delight, but with a squawk the bird disappeared.

Mr Darcy looked at her with some amusement before he began mounting more spells, one on top of the other, causing Elizabeth more and more trouble to eradicate them. Her frustration grew as she dismantled fire, thick rosebushes, and wind spells (one that blew her bonnet away, causing her to put up her shield). No longer assaulted bodily by the spells, Darcy continued to apply enchantments that swirled about her with increasing skill. Her senses overwhelmed, and feeling increasingly vexed, Elizabeth was nearing surrender when she let out a small cry and fell to the ground, grasping at her ankle. Half of Mr Darcy's spells burst to nothingness in an instant, the others abandoned as he rushed to her side. But Elizabeth, not at all harmed, sat up, laughing, and within a few seconds had done away with all of his remaining spells.

"You see, Mr Darcy! Where went your 'concentration'?"

Without a reply, he pulled her back onto her feet.

Seeing the cross look upon his face caused her laugher to cease and Elizabeth's brows drew together in puzzlement. "I do not understand your look of vexation, sir."

"I am not vexed."

"Indeed, you are," she insisted, somewhat mystified as to why she should care.

"I am not." His eyes blazed. "You should not laugh; your unravelling was not so expert as I had expected it to be."

Elizabeth's temper flared. "Perhaps that is due to my inexperience, as you call it, Mr Darcy; but you may not discount my resourcefulness."

"Your resourcefulness was entirely dependent upon the fact that I would react as a gentleman."

"Was it?" Elizabeth countered, suddenly feeling a desire to be rid of the man.

"You should practise more," he said after a moment's silence.

"And you should practise greater concentration!" she replied.

Mr Darcy smiled ruefully. "I speak in earnest, Miss Bennet. I will provide the spells, if you should desire to practise."

Elizabeth's breath caught in surprise. She had often longed for the opportunity to perfect her skill—to put it to greater use than the checking of her younger sisters' love enchantments. "I do not know that my father would approve," she said hesitantly.

When Mr Darcy did not reply, she thought for another moment. "But I would improve myself. Who better to practise counter-magic upon than a member of the Wizarding Court?"

Mr Darcy's eyes searched hers. "I have never spoken of the Wizarding Court, Miss Bennet. It would be best if you did not assume."

Tossing her head, Elizabeth laughed. "Well, then, Mr Darcy, if you must be disagreeable, I will bid you good day." She turned to walk back towards the parsonage.

"Tomorrow"—his voice halted her steps—"I will be walking in the birch grove."

She turned to acknowledge him with a nod of her head, and then continued walking.

Staring at the darkened walls, Elizabeth turned first to one side and then the other on her bed. He was by far the most disagreeable man she had ever met—abominably rude and conceited. And yet she could not account for his interest in her, or the gallantry he had displayed on several occasions. He saw something in her skill that could be harnessed and put to good use, even encouraged her to use it! Was she wise to trust him?

Had he not protected her from exposure to his relations, and her friends? He had kept her secret—even when it might have been advantageous for him to reveal it. Most puzzling of all, Elizabeth realised that her father trusted him—to a point—with the knowledge that she could work disenchantment.

Falling into a restless sleep, Elizabeth rose and walked into the Park as soon as would be deemed proper. She stood for some time at the grove, thinking herself too early, but as the sun drew higher and Mr Darcy did not appear, Elizabeth began to doubt him. He had rethought his offer—come to his senses. Why should he not have? She was nothing to him if not for her ability; even then, Mr Darcy had much more to concern himself with. Practising magic on a country girl of little consequence and no talent would be seen as ridiculous. And yet, Elizabeth could not dismiss a feeling of bitter disappointment—not because of the absence of his company!—but because she had longed to improve her skill in some small way.

The remainder of the day at the parsonage was spent in idleness. Elizabeth reread Jane's letters, which in no way improved her spirits for, despite her attempts, Mr Bingley had not even come to see her. The Gardiners had not yet written, but Jane promised their aunt would at the next opportunity; they were very busy with matters concerning the new-found Merchant Court. Its success was great, but Jane assured her that further details would be provided when her aunt could spare a moment to write.

Later in the afternoon, Colonel Fitzwilliam called on the ladies at the parsonage to inform them that Lady Catherine was obliged to cancel their invitation to dinner since she was feeling in poor health. When Charlotte enquired after Mr Darcy and the rest of the household, the colonel replied that they were all well, and Darcy had been detained on matters of urgent business. Elizabeth raised a brow at this but did nothing to further promote the conversation.

A merry hour was spent in the colonel's company (whom Elizabeth and Maria thought very agreeable indeed), but after that afternoon, they did not see anyone from Rosings for a week. Lady Catherine continued to be unfit for company, much to Mr Collins's distress. The week was dull; there was little news to be got, neither Jane nor her aunt sent any letters, and the weather turned dark and gloomy. Elizabeth found herself so bored that, in spite of her earlier feelings, she invented a name for herself as Mr Darcy had requested. She did not know why; she was not certain he would ever mention it again. But if the code had something to do with the Wizarding Court, Elizabeth desired answers—and if a name was what was required, she would produce it.

On Thursday afternoon, six days after Elizabeth had last seen Mr Darcy in the woods, the idleness was broken abruptly. Mr Collins, out of breath and distressed, hurried into the sitting room where Charlotte sat with both her guests.

"What is it, Mr Collins, are you ill?" Charlotte said in alarm.

Her husband shook his head violently. "No, indeed, but it is most distressing, most unfortunate!"

"Mr Collins, do have a seat. It will steady your nerves," Elizabeth said, and her cousin bowed gratefully, moving to sit across from them.

"There has been another attack—the first in four months!" he said. "In town, as before. And I am afraid that this time there has been a casualty."

All three women gasped, and Mr Collins took the opportunity to catch his breath before continuing. "It has been whispered for some time that the Thief's only successful opponents have been members of the Wizarding Court. These rumours seemed to have been confirmed, for it has been announced officially that a gentleman involved was a member. It is for these very reasons that my patroness Lady Catherine has impressed upon us the need to abstain from magical practices—otherwise I fear we might be in great danger, and—"

"Mr Collins!" Elizabeth cried. "You mentioned a casualty. What became of the gentleman?"

"Do you know his identity?" Maria's voice trembled.

Mr Collins hesitated. "I fear the outcome is too distressing."

"It would be far better coming from you than hearing it on our next outing," Elizabeth insisted.

"The gentleman in question—not identified as of yet—is dead."

OF THINGS SEEN AND UNSEEN

PENDRAGON SAT ON THE MOOR, HIS HEAD IN HIS HANDS, MIST swirling about him.

A few feet away, Fortinbras stood with another young man. Known by the name of Tree, he stood some four inches shorter than Fortinbras, his hair wind-swept and his eyes red.

Fortinbras began to pace.

"I have never seen him like this," Tree said in hushed tones. "He is not himself—but it is no wonder."

"What happened?"

"Nothing went according to plan." Tree sighed, running a hand down his face. "The attack was unexpected—in Benedick's own home. He is dead, and his wife nearly so. Pendragon was his first avenue—and I his second. By the time I arrived…"

"You did well to move here," Fortinbras said. "This is one of our only secure places left, although I am sure he was difficult about leaving." They both turned to look at Pendragon, who had not yet moved.

"Yes." Tree almost laughed. "But I could not very well let him stay. The connexion is too strong as it is, there are bound to be suspicions."

Fortinbras looked to the east, where the sun was rising. "You have done what you could, my friend," he said to Tree, "but you may rest assured I will take care of him from here."

Tree looked once at Pendragon's solitary figure before squaring his shoulders resolutely and clasping Fortinbras's hand. "Until we meet again," he said, and moved westward, disappearing into the fog.

Motionless, Fortinbras stood in thought for a moment before kneeling at Pendragon's side. "We must return," he urged him, putting a hand gently on his shoulder. "I came as quickly as I could. Would to God I had come sooner."

Pendragon shook his head miserably. "He is dead."

"Yes, he is dead, but you are alive, and we must return." Taking Fortinbras's outstretched hand, Pendragon pulled himself to his feet until, gasping, he fell back to the ground. "Why did you not tell anyone you were injured!"

"No one asked," Pendragon replied, grimacing in pain. "It is worse than before."

"That same wound?"

"The same."

"What are you to do? We must return, or everyone will suspect." Fortinbras raked a hand through his hair. "Ordinarily I would mask it for you, but under these circumstances... We should never have gone there, and now there is nothing—"

"There is something. Put on the masking spell and take me to the parson's house. Leave me there and proceed as planned. I will join you within the hour."

Fortinbras paused. "The parson? What has he to do with anything?"

"He has nothing to do with it."

"Then?"

Pendragon sighed. "We are wasting time, Fortinbras."

"You and your confounded secrets!" Fortinbras cried, his face flushed with anger. "If you had been more open with me, then—"

"Then what?" Pendragon growled. "None of this would have happened?"

Fortinbras's mouth hung open for a second before he closed it without saying a word. Pulling Pendragon to his feet, he layered the enchantment, covering first the open wound, stopping up the blood and giving it the appearance of mobility. "Do not walk on it for long. The enchantment will not last, and I will not have you bloodying up the parsonage sitting room."

"I will not be going inside," Pendragon said with irritation while Fortinbras pulled his arm over his shoulders. With Pendragon leaning his weight against him, they moved up the hill towards the sunrise, cold air biting against their faces until, falling into darkness, they were swallowed up in mist.

~

Elizabeth stirred in her sleep, opening her eyes to see the light creeping through the closed curtains. Had she heard a noise? Straining her ears, she listened intently before turning over to the other side. It was early, barely light, and she must have been dreaming.

Something hit the window with sudden force, causing Elizabeth to throw the covers off in alarm and move to the curtains. Brushing them aside, she gazed down into the dusky garden where the figure of Mr Darcy stood alone, his arm raised to throw another pebble. Gasping in indignation, Elizabeth dropped the curtain and put a hand to her throat. Suppressing her relief at seeing him alive, she felt a flush of anger spread across her cheeks at the impropriety of his actions. She would not answer him, it was unthinkable.

"Miss Bennet!" he called. His voice was hoarse but spoke with enough clarity that Elizabeth feared he would wake Maria in the next room. Elizabeth threw her shawl about her shoulders and slipped into her shoes, moving out into the garden as silently as possible.

"Mr Darcy," she hissed as she drew near. "What are you doing!"

"Do not look so alarmed," he said wearily, as—to her astonishment—he lowered himself to the ground. "No one else can hear me but you, although they might see you, since I am unable to cast an invisibility spell over you. Are you satisfied?"

Comprehension dawning in her eyes, Elizabeth crouched next to him. "You are injured."

With a grimace, Mr Darcy used both hands to move his right leg in front of him. "It is quite useless. And in a moment the wound will open again, and I shall be in all manner of trouble."

Elizabeth squinted. "Practising again?" she said, while in the same moment concentrating to discover the core of the hex. It was layered deep beneath other spells, some more powerful than others.

"I have told you before," Mr Darcy said, welcoming a distraction from the pain by the sight of her plait running down the side of her shoulder. "I am not at liberty to reveal how and where I was injured. It is an enchantment of my own making—and others—that will not allow me to speak of where I have been."

"I could undo it for you," Elizabeth said.

"I beg you would not."

Sitting back on her heels, Elizabeth folded her arms across her knees. "If I were to give you my chosen code name, would you tell me?"

Mr Darcy looked at her with surprise, but shook his head. "No, I could not."

Her eyes flashed in anger. "Then why should I help you?"

Mr Darcy looked down at his lifeless leg hopelessly. "My aunt —I would never have come to you if not for the fact that I cannot— I cannot conceal my injury from her without exposure. Under ordinary circumstances I could mask it and wait for it to heal on its own, as I did the last time," he said with a pointed look. "But no one knows I have even left Rosings. To return with an injury such as this... I beg you, Miss Bennet."

Elizabeth nodded, moving to hold her hands above his leg. She hesitated, blushing, before raising her eyes to meet his gaze. "It would help me, Mr Darcy, if you would remove the masking spells you have employed. And if you will permit me—" She moved one hand to his knee, wincing as he gritted his teeth.

Closing her eyes, Elizabeth unraveled each layer from front to back, as if pulling the thread out of knitting. As she moved deeper into the spell, she felt a chill spread from her fingers to her very heart; she had not encountered magic of this sort before, and more than once she nearly slipped. After several long minutes, a shock emitted from between her fingertips and where the wound had been. Mr Darcy's leg twitched and he moved his hands along the sides of it before standing. Walking down the lane and back again, he looked at Elizabeth in delight.

"You have mended it completely," he said with wonder. "It is better than it was before."

Elizabeth almost smiled, her hands still trembling from the chill, but her stomach lurched. Scrambling to her feet, she ran to the cover of the garden hedgerows before retching onto the ground. She wiped her hand across her mouth and fell to her knees, tears streaming down her cheeks as her shoulders shook with cold.

Feeling Mr Darcy's warm hands at her shoulders, Elizabeth did not answer his calls of alarm until her tears had ceased. "I am sorry," she whispered, and then looked up at him, almost laughing. "I must look a fright."

Mr Darcy's face was pale, his hands hanging limp at his sides. "You are ill—I should never have—"

"No, no." She rose to her feet shakily. "I am well now, it has passed. I have never countered such a spell before," she said, looking into his eyes, "It was frightening. You said you are better than before—yes, I removed the remainder of whatever had been left behind from the first incident. That spell was not acquired while 'practising,' Mr Darcy, and it was inflicted by the same enchanter as the first one."

His eyes met hers with remorse. "Words cannot express my gratitude."

"You are welcome," Elizabeth replied, holding his gaze. She thought how well he looked now, with nothing but the invisibility enchantment clouding his person, his hair tousled, and the blood creeping back into his cheeks. He did not seem nearly so disagreeable as he ordinarily did. Her earlier sickness almost forgotten, Elizabeth opened her mouth to tell him of the name she had chosen for herself—hoping to discover as much information as she could—but Mr Darcy blinked and spoke first.

"I must leave, Miss Bennet," he said, moving his hands from where they had rested at her arms. With a flash he disappeared, leaving Elizabeth in the garden alone.

～

My Dearest Elizabeth,

No doubt by now you have learned of the terrible tragedy that occurred just two days ago in London. The gentleman concerned did not move in the same circles as ourselves, but his loss is grieved by us all. Be assured that we are well; the children are with my relatives in the country. We thought it best for them to be hidden for a time, although your uncle and I are not as yet considered targets. That is one favourable aspect of our class—we do not receive the attention of our wealthier peers.

Your father has written a hasty sort of message, asking whether or not Jane ought to be sent home. We replied that she should remain in town with us until your return three weeks hence. Jane is always useful, but her skill and expertise grow with each passing day. The distraction from matters of the heart is good for her; otherwise I fear she would have felt the loss of Mr Bingley, and the slight of his sisters, acutely.

But here I must come to my purpose, which is to issue a warning. You have heard negative rumours surrounding a certain gentleman and his connexion to the W. Court. I will not mention names, that is far too dangerous (I trust you will destroy this letter as soon as possible), however you know of whom I speak. You do not like him. It concerns not the gentleman, but rather his court—perhaps you would be so good as to pass this information along to him? We have recently acquired a connexion (by way of a different member) who supplies us with inside information.

Rest assured, this has all been approved at the necessary levels; based upon new information, the M. Court is concerned over the possibility of a leak in the W. Court—one that has not been approved by anybody, and is transpiring at the highest levels possible. We have no notion of the identity of this informant. The true names of W. Court members are most difficult to come by; half of them do not even know the actual names of their own members. But do warn him—and be wary. The recent attack occurred within Mr Robert's own home. The only possibility of the Thief knowing where to attack would have been through an informant—there are no other possibilities.

Please write to me, Lizzy, and tell me how you are. I think of you often, and look forward to your joining us soon— although it means that Jane must soon depart! I hope that I have not confused you further, but fear for you being in Kent. I will rest easier once I can see you with my own eyes.

Yours affectionately,
M. Gardiner

Elizabeth folded the letter thoughtfully, running her fingers along its edges before tossing it into the fire. It had been two days since her encounter with Mr Darcy in the garden, and since then he had not come to call, or ventured into the Park. Lady Catherine was now feeling herself in better spirits and had extended an invitation to tea the next afternoon, where she might at least catch a glimpse of him. With a sigh, she straightened, standing to stare out the window. She longed to understand his mysterious injuries and behaviours. Perhaps he would speak to her of it again, the next afternoon, and she might receive overdue answers.

Walking out in search of Charlotte, she found her, along with Maria, picking flowers in the garden. After spending an hour in the spring sunshine, they set off on a short walk down the lane. With surprise, they were passed by Miss de Bourgh (and Mrs Jenkinson) in her phaeton; they did not stop but slowed their pace to wave graciously. Charlotte was pleased to have confirmation that, indeed, the household at Rosings seemed returned to their former state of health (such as it was), and Maria sighed to think of owning such a splendid carriage.

Walking farther into the Park, Elizabeth was distracted when she noticed a small, round stone building hidden within a cluster of trees. Unlike the rest of Rosings, it was overgrown with vines and bushes, barely visible but there nonetheless. She had never noticed it before; it pulled at her, as if by magic. Indeed, she almost caught the strains of magic about it, but not of a familiar kind.

"What are you looking at, Lizzy?" Charlotte asked, peering into the trees.

"There." Elizabeth pointed. "Do you see that?"

Charlotte wrinkled her brow. "What? The trees?"

"No, no—" Elizabeth stopped short. "Do you see anything, Maria?"

"I do not know what you are talking about, Lizzy. Is it a wild animal?" Maria gasped in alarm.

Laughing, Elizabeth turned away. "Not a wild animal—as if there would be in this Park! I must have been mistaken, for it seems there is nothing there at all."

Charlotte gave the area another squinting glance before moving back into step with Elizabeth. "You always notice the strangest things," she remarked with a smile.

Elizabeth longed to tell her what she had seen but, remembering her father's admonition, only laughed. She would return to it when she had the chance. Perhaps then she might discover what sort of magic kept it hidden from everyone else.

~

Mr Darcy did not speak to her again at their next meeting, nor the one after that. Elizabeth was affronted by his behaviour. Walking now without the slightest limp, he stayed mostly in the company of his aunt, saying little, and refusing to catch Elizabeth's eye.

"I do not understand your cousin, Colonel," Elizabeth said in a confidential tone. It had been three days since MrDarcy's injury; he and the colonel had come to call again at the parsonage, but Mr Darcy stood awkwardly with Charlotte and her husband, engrossed in Mr Collins's discussion of tomatoes. Elizabeth glanced in his direction. "He has not seemed himself."

The colonel looked uncomfortable for a moment before flashing a brilliant smile. "Darcy has always been mysterious. After the recent attacks...well, I am sure, Miss Bennet, you heard the name of the gentleman. He was a great friend of Darcy's, they were at university together."

Elizabeth glanced at Mr Darcy in concern.

"Under usual circumstance, we would have left Rosings by now to be with Darcy's sister, of whom we share joint guardianship. He worries over her a great deal, as do I, and after recent events—well, families are staying close. But we are obliged to stay as long as he chooses, and he chooses to remain."

"You are obliged to do as Mr Darcy says?" Elizabeth lifted a brow.

"Naturally! Do not we all?"

She pursed her lips. Thinking of making lighter conversation, she remarked with some amusement, "I understand. You are here at his disposal! You must wish for him to marry, then, to secure a lasting convenience of that kind. Then he will have no use for you, and you may come and go as you please!"

"Marry?" Colonel Fitzwilliam was himself relieved to turn the conversation to more pleasant topics. "As scrupulous as he is with his friends, I cannot imagine how he might choose for himself!"

"His friends?"

"Of course. He congratulates himself on saving one such recently from a most imprudent marriage. He did not mention names or particulars, but I suspect it is one Mr Bingley, with whom I believe you are acquainted. I only think so, because he is the kind of young man who gets into scrapes of that sort." He laughed, not noticing the flush spreading across Elizabeth's face.

"Did Mr Darcy give you his reasons for this interference?"

"I understand that there were some very strong objections against the lady."

"And he the judge?" Elizabeth said, her voice rising. "Pray tell me, did he use his arts to separate them?"

Colonel Fitzwilliam gave her a curious look. "Darcy would never use enchantment to such an advantage. You are rather disposed to call his interference officious?"

"For Mr Darcy to determine and direct the happiness of his friends? But, as we know none of the particulars, it is not fair to condemn him," she said, forcing a smile. "It is not to be supposed that there was much affection in the case."

"Although less of a triumph for him in that circumstance." Colonel Fitzwilliam glanced at his cousin before turning back to Elizabeth. "It may be that he is at fault in his direction, but I hope you will look on it with a forgiving eye, Miss Bennet. For one who has lost much and endured—perhaps officiousness is not so great a sin."

Elizabeth did not agree, and so could not trust herself to reply. After a moment of looking at her hands, she gave the colonel a smile to reassure him. For the rest of the afternoon, Elizabeth's relief at Mr Darcy's avoidance of her was profound. The anger she felt at this discovery was so great that she was ready to excuse herself by claiming fatigue, but the gentlemen anticipated her by taking their leave.

The next morning, a headache that had begun the afternoon before worsened in the extreme. Elizabeth remained in her room, occupying herself, perhaps unwisely, by rereading her letters from Jane. In them she felt every disappointment of Jane's as a disappointment to herself, and more. Elizabeth realised through her tears that this circumstance confirmed what she had long suspected to be true.

How fortunate Mr Wickham's warning proved to be now! How had she allowed herself to forget his pride? Indeed, over the past two weeks, Mr Darcy had often dismissed her—only once asking her aid when in dire need. He never had any intention of bringing her into the Wizarding Court—however useful she might have been. Mr Wickham's information had done well by preventing her from feeling more pain than she ought. What if she had allowed herself to believe in him more completely? And yet, Elizabeth's tears did not cease for some time. That afternoon she asked Charlotte to make her excuses for her when they dined at Rosings, for she felt herself unfit for company.

❧

"I have been a very patient man, but this must come to an end," Fortinbras said, following Pendragon's pacing about the grove. He sat perched in the low branch of a great tree, illuminated by the moonlight shining above them.

"Do you suppose she is ill?" Pendragon said, not bothering to look up.

"What?" Fortinbras exclaimed.

"Ill. She might be, she has not seemed well, and it would be entirely my fault," Pendragon said, running a hand through his hair.

"You must stop this, Pendragon, you will drive me to insanity," Fortinbras said, leaping from his perch to stand directly in front of his companion. "Now," he continued with a sigh, placing his hands on Pendragon's shoulders. "I have not asked because there was no opportunity, but you must tell me. How have you been so thoroughly healed?"

Pendragon's brows rose. "You should have suspected by now that I am not at liberty—"

"To reveal any information of any kind? Rubbish!" Fortinbras snapped, beginning to pace on his own. "If you will not answer, then I shall be forced to guess—which, I believe, is a far more risky business."

Pendragon folded his arms expectantly.

"All right," Fortinbras said. "She is the same person you spoke of before and have been in love with since the summer. She has something to do with your miraculous recovery. I have not the slightest idea what or why—but if she was the cause of it, I am astounded by her talent."

Pendragon scowled. "I am not in love with her."

At this, Fortinbras let out a roaring laugh. "Do not play the fool, it does not become you," he said, wiping the corners of his eyes. "What I cannot understand is why you do not declare yourself and be done with it."

Pendragon clenched his jaw. "If you know not why, then you are the fool, Fortinbras."

Fortinbras's laughter died down to a chuckle. "We are all in danger now, Pendragon. You will not bring her greater danger by revealing yourself. And if her ability is what I suspect it might be— although how it is kept hidden, I cannot imagine—then she is likely to offer you greater protection than you may offer her."

"You do not understand the nature of her abilities, whatever they are—if they are. They are not as you imagine them."

Fortinbras shrugged in resignation. "I do not know what I imagine. I am often wrong—but you are not always right."

Pendragon smiled. "She would agree with you, at that."

Fortinbras laughed again, and with a shake of his head, left Pendragon to his thoughts. He sighed, climbing up to sit on the branch Fortinbras had occupied earlier, and gazed up at the bright stars.

"No more of this," he muttered. "What if, perchance, you are right, Fortinbras? How should I act?" He shook his head. "I will speak to her then, tomorrow. If it must be done, it must be done. I cannot go on like this."

POURING RAIN

WHEN ELIZABETH WOKE THE NEXT MORNING, HER HEADACHE HAD diminished, but not her annoyance. Hoping to avoid Mr Collins's company and Charlotte's questioning looks, she languished about in her room before breakfast and tried to think of what to write in reply to her aunt's message. At length, after blotting the page one too many times, she descended for a quick cup of tea, afterwards making her way out to the Park.

Walking briskly in an attempt to put Darcy from her mind, Elizabeth moved straightaway to where she remembered having seen the stone hut a few days before. At first, Elizabeth thought perhaps she had not walked far enough; then, as she went farther and saw nothing, she wondered if perhaps she had gone too far. Turning back, she circled the area where she was certain the building had stood before. Finding nothing, not even a trace, her search spread across more ground, taking her off the path and through the wild sections of the woods.

As the sun climbed higher, the air grew warm. Elizabeth took off her bonnet to fan herself, recalled where she was, and reluctantly found her way back to the lane from which she had drifted a long distance. Hot and disgruntled at having lost track of the time, Elizabeth turned her steps back towards the parsonage. Mr Darcy was the last person she had expected or wished to meet, and so it was with annoyance that she came upon him, sitting on the ground with his back leaning against a tree, hat off, feet stretched out before him. His eyes were closed, and he was not far from where she had first strayed off the lane. Hoping to creep by him unawares, Elizabeth moved softly but to her dismay, Darcy opened his eyes at the moment she was in front him.

"Who's there?" he said, smiling.

"I will not play at your game today, Mr Darcy." Elizabeth sniffed.

He scrambled to his feet. "You said you had invented a name for yourself," he said, stepping closer. "I would hear it."

She stepped back. "It is of little consequence."

"On the contrary. Will you not tell me?"

"No, Mr Darcy, I think not," she said, and began walking forward.

He moved in step alongside her. "You mentioned it to me before, might I ask why now you will not give it?"

"Need you ask?" She refused to glance at him as she walked ahead.

"Will you stop for a moment, Miss Bennet?" he said abruptly. "I must speak with you."

"There has been little said between us recently, Mr Darcy." Elizabeth raised a brow but halted her steps to face him. "What makes today the exception?"

"You must know of what I speak."

"Your Court?" Elizabeth said, crossing her arms. "I have heard enough of it from—"

"It is not of the Court," he said. "Not entirely. I cannot blame you for being disappointed in me the last few days, but it was for your protection."

"My protection?" Her brows creased in confusion.

"Or perhaps my own. It was not what I would have wished but it can no longer be repressed." Mr Darcy's face was pale.

"I do not ever understand what you mean," Elizabeth cried in frustration.

Mr Darcy blinked. "Not understand? Miss Bennet"—he took a breath and stepped forward—"you must know that I love you."

Elizabeth was astonished and remained silent.

He took this to be a sign of encouragement and continued. "You cannot be surprised—indeed, you must have wondered at my attention to you and subsequent dismissal over the past week. But you must understand that I had no intention of pursuing what I felt could never be. Until yesterday, I had not allowed myself to consider the possibility. I believe I have loved you almost from the first—I cannot remember where it began—and although I have fought against it, I cannot now continue without telling you how dear you are to me."

Elizabeth's eyes widened in shock, but the gentleman did not notice as he paced about.

"The disparity between our stations was difficult to overcome," he continued, "not only this, but also the long history of magical talent associated with my family, and the lack of it in yours. Naturally, it would cause any wizard of repute to pause—but that is of no consequence. My affection for you, and admiration of your abilities, has grown increasingly since I have known you. The strength of my attachment has conquered every endeavour to suppress it, despite my better judgment. I have feared—and I hope.

"Would you"—he stopped, moving to stand directly in front of her—"give me the honour of accepting my hand in marriage?"

There was a long and dreadful pause. Elizabeth looked into his bright eyes without wavering; he spoke of fear but did not display any. She must refuse him. While she was flattered that he should admire her—love her!—there was no other option.

"I have no desire to give you pain, and would express gratitude, were I able to feel it. But it is impossible for me to do so. I cannot accept you, Mr Darcy. I had no idea of your sentiments—but am certain that the other feelings you have expressed will prevent disappointment from being long-lasting."

Mr Darcy blinked, then stepped back, his face flushed. After another pause, he spoke in a voice of forced calmness. "Do I mean so little to you that I may be brushed aside without even an attempt at civility?"

"I might as well ask whether I mean so little to you, to be insulted and courted in one breath? That you like me against your better judgment? Comparing our ancestry! Yet you know very well that our fathers were contemporaries!" Elizabeth's eyes flashed. "But that is not the true reason for my incivility—if I was uncivil. Could you possibly imagine that I would accept you—you who have ruined my sister's hope for happiness perhaps forever! Will you deny it?"

"There is no reason for me to deny it," he replied, his voice low. "Towards him I have been kinder than towards myself."

Elizabeth laughed. "Kind to separate two people in love?"

"That is your perception. I acted in the best interest—and protection—of my friend. There are reasons behind my actions that you could not fathom."

"Protection from my sister? The degradation of a connexion between our families is so dangerous!"

"There is nothing dangerous about your family. Do not make assumptions based upon information that you do not understand," Mr Darcy said, his voice rising.

The sun still blazed through the trees upon their heads. "Assumptions are all that are possible with you, Mr Darcy," she retorted, stepping back further. "You led me to believe that I would be given the opportunity to understand certain pieces of information that were hinted at. But I should not have been surprised that you prefer—still!—to keep such information to yourself. Your character was unfolded to me in the recital which I received many months ago from Mr Wickham."

"You take an eager interest in that gentleman's concerns," said Mr Darcy in a less tranquil tone.

"He gave me more useful information than you have in the entirety of our acquaintance!"

"I have no doubt of it—although whether or not his information is 'useful' may be questioned."

"And you disdain him—denied him what was intended to be his, and reduced him to his present state of comparative poverty!"

Elizabeth took a deep breath, returning the intensity of Mr Darcy's gaze. "How, exactly, did you receive that wound? Was it defending your friend against the Thief? Or was he defending himself against you?"

Mr Darcy staggered back. "What?" he said, his eyes darkening.

"I know more than you think, Mr Darcy—I know of your uncle's true identity! You are a member of the Wizarding Court—but do you know that there is an informant within it? Your secretiveness, your lies—I was warned of it all."

"You suggest that *I* am the Thief?" Mr Darcy's voice constricted. "And this is your opinion of me! This is the estimation in which you hold me! I thank you for explaining it so fully. I have been secretive, but only out of the utmost necessity. You claim that you understand my role in the Wizarding Court—then by all means, you must understand also that the lives of my friends at times rest in my hands. Had I revealed all to you, in spite of my reservations, and flattered you—these accusations would not have been made."

"There is nothing you could have revealed, Mr Darcy, to aid you in your case," Elizabeth said, struggling to keep her voice from shaking. "Had we lived in a world without threat of evil, or such dangerous circumstances, you could not have made me the offer of your hand in any possible way that would have tempted me to accept it. The fundamentals of your character—that you are proud, caring little for the feelings of others except when convenient to yourself—remain the same and have been impressed upon me from the earliest moments of our acquaintance. You are the last man in the world whom I could ever be prevailed upon to marry."

The silence stretched quivering between them. Mr Darcy's eyes met hers with barely concealed astonishment and mortification. "I understand you, Miss Bennet. I am sorry, then, for what I have felt. Forgive me for having taken up so much of your time."

Elizabeth nodded, and both turned to walk swiftly in opposite directions. It was not until she was safely locked inside the comforts of her own room that she gave way to her tears.

⌇

When her tears had subsided, Elizabeth moved to sit at the open window and allowed a cool breeze to play across her cheeks. Even in all of her imaginings about Mr Darcy's secrets, she had never believed him to be in love with her. She did not pity him—she did not think his affection would last long enough to deserve it—and his treatment of her, of Jane, and of Mr Wickham drove away any she might have felt. But she regretted even the implication that he was involved with dark magic. She knew he was not and should have checked her anger.

That evening, they were fortunately not expected at Rosings for dinner. Elizabeth was subdued for the remainder of the day, and Charlotte expressed concern over her friend's health. Mr Collins wondered if she might ail from the same sickness that Lady Catherine had suffered, and Maria whispered that she was sorry she could not make her a cup of enchanted tea to raise her spirits. This brought a faint smile to Elizabeth's lips, and she assured them all that she was in good health, but perhaps tired from her overexertion in the Park earlier that day.

Charlotte put her to bed early after several cups of tea, with admonitions not to walk out the next morning. But Elizabeth rose early and could not prevent herself from walking out. They were expected at Rosings that afternoon, and she could not face the prospect of seeing Mr Darcy without the calm of the morning air to sustain her.

Thinking again of Mr Darcy (whom she had not stopped thinking of since their previous encounter) reminded her to avoid the birch grove where they met before. She had not walked very far, and was planning to return to the house when something caught the corner of her eye. Looking over with surprise, Elizabeth saw the stone building, this time almost entirely covered with vines, nestled some distance into the wood.

Now certain that this was an enchantment, Elizabeth felt the thrill of magic as she drew nearer; this was a different location than where she had spied it before. It took her much longer than expected to reach it, for the brush was dense and full of prickles that pulled at her skin and clothes. Several times, at the moment she thought she had arrived, she would look away only to look up again and see that the structure was further along than she had supposed. At last, tired and breathless, Elizabeth stood on the door-step, peering through a doorless arch into darkness. The light did not penetrate into the black. Elizabeth shivered, hesitating.

"Miss Bennet!" a voice called some distance away.

She turned her head and saw Mr Darcy approaching fast. Flushing, she straightened her bonnet.

"What do you do off the path, Miss Bennet?" he asked when he reached her, puzzled. "I have been walking for some time in the hope of meeting you."

Elizabeth swept her arm towards the stone hut behind her. "I found it intriguing—it is not the sort of magic to which I am accustomed, and came to investigate. I did not think to cause you trouble."

It was now Mr Darcy's turn to blush. "That was not my implication. What did you find intriguing? There is no particular magic here."

Elizabeth pursed her lips. "I cannot sense magic if there are no spells in effect, but this structure is filled with them. They are hazy to me, but I can just make out—" She paused, and then almost laughed at the look on his face. "I understand," she said, motioning back towards the darkened arch. "You cannot see it."

His brow creased. "See what?"

"This building."

"Where?"

"Mr Darcy, I am standing on its door-step!"

He moved to stand closer, frowning. "You must be mistaken. Were there a building here, I would certainly be able to detect it."

"No magic too difficult for you, then," Elizabeth said coldly, stepping away from the hut. "And you insist upon insulting me at every turn."

Mr Darcy looked pained. "I do not insult you, but it is impossible—"

"Look, in front of you." She held out her hands and closed her eyes in concentration. Through the haze of magic buzzing about, she located the correct spell and pulled at it. Reluctantly, slowly, but with greater ease than the spell she had unravelled before, it came undone.

Mr Darcy's eyes widened.

"You see, I did not imagine it," she said, moving forward.

"Do not go there!" Mr Darcy cried, taking hold of her arm.

Elizabeth was about to reproach him when the earth rocked beneath their feet, sending them sprawling to the ground. There was an explosion of sound, and for a moment she could not see anything but blinding white—followed by darkness. Mr Darcy held onto her arm tightly; when at last their surroundings returned to visibility, the stone building was gone, and a row of hedges encircled them. The sun was covered by a cloud and drops of rain began to fall from the sky.

Pulling her to her feet, Mr Darcy took hold of Elizabeth's shoulders. "Elizabeth, you must run to Mrs Collins and tell her that there has been an attack at Rosings. After which you must depart for London to be with your Aunt and Uncle Gardiner. Do you understand me?"

"What have I done?" she gasped, unable to meet his gaze and instead closing her eyes in an attempt to sort out the enchantments building around them.

"I do not know what has happened—please understand—I am telling you the truth. But I recognise this enchantment—I have battled it far too often."

"I cannot find the point at which it begins!" Elizabeth cried. "I do not know how to break it!"

"This is magic far more powerful than you or I could unravel. There is no hope of escape for me, I must wait until he comes—and he will come, although it might take some time. Elizabeth," he said again, urgently, with a slight shake to her shoulders. "You must go to your aunt and uncle in London, and you must hide. Put the shield on that you employed when we first met and walk out of here. I will follow as soon as possible."

"I will stay and help you fight him. I might be able to—"

"No!" he said, his hands gripping hers. "You will not stay."

"You cannot make me leave," she said, raising her chin.

"I beg you to leave," he said, releasing his hold on her arms.

They faced each other in silence as the rain fell harder, drenching them. "There is not much time! All of your father's worst fears have been realised in this moment. The Thief knows of you now—and that someone was able to work disenchantment. Do you have any idea of how strong the attraction of such power is to a Necromancer?"

Elizabeth did not reply but spread a barrier between themselves and the falling rain. "If you stay close to me, we could walk out together," she said, wiping the water from her face.

"And have the Thief follow you to London? Your shield is not powerful enough for me to escape the enchantment that holds me here in any case." He reached into his coat, pulling out two items. "Here," he said, pressing a watch into her hands. "Leave this on the ground just outside the Park. Do not remove any enchantment from it—it will work on its own, and it will bring me the aid I need. Will you do this for me?"

She nodded, shivering from the cold, and glanced up at the dark clouds amassing above them.

"And will you go to London? I will come there as soon as I can. I give you my word," he said, his eyes pleading. He pressed the second item, a letter, into her hand. "Take this. Do me the honour of reading it. It explains much—much of what should have been explained long before. Can you forgive me, Miss Bennet?"

"I am sorry for accusing you of such dark arts, Mr Darcy, and pray to God that you will be spared."

"There is no fear of that," he said, with the ghost of a smile. "My insufferable pride will not permit me to die. Will you go?" He pressed her hand. "You must hide yourself, you must be safe. Trust no one, not even if they resemble a close acquaintance, except your aunt and uncle, and Jane. Even then, test them with questions that only they could answer."

"Your code," Elizabeth said, returning his earlier attempt at a smile. "That is what it was for."

He nodded. "If someone approaches you in my form, if you are not greeted with the code, then it is not me. Protect yourself. And my cousin, Colonel Fitzwilliam—he is a part of this, too. He will identify himself as Fortinbras. Can you remember it?"

"And you are Pendragon?" Elizabeth said.

"No," he replied with a short laugh, moving her towards the edge of the enclosed circle. "That is only what I call myself. But in the Court, I am officially called the Poet."

"The Poet?"

"It was not a name of my choosing," he said gruffly.

Turning to him, Elizabeth took his hand. "I will do as you ask, with your promise of return," she said, dropping his hand as she pushed through the hedgerow.

"Your name!" Mr Darcy called urgently.

"Rosalind," she replied, and then was gone.

Alone, with the rain now dripping onto his head, and lightning crashing about him, Darcy spoke softly, knowing that he could not be heard. "Rosalind…would that I had been your Orlando."

CONCERNING MR DARCY'S LETTER

ELIZABETH RAN. HEART POUNDING IN HER CHEST, SHE CARED NOT that the rain soaked her hair or that branches tore at her dress. She forgot what she carried until she stumbled, and it flew out of her hand onto the ground. The silver metal of Mr Darcy's watch burned bright blue on the ground, leaving a red imprint on her hand where she had clenched it too tightly.

In an instant Colonel Fitzwilliam stood before her, the rain pelting down upon his head. He pulled his own watch, blazing red, out of his smoking waistcoat pocket. "This had better be important, Darcy. This is the third jacket burnt, and the last time—" He met Elizabeth's eyes in shock. "You are not my cousin."

Elizabeth shook her head, gasping for breath, her cheeks red. "There has been a terrible accident. Mr Darcy is trapped in a circle of hedgerows."

"He cannot hack his way out, then?" The colonel smirked.

"I am serious," Elizabeth cried.

He blinked. "What do you mean, trapped?"

"By enchantment. The Thief, Colonel! He is under attack! Mr

Darcy gave me that token"—she pointed to the watch—"and said it would bring him aid."

"He is trapped, and yet you are here? How do you know of this?"

"I cannot explain," Elizabeth said. "But before I point you in the right direction, I must ask you one thing."

The colonel's eyebrows rose.

"Your code name," she said.

His mouth gaped. "I cannot give it to you— Not unless—"

"Who's there?" Elizabeth said impatiently.

He started. "Nay, answer me. Stand and unfold yourself."

"Long live the King."

The colonel paused, his eyes narrowing. "Fortinbras," he said at length. "I am known by the name of Fortinbras."

"There." Elizabeth pointed. "In the woods, off the path." There was a rumbling beneath their feet and a flash of blue light from the Park. Colonel Fitzwilliam was gone without a word of farewell, and Elizabeth ran on to the parsonage.

She found Charlotte and Maria in the parlour, laughing over a bit of news sent from Mrs Lucas. At the sight of Elizabeth's pale face and soaked dress, their laugher was cut short.

"We had wondered what happened to you," Maria giggled.

Elizabeth stood gasping for breath as water dripped onto the carpet.

"Lizzy?" Charlotte rose, puzzled by her friend's appearance. "Is something the matter?"

"There—has been an attack at Rosings," Elizabeth said. Maria shrieked and dropped her embroidery, spilling many coloured threads across the floor.

"An attack?" Charlotte swayed, gripping the back of a chair to steady herself. "What are we to do?"

Elizabeth moved to take Maria's hand. "I spoke hastily. The attack has not yet occurred—or rather, is commencing as we speak in the woods of the Park. I do not have time to explain now, but we must fly to my aunt and uncle in town. It is not safe to remain here."

Maria burst into tears. Elizabeth attempted to comfort her, but Charlotte frowned.

"We will have none of your tears now, Maria," she said, moving to pull her sister to her feet. "Go up to your room and pack your things as quickly as you can."

As Maria scuttled past them, snuffling, Charlotte turned her eyes searchingly to Elizabeth. "And your mode of escape? We have no carriage, Lizzy."

Sinking into the chair Maria had vacated, Elizabeth said, "The thought had not occurred to me."

"Then I will speak to Mr Collins." Charlotte nodded, moving to the door.

"You are coming with us, Charlotte," Elizabeth called.

Her hand on the doorknob, Charlotte paused. "I think not, Lizzy. This is my home. You must not worry for me." So saying, she left the room to find her husband.

Elizabeth sat staring in a daze, her mind imagining a thousand possibilities before she started, jolting into action. Dashing up the stairs, she pulled off her wet clothes, kicking them into a corner. Fastening into her travelling gown, Elizabeth tossed all remaining personal effects into her trunk.

Pausing for only a moment when her hands fell upon the volume of Hamlet left for her by Darcy, it was packed along with the rest of her things; his letter, miraculously dry, she folded and put into her pocket. Willing her hands not to shake, she pulled the trunk into the hallway where she met Charlotte.

"Mr Collins is gone to Rosings to warn the household—and to seek assistance. Perhaps if Lady Catherine and her daughter are to depart, you might travel with them."

Elizabeth's brows rose, but she said nothing.

Moving into Maria's room, where the girl sat on her bed wretchedly sobbing into a handkerchief, Charlotte whispered, "Do not look so apprehensive, Lizzy, we will find other means if need be. If only we were more magically capable—then you might be transported. Perhaps Mr Darcy—"

Elizabeth shook her head. "Mr Darcy, along with his cousin, is battling against the Thief as we speak. They can be of little assistance to us now." As if to underscore her words, the floor lurched and both Elizabeth and Charlotte were thrown onto the bed.

While Elizabeth calmed Maria's wailing, Charlotte flew about the room packing her things. Both she and Elizabeth dragged the two trunks down the stairs to the front hallway. Mr Collins burst through the door, the rain still pounding outside behind him.

"Lady Catherine is most distressed—quite ill. She is in a swoon and was taken up to her rooms. But her daughter graciously sends the use of her carriage." He swept his arm behind him just as two long-faced footmen stepped onto the door-step and took up the small trunks.

Her eyes filling with tears, Elizabeth begged Charlotte and Mr Collins to depart with them, but to no avail. Mr Collins could not be prevailed upon to leave his parish at such an hour, and Charlotte would not part from her home.

"Watch over Maria, Lizzy." She clasped Elizabeth in a close embrace, another flash of blue light mingling with red and yellow in the distance. "That is all you can do for me."

"Maria will be safe with me, you may be certain," Elizabeth said, wiping the tears from her eyes. After a short farewell to Mr Collins, who was rambling almost uncontrollably, she and Maria were pressed into the carriage. Lurching forward against the rain, they hurtled towards London at break-neck speed.

Not ten minutes after their departure from Hunsford, the rain suddenly and completely ceased. Elizabeth, who sat with Maria's head against her shoulder, strained to see out the window, but at length resigned herself to staring at the dark red of the cushions across from her. The carriage was not one of Rosings' finest, but it seemed enormous to Elizabeth for two such small travellers. The sounds of Maria's whimpering, along with the steady rocking of the carriage, did little to ease her unsettled mind.

After what seemed to be half an hour (but was in fact only fifteen minutes), Maria's tears stopped when she dozed off. Elizabeth, trying to be as quiet as possible, adjusted Maria's head across her lap. She pulled Darcy's letter out of her pocket and broke the seal with shaking fingers.

Miss Elizabeth Bennet,

You need not be alarmed that this letter will contain any repetition of the offer which was, yesterday, so disgusting to you. But I cannot rest until the charges against me have been met—and you are told what should have been explained long ago.

I am a member of the Wizarding Court. As you have no doubt been informed, it was founded by my father nearly thirty years ago for the purpose of combating rising evil in this country, first and foremost, but also around the world. Magic in those days was far less regulated than it is today, even with so much left to be desired. He was aided in this resolve by several of his closest peers—your father being one of them. This may astonish you or it may not; it is of little consequence. Suffice it to say that Mr Bennet is no longer an active member, and therefore at liberty to reveal his former affiliation. His reasons for not informing you of the Court and his own involvement in it I can only speculate, and so recommend that you speak with him on the subject as soon as possible yourself.

The Wizarding Court by and large has been successful. The Court defeated the Necromancer, my own uncle, as you know, some twenty years ago. Naturally, I had no involvement in that particular case whatsoever but the reverberations of it are enormous. The Necromancer, once a member of the Wizarding Court himself, was barely overcome. The Thief, in all of his machinations, operates upon a similar basis. The newspapers have correctly identified him as a mimic of a greater mind. The Thief's targets are sporadic, without any particular pattern. He strikes always at those with magic he means to acquire for himself—but the motive, other than the obvious acquisition of power, is unknown. What I mean to say is that we know he is amassing power, but to what eventual purpose is unclear. World dominance? Governmental control? We know only that the Thief must be stopped. Several of the recent attacks were not accidental—they were ploys to draw the Thief out and defeat him. We have only been successful in drawing him out, but obviously not in defeating him.

What I tell you now must never be mentioned to anyone until you are given explicit permission by the gentleman himself. Mr Bingley is also a member of the Court and operates under the code name 'Tree.' He is my second line of defense, after Fortinbras, and I, his first. His membership in the Court is the first and foremost reason for my discouragement of a match between him and your sister—or, indeed, any lady. Men in our position, in all truthfulness, had best not marry for it is far too dangerous. Bingley was distracted from his work, which must hold priority over all.

With regard to his particular inclination, I must state that I have the highest regard for your sister; were you and she of a different family, the above would have been my only objection to such a match. As it is, the position of your family was only partly to blame for my disapproval. The behaviour of your mother and younger sisters on more than one occasion exhibited a complete lack of propriety. Your father is not excluded from this, however you and your elder sister must be. You were both always above reproach.

You mentioned dividing two people in love—that was not my intention. I observed your sister with impartiality and was unable to detect any traces of particular attachment to my friend. I concluded that the match was being encouraged from other areas, and that it would cause greater harm than good for all parties concerned. But Bingley has great natural modesty, with a stronger dependence on my judgment than on his own. To convince him, therefore, that he had deceived himself was no very difficult point. To persuade him against returning into Hertfordshire, when that conviction had been given, was scarcely the work of a moment. I cannot blame myself for having done thus much.

I will confess that I concealed from him your sister's presence in town this past winter. Perhaps this concealment, this disguise was beneath me; it is done, however, and it was done for the best. On this subject I have nothing more to say, no other apology to offer.

Now I must turn to a painful subject. I do not know what sort of lies Mr Wickham employed—but you may rest assured that you are not the first to have believed him. Most of what he related is full of half-truths, but what I shall relate can be backed by more than one witness. Mr Wickham is the son of a very respectable man, a moderately talented wizard in his own right. He was also the steward of my father's estate, and a member of the Wizarding Court (although not in the topmost circle). Mr Wickham, in his youth, displayed some natural aptitude towards magic, and my father, in part due to his affection for his father, supported his education. By an unfortunate circumstance of life, Mr Wickham's abilities did not mature as he grew older. His magical capabilities remain stunted, although in one area he grew particularly adept: slipping out of enchantments.

In spite of my opposition (for I had long since ceased to trust him), my father began the process of Mr Wickham's admittance into the Wizarding Court, in hopes that he might be of some use there. My father's premature death prevented the completion of these processes—but not for the reason you might think. The circumstances surrounding my father's death are generally known as 'mysterious,' but there was nothing mysterious about it—I was there. My father was attacked by an unidentified magician. He died, and I was too inexperienced to discover the clues that might lead me to the attacker's identity. I have my suspicions that the Thief who attacks others today is the same person who killed my father.

I do not know; I cannot know until his attacker is discovered and defeated.

Mr Wickham's involvement in my father's death was unintentional, but devastating. He revealed information—information meant to be kept amongst those in the Court only—to an aide of the attacker. We never discovered the identity of the aide, and Mr Wickham was punished far less severely than my personal feelings might have allowed. He is barred from the Wizarding Court forever and had been placed under several enchantments that would prevent him from speaking of it to anyone again. As you can see, his one ability shines forth—he has been able to slip out from under these restrictions and is again spreading tales in order to benefit himself.

While it is difficult for me, I must speak a word in Mr Wickham's defense: that is, that he was innocent of any involvement in the attacker's scheme to murder my father. Mr Wickham loved my father, in his own way, almost as much as his own—perhaps more.

After this, I thought (and hoped) that I would never see Mr Wickham again. I was mistaken. I have a younger sister, then fifteen years old and more than ten years my junior. She is my closest living relative and, due to the nature of my work, is moved often for her own protection. About a year ago, she was placed at Ramsgate for the summer under the care of a Mrs Younge (in whose character we were most unhappily deceived). Mr Wickham was also there and, make no mistake —by design.

He so far recommended himself to Georgiana, whose affectionate heart retained a strong impression of his kindness to her as a child, that she was persuaded to believe herself in love, and to consent to an elopement. I joined them unexpectedly a day or two before the intended elopement; my sister could not bear the thought of causing me pain and confessed the entire scheme. You may imagine how I felt, and how I acted.

For the sake of my sister, I could not risk public exposure. I wrote to Mr Wickham, who left immediately. Mrs Younge was, of course, removed from her charge. Mr Wickham's chief object was unquestionably my sister's fortune, which is thirty thousand pounds; but I cannot help supposing that the hope of revenging himself on me was a strong inducement. His revenge would have been complete, indeed.

He has never forgiven me for his exclusion from the Court, however justified. He insists to this day that he was not to blame for the slip—that he was under enchantment, or other such inducements, and that one such mistake should not bar him forever. I could not agree, and neither did my colleagues in the Court. The vote to exclude him was unanimous. His character tended towards such habits that would cause too great a danger for our organisation and its members.

Now you know the whole of it, or as much as I am able to relate in this letter. I do not know in what manner Mr Wickham imposed upon you, but you may be assured that concealment enchantments were unnecessary for him—he does well enough without them. You could not have known— detection could not be in your power, and suspicion certainly not in your inclination.

I apologise for not having relayed this information to you sooner, and in person. I should have spoken last night but was not then master enough of myself to know what could or ought to be revealed. For the truth of everything here, I appeal to the testimony of Colonel Fitzwilliam who, as a fellow member of the Wizarding Court, would be able to give any details you might desire of him.

I would ask that you not tamper with the enchantment I have placed upon this letter; the first conceals the true contents from any other person reading it, save yourself. The second will cause it to inflame after you read the last lines, and so I would suggest that you put it away from yourself as soon as possible.

I will only add, God bless you.
Fitzwilliam Darcy

THE MISSING ADDRESS

TOSSING THE LETTER ONTO THE SEAT ACROSS FROM HER, ELIZABETH watched the familiar blue flame consume it slowly. As much as she longed to keep it—to read it again—she knew it must not find its way into the wrong hands. There was no danger of her forgetting its contents; the words were now seared into her mind as if written with that blue fire itself.

Not wanting to wake Maria, Elizabeth wiped the persistent tears from her eyes. It was right that she should feel pain—humiliation! She, who prided herself on her own judgment, had been so free in her disapproval of one, and approval of another. It was dangerous to make such a mistake in such times or, indeed, at any time.

He had been proud, but his assessment of her family she found accurate and shameful. What would her mother think to learn that her behaviour, and that of her younger sisters, had contributed to the loss of Mr Bingley?

Maria stirred, turning to see Elizabeth's tear-streaked face. "Oh," she cried, "you are frightened too, Lizzy!"

Sniffing, Elizabeth did not contradict her, and the two held onto each other for the remainder of the journey. She was not frightened in the way Maria supposed her to be. She would have willingly returned to fight against the enemy. She feared, instead, for the life of the man she had rejected—and who had afterwards stood between her and great peril.

⁓

Dusk was falling as they arrived at Gracechurch Street. The way familiar to Elizabeth, she sat forward in anticipation of the carriage's halt. Unexpectedly, instead of stopping at the bright windows of the Gardiners' townhouse, the carriage drove forward and then circled about the street. Puzzled for a moment, Elizabeth called to the driver, but was not heard. She was therefore obliged to wait until they had gone about the street thrice before the carriage rolled to a stop, and a footman opened the door. Looking agitated, he stated in no uncertain terms that the address given to the driver was incorrect.

"I can assure you it is not," Elizabeth said, stepping out of the carriage and motioning for Maria to join her. "You have been most kind. Express our thanks to Lady Catherine and Miss de Bourgh, but if you would be so good as to unload our things, we will manage from here."

The footman squared his shoulders, protesting that they could not leave two women on the street after dusk at a non-existent address. The driver soon joined him in his exclamations. It took the last strands of Elizabeth's patience to assure them, as well as the remainder of her pocket money, before they were persuaded to leave. Maria, upset by the entire matter and at a complete loss as to why the Gardiners' house did not seem to exist, burst into fresh tears.

"Do not cry again, Maria," Elizabeth said, marching back to the house, which stood some one hundred yards away from where the carriage had stopped.

"But the driver was right—there is no such address, Lizzy! I counted the numbers as I went by," Maria protested, skipping to keep up.

"Maria, my aunt and uncle are wizards—and we were sent here

for our protection. Did you think their house would be visible to all passers-by?" Elizabeth said in clipped tones, stopping short in front of the steps. "Now, look there. The light is twinkling through the windows."

Maria sniffled and looked up obediently, her eyes widening as she discerned the cheery building. Taking her arm, Elizabeth hurried up the steps, the door opening for them immediately. It was with great disappointment Elizabeth was informed that Mr and Mrs Gardiner, along with their niece, had gone out half an hour before. A manservant was sent to retrieve their trunks, still sitting on the pavement where the footman had left them, while Elizabeth situated Maria in a room upstairs. She was soon put to bed with a cup of tea and a book, and Elizabeth removed to wait for her aunt and uncle in their small upstairs sitting room.

The wait was excruciating. Elizabeth paced for some time until at last she sat, exhausted, on the rug by the fire, her back supported against the leg of a large armchair. She could not stop thinking of Mr Darcy's face as he pulled her towards the edge of the hedgerows, rain dripping into his eyes.

"His pride will not permit him to die," she whispered to the fire.

Mrs Gardiner found her there some time later, fast asleep.

Kneeling down next to her niece, she shook her gently. "Lizzy?" she said, brushing a curl from her forehead. "What are you doing here?"

Elizabeth sat up with a start, her eyes sweeping the room to take in where she was. Seeing her aunt's alarmed face, she clasped her in an embrace. "There has been an attack at Rosings," she said, her voice trembling. "I came here to be safe."

Mrs Gardiner pulled back, holding Elizabeth's shoulders. "An attack? Are you hurt? And your friends?"

Elizabeth shook her head. "I am well, but I do not know anything as to the state of my friends."

Her face pale, Mrs Gardiner moved Elizabeth to sit on the sofa before leaving to seek her husband and Jane. The meeting between the two sisters was met with tears on both sides (which Elizabeth surmised to mean that Mrs Gardiner had informed Jane of the attack). But pleasantries were brief, as Mr Gardiner could not contain his questions for long.

"Everything," he said, sitting in his chair across from the three ladies. "You must give me every detail."

Elizabeth smiled weakly, knowing that she could not reveal everything. She wiped her tears. "Upon arriving at Hunsford, Mr Collins informed me of his patroness's eccentricity—she forbids the use of magic upon her property. Her reasons for this, you might guess, stem from the fact that her husband misused the practice"— here Mr Gardiner interrupted with a snort—"and was subsequently killed. I was sceptical at first, but I walked often in Rosings Park and was astonished to discover that it was, indeed, true: magic barely exists within the pales of Rosings."

"Was Lady Catherine the intended victim of the attack, due to her association with her husband?" Mr Gardiner asked.

"Not that I am aware, but you must not move ahead of me," Elizabeth said, exchanging a smirk with Mrs Gardiner. "On my walks, I discovered two areas which still contain magical properties. One was of an ordinary sort, among a patch of trees. The other—it was a small stone structure that changed locations from day to day. No sooner had I seen it than I was eager to explore it. Imagine my astonishment when I returned the next day, only to discover that it was no longer there. It would be several days before I discovered it again. Mr—Mr Darcy was with me, and he could not see it. So I—I did something foolish. I removed the concealment spell, and attempted to step in. Instantly, we were enclosed by a barrier of hedgerows; the hut had disappeared, and we were beset by hostile enchantments."

"Lizzy." Jane trembled, clutching her hand. "It is unbearable! How did you escape?"

"I was unhindered by the entrapment spells. I escaped—but Mr Darcy did not. He insisted that I come here, rather than wait for what was coming."

"Which was?" Mrs Gardiner probed.

"The Thief. I did not meet him myself." Elizabeth paused. "You know that Mr Darcy is—"

"Yes, yes." Mr Gardiner waved her on. "A member of the Wizarding Court. How could you have known it was the Thief?"

"By the enchantments—they are always particular to the enchanter."

Mr Gardiner rubbed his hands across his face. "It was right for you to come here. But I do not know how long we can keep you safe—I do not understand any of this, Lizzy." He sighed. "My first instincts tell me that it could not have been an attack in the Thief's ordinary style—it seems as though you stumbled upon something accidentally. The association of this structure with Rosings is alarming to me. Most alarming."

Elizabeth's eyes widened. "Because of the Necromancer?"

"Precisely. But I could be wrong. You say you were with Mr Darcy? It could have been a trap intended for him that you stumbled upon."

Mrs Gardiner turned to her husband. "What are we to do, Edward? In any case, the Thief now knows of Elizabeth's ability. No doubt that was the reason Mr Darcy sent her here."

"The Thief knows of her power, perhaps...or rather, knows that someone used disenchantment to break his concealment spell. But if Elizabeth left before he arrived, there is no possibility he has acquired knowledge of her identity. Darcy was wise in sending her away—although I am sure you did not agree to the plan immediately, Lizzy?" Mr Gardiner said with a half-smile.

Elizabeth blushed.

"And you do not know..." Jane faltered. "If he is still alive?"

"No." Elizabeth's voice broke. "I do not."

They sat in silence, each lost to their own thoughts. At length, Mrs Gardiner tilted her head, brows drawn together in uncertainty. "Was that a knock at the door?"

All four listened, hearing nothing at first, until the knock grew more insistent. Suddenly, they heard the sound of the door opening. A man shouted something up the stairs.

"That is Barnaby," Mr Gardiner said, springing from his chair and hastening out the door.

"Mr Barnaby is our contact between the two Courts," Mrs

Gardiner explained to Elizabeth just before her husband reappeared in the doorway.

"Come down at once, all of you," he said, before disappearing again.

Elizabeth bounded down the stairs, stopping short at the sight that greeted her in the hall. Three men in dark cloaks stood in the doorway, the light barely illuminating their faces. Gasping in surprise, her eyes met Mr Darcy's bright ones. He was by far the tallest of the three; next to him, Elizabeth recognised first the unusually sombre face of Mr Bingley; the third man, Barnaby, she knew as Darcy's valet. Her uncle was crouched down next to the form of another man, stretched out across the floor. With a cry she knelt next to her uncle, taking Colonel Fitzwilliam's hand.

"Edward?" Mrs Gardiner called. She and Jane now stood at the foot of the stairs.

"We must move him into the study, quickly," Mr Gardiner said. The three men hoisted him up, following Mr Gardiner.

Elizabeth addressed Mr Darcy. "He is not dead?"

His eyes met hers only briefly. "Nearly so. I know we should not have come here because of the danger, but I did not know who else could unravel the enchantments in time."

Mr Gardiner shoved piles of paper and writing utensils off his desk onto the floor, and Colonel Fitzwilliam was laid across it. "Now, Jane," Mr Gardiner said. "Can you help me—"

"No." Mr Darcy pulled the hood from his head. "Miss Elizabeth must remove the spell."

"Lizzy?" Mr Gardiner blinked. "But she has no experience—"

"Jane will assist me, Mr Darcy," Elizabeth said. Both sisters moved forward, each taking one of the colonel's hands. "I do not know the nature of the injury," Elizabeth murmured. "But if we work together—"

"Of course." Jane nodded. They worked for some time in silence, while Mr Darcy paced. Suddenly the colonel bolted up, his eyes bright, and began to sing boisterously.

"Hold him," Mr Darcy called, and the two other men moved forward to push Colonel Fitzwilliam back into the desk.

"His wits are addled too," Elizabeth said through clenched teeth.

The difficult work at last came to an end. Elizabeth was exhausted, but able to control the shaking of her hands. Jane spent several additional minutes bent over the now sleeping form of Colonel Fitzwilliam.

"When he wakes, he will be hungry," she said, stepping back and brushing loose strands of hair from her face. "But I have added several spells to increase his comfort. I think he will find himself feeling better than he does ordinarily for a few hours."

Mr Darcy almost rolled his eyes. "I am not sure that was advisable—Fitzwilliam is difficult enough as it is, ordinarily."

"You did marvellously, Miss Bennet," Mr Bingley said, removing his hood.

An awkward silence fell upon the room. Jane was too shocked to reply, not having recognised him before, and Mrs Gardiner could not help but notice Mr Darcy and Elizabeth stealing glances at each other when each thought the other wasn't looking.

"Tea is in order, shall we all take tea?" she said briskly.

～

"Let me see if I can begin, and you may pick up where I leave off?" Mr Gardiner said, raising a brow at Mr Darcy.

Mr Darcy, the only one of the company who had chosen to remain standing, looked up from staring at his tea long enough to reply, "Proceed."

Mr Gardiner took a breath. "You, along with Elizabeth, were walking in Rosings Park when you came across a small stone structure."

"No."

"No?"

"Miss Elizabeth came across the structure. I could not see it."

"Ah, yes." Mr Gardiner took a sip of tea. "And since you could not see it, she chose to disenchant the concealment spell. Why you should do something of that sort, Lizzy—"

"My dear," Mrs Gardiner interrupted, "that is not relevant to the chain of events."

Mr Gardiner scowled. "After which, Elizabeth attempted to

enter the structure, but it promptly disappeared, you found your-selves encircled by hedgerows and beset by unpleasant spells."

"That is correct."

"Well." Mr Gardiner sighed. "That is where I leave off, and you must begin. Elizabeth escaped, and yet you remained. Why?"

"To prevent the Thief from following."

Mr Gardiner looked from Mr Darcy to Elizabeth, and then to Mr Bingley and Barnaby, who both sat by the fire, listening intently. "Would you leave us for a moment, gentlemen."

Barnaby stood, with Mr Bingley following somewhat more reluctantly, closing the door behind them.

Elizabeth sensed the addition of four muffling spells cast at once. "Must you all provide your own variation on a theme?" she grumbled, holding her head.

Mr Darcy immediately removed his spell, followed by Jane and Mr Gardiner.

Mrs Gardiner smiled. "Mine was, by far, the superior of the four in any case."

"It was imperative that Elizabeth—Miss Elizabeth—not fall into the hands of the enemy. Her ability is too great a power for one such as the Thief to resist," Mr Darcy said, moving to take the seat Mr Bingley had vacated by the fire.

"And your ability is not as equally dangerous?" Mr Gardiner raised a brow. "Do you believe it was a trap intended for you—or for Elizabeth?"

Mr Darcy considered. "Not for Miss Elizabeth. I am certain that until today, the Thief had no idea any such person existed."

"I do not understand why my ability should prove such a temp-tation to anyone," Elizabeth protested. "I can unravel magic, but I cannot wield it. In all of history, there has never been a case of a disenchanter who was able to use the magic he removed!"

The room fell silent, and Mr Darcy reluctantly met her gaze. "That is true, but we must always err on the side of caution. I am not certain," he said, turning back to Mr Gardiner, "that it was an attack at all. I believe that Miss Elizabeth unwittingly discovered a point of return for the Thief—we have many such portals ourselves —or perhaps something greater."

"And the reason for its being found at Rosings?"

"I cannot know until there has been further investigation. I was unable to examine the area properly, as you might suppose. The enchantments already in place continually assaulted me as time progressed until the Thief's arrival. At that point, my cousin arrived, having received the message I relayed with Miss Elizabeth's help. He was unable to break into my prison for some time, which was perhaps better, for as soon as he did—" Mr Darcy's voice wavered for a moment. "My cousin is a brilliant wizard, but his rashness in this case got the better of him. He was unprepared for what he found."

"Yet you are both here, alive," Mr Gardiner replied, "and the Thief unconquered."

"It was most curious," he replied, his brow furrowed. "The Thief was also less prepared than in our previous battles. I might have won—except that both Fitzwilliam and I were cast out of our prison, with no means of finding a way back in. Everything seemed as it was before Miss Elizabeth removed the spell, and there was no possibility of pursuit. I called for Bingley, and then Barnaby, since he would be able to direct us to you."

"Cast out?" Mr Gardiner said.

"What will you do now, Mr Darcy?" Elizabeth ventured.

He turned his eyes to her again. "Tomorrow, I will return to Rosings under the guise of comforting my aunt and cousin. But I will, of course, be attempting to rediscover the location of the hut— or gather clues as to where it might have disappeared."

Mr Gardiner cleared his throat. "Are you certain that is the wisest course?"

"It is the one I have chosen," Mr Darcy said in a low voice.

"You will not find it again without my aid," Elizabeth said. All four of her companions turned incredulous gazes upon her.

"Absolutely not, Lizzy!" Mr Gardiner protested, with Mrs Gardiner nodding in agreement.

"You must not put yourself in danger, Elizabeth," Jane admonished, and then turned her gaze on Mr Darcy. "Or you."

He rose. "I am determined, Miss Bennet. If I may be so bold,

Mrs Gardiner, as to join my cousin—" He swayed slightly, causing Elizabeth and Jane both to rush to support him.

Mrs Gardiner shook her head. "It is nearly morning. It was foolish of us to keep you up for so long. I am sorry for the accommodations, but Maria Lucas is asleep in the guest room, and the nursery was the most comfortable alternative."

"We will meet again in the morning," Mr Gardiner called, as the women hurried Mr Darcy out of the room, "but not too early."

They found Barnaby and Mr Bingley in the hall, both sound asleep but quickly roused by a firm stamp of Mrs Gardiner's foot. Ushering all up the stairs, she first sent Elizabeth and Jane to bed before settling the gentlemen on mattresses conjured for the occasion, with Colonel Fitzwilliam in the nursery.

Elizabeth felt fatigued, but her mind raced with concerns from the evening. She longed to talk to Jane but knew by her sister's trembling fingers as they unbuttoned the back of her dress that Jane's thoughts were as jumbled as her own.

Elizabeth awoke to the sound of birds singing at her windowsill. She could not have been abed for more than four hours but, recalling the events of the last evening, threw the covers off and rushed to prepare herself to go downstairs. Jane was asleep, so Elizabeth slipped out of the room and turned her steps to the breakfast room.

As she expected, Mr Darcy sat at the table, his face pale but his eyes alert, sipping a cup of coffee.

"Good morning, Mr Darcy."

"Miss Bennet."

She sat across from him, unsure where to begin. "You do not wear your customary façade this morning," she said, noting his ruffled hair. "Why is that?"

He cleared his throat. "I am sure it is of little consequence to you."

Elizabeth looked down, feeling the bitterness behind his words but unable to fault him for it. She busied herself with pouring a cup of coffee and buttering a roll.

"However, if I do knock over my coffee, you must forgive me," he ventured in a softer tone, but still not meeting her gaze. "I have relied upon a counter-clumsiness spell for far too long."

Elizabeth laughed. "You are forgiven then." She sobered. Their eyes met for a moment. "I am glad that you are…all right."

"Not dead, you mean?" He smiled wryly.

"And not cursed with more painful spells for me to unravel." Elizabeth smiled in return. "Very glad."

"Are you?"

"Glad of what?" Colonel Fitzwilliam beamed, bouncing into the room. "Oh yes, of course, glad that I am miraculously recovered! All due to you, I understand, Miss Bennet?"

Elizabeth, startled, almost overturned her cup. "And my sister, Jane. I did not work alone."

"I feel superb!" the colonel exclaimed. "Never better in my life! Famished, though."

"We will soon remedy that," Elizabeth said, laughing. "I will fetch my aunt, I am sure she is having something prepared especially."

Escaping from the room, Elizabeth leaned against the wall in the hallway to catch her breath. She admonished herself not to forget that in that room sat the man she had rejected, not one she had accepted. She could not forget—however glad she was of his safety, however much she longed to defeat the Thief alongside him. In spite of everything, she had made her choice…and she did not regret it. Why would she?

A PARTNERSHIP

MRS GARDINER HAD WELL PREPARED THEIR COOK FOR THE additional guests that morning. Breakfast was perhaps not as fashionable as some in the party might have been accustomed, but it was hearty. With the morning had come new light and better cheer for the entire company. Mr Darcy was silent—but then, he was almost always silent. Jane descended into the breakfast room with calm serenity and a ready smile that she could not help but direct towards Mr Bingley's eager attentiveness. Only Elizabeth and Mrs Gardiner could have known what disquiet she must have felt the night before.

Mr Gardiner did not breakfast with them, for he had eaten some time earlier. Instead, he locked himself in his study with strict instructions not to be disturbed until after he had sorted through the mounds of papers strewn across the floor. Conversation at the table was carried by Colonel Fitzwilliam, who was in remarkable spirits. He was eternally grateful to Jane and Elizabeth, had never felt better in his life, and could not resist regaling them with further tales of his mishaps in the line of duty. No one particularly minded the colonel's jovial ramblings, as it allowed each to keep to his or her own thoughts.

At exactly ten o'clock, Mr Gardiner entered the breakfast room to request Mr Darcy's presence, along with that of Barnaby, in his study. Seeing Elizabeth's enquiring look, her uncle smiled. "Do not make yourself uneasy—we shall not discuss matters that pertain to you or Jane without your presence."

Elizabeth was uneasy, but she did not protest further. Mrs Gardiner suggested to Jane that Mr Bingley might enjoy seeing the garden, where she hoped he might tend to a hydrangea that had not bloomed properly. Elizabeth was concerned for her sister, but did not follow after catching a look from Mrs Gardiner. Soon afterwards, the colonel was again overcome with drowsiness and chose to return to his bed.

"Are you all right, my dear?" Mrs Gardiner enquired once they were alone.

"As well as may be expected." Elizabeth smiled. "Has Uncle Gardiner written to Papa? I should like to know what he would say to all of this."

"Apparently, Mr Darcy sent him a message last night after the rest of us had already gone to bed, explaining the whole of the circumstances," Mrs Gardiner said, watching the expression on Elizabeth's face.

"Oh?" was the only reply, and Elizabeth moved to sit by the window.

"I was greatly surprised by his cordiality," Mrs Gardiner said.

"Whose?"

"Mr Darcy. After the account we heard of him in Hertfordshire —and even from you!—we did not expect any kind of cooperation between the Wizarding Court and our own. And yet, as it seems, Mr Darcy has orchestrated the contact between the two."

"Did he?" Elizabeth's cheeks felt slightly warm. "I am surprised."

"He was far more withdrawn this morning, to be sure." Mrs Gardiner nodded. "I could be wrong. We may not have known him long enough for his disagreeability to appear."

Elizabeth laughed. "In truth, I am not enough myself this

morning to answer you. His behaviour in Hertfordshire and what I thought of him then—or even yesterday—is much altered."

"Experiencing such danger can alter how we view a person, or change it completely. At times, those you would least expect prove to be the greatest friends in time of need."

Elizabeth did not answer, and Mrs Gardiner did not press. Nearly an hour later, the gentlemen emerged from Mr Gardiner's study and joined them in the downstairs sitting room.

"It is official," Mr Gardiner said, unable to hide his grin. "The Wizarding Court and our Merchant's Court will operate on a joint basis."

"It is a great loss to the Wizarding Court that you are unable to be a member," Mr Darcy said, returning the smile with a hint of his own. "But I believe that with a partnership, we can perhaps be of better use to one another."

"Mr Darcy will return to Rosings, along with his cousin," Mr Gardiner continued, turning to Elizabeth.

"But you will not permit me to do so," she finished.

"You must understand that the danger is too great," Mr Gardiner said. "And your father—"

"Would not permit her to go in any case."

Turning in surprise, Elizabeth saw her father standing in the doorway, Jane and Mr Bingley not far behind him. Springing up, Elizabeth rushed into his warm embrace.

"He arrived only two moments ago," Jane said to the rest.

"And not a moment too soon." Mr Bennet did not bother to remove his travelling cloak before sitting down across from Mr Gardiner and Mr Darcy. "I thank you for your letter," he said, nodding to the latter, "although I must say it was unexpected."

"None of this is expected," Mr Darcy replied.

"I think it best that my daughters return to Longbourn with me. They have been away for too long as it is," Mr Bennet added, seeing Elizabeth's look of protest.

"Is your home adequately secure?" Mr Darcy asked, not blinking at Mr Bennet's look of incredulity.

"Dare you ask such a question?" he said, his voice hoarse.

"Even if the rest are ignorant of my situation, I know that you are not."

"Then you must understand why the question was asked, sir," Mr Darcy replied, his gaze unwavering.

Mr Bennet's eyes crinkled slightly as he smiled. "Yes, I understand. But you have been to my home, Mr Darcy, and if I am not mistaken, added to its fortifications—without my permission—following news of the first attack."

Elizabeth looked at Mr Darcy in surprise, but his eyes did not move from her father's. "It will be adequate. But may I suggest that Miss Elizabeth not remain in one location for long? Such has been my practice, and that of the Court, for several years."

Mr Bennet sighed. "I will consider it, Mr Darcy, but not today. Today, I must return my daughters to their mother before she hears of the attack in Kent. And she will hear of it—it is only a matter of time."

Mr Darcy nodded, satisfied. Jane removed with Mrs Gardiner to pack her things, while the rest were invited to join Mr Gardiner for a small dinner. Mr Bennet and Barnaby accepted his invitation, and Elizabeth was moving out the door when she paused, hearing Mr Bingley address his friend.

"Do you know, Mr Darcy, Miss Bennet has been in town for these past few months, and I had no idea of it!"

Mr Darcy did not reply.

"It is strange—or perhaps not so strange—that Caroline failed to mention her visit to me. Did you?"

"Did I what?"

"Know of Miss Bennet's presence in town?"

Mr Darcy's eyes met Elizabeth's briefly. "I did."

There was a dreadful pause. Mr Bingley's face flushed, and after several moments of silence he left the room. Mr Darcy turned away from Elizabeth and moved to look out the window.

"Will you rebuke me now?" he asked, his face still hidden from her.

"Mr Bingley's silence was rebuke enough," she replied.

"I am sorry—my presence must disturb you. Were it not necessary, I can assure you that—"

"You do not disturb me," Elizabeth said, moving to join him at the window. "We have both been wrong."

Mr Darcy took in a sharp breath.

"How do you intend to locate the stone hut again when you were not even aware of its presence until I revealed it to you?" Elizabeth said, feeling that she must change the subject.

He smiled slightly, looking down at his hands. "There is the possibility that I might be able to detect it now that I am aware of its existence. But in complete truth, I do not know, Miss Elizabeth. I doubt that it even remains at Rosings, but I am determined to discover what I can."

"And I must go home to be useless; this, the only consequence of my discovery," Elizabeth said, willing her tears not to rise.

"Your safety, and that of your family, is of the utmost importance."

"There will be little safety for anyone if no one is willing to accept the aid I can give." Elizabeth moved towards the door.

"Have you forgotten already the code that I gave you?" Mr Darcy turned and met her gaze for the first time.

Elizabeth nodded.

"You will remember it, in the future," he said, his eyes softening, pleading. "I would beg you to use it if ever there is a question of your safety. And remember that I have always sought your aid when it was most needed. I would ask nothing more of you."

Elizabeth waited until he had turned his gaze back towards the street below to look over at the lines of his face and resisted the urge to smooth back his hair from his eyes. "I will remember it," she said, before quitting the room.

~

Elizabeth stood with her back against her father's study door, chewing her lip. Their journey from London to Longbourn had been uneventful. Mrs Gardiner had promised to write every possible detail she was able as news came in. It was small consolation, but Elizabeth appreciated her thoughtfulness. Now home, her main concern was to speak with her father, and to her sister. Jane was in her room, resting from the long journey and fatigued from the events of the past day. But that was best—Elizabeth would speak to her father first.

Her soft knock was answered by an immediate call to enter. Walking in, Elizabeth moved to sit at her customary chair before Mr Bennet's desk. "Well, Papa, why have you never told me that you were a member of the Wizarding Court?"

Hands shaking slightly, he pulled out his pipe. "You will forgive me the liberty, Lizzy," he said with a smile, "but I must think."

Elizabeth laughed, drawing her feet up onto the chair and resting her head against her knees. "You need not even ask!"

Mr Bennet rose, pacing in front of the window, his pipe smoking in shades of orange, yellow, and then blue. He took in a deep breath. "What I am about to tell you, you must never speak of to anyone else—with the exception of Mr Darcy."

Elizabeth nodded, placing her feet back to the floor.

"I say the exception of Mr Darcy, because I know that he spoke to you of it first—and because he revealed a secret that few know."

"Papa, I—"

"I am—or rather, was—a member of the Wizarding Court. The details of what you know or do not know are unclear to me—but I understand that you have been made aware of a code."

Elizabeth nodded.

"Allow me to test it, if you will," Mr Bennet said, clearing his throat. "Who's there?"

"Nay, answer me. Stand and unfold yourself."

"Long live the King."

Elizabeth paused. "I do not know your code name."

"Never mind that. It was long ago. I was what they might call one of the 'founders'. I knew Mr Darcy's father—quite well. My circumstances, for various reasons, are different at present. I have not been capable of active participation in the Court for these twenty-three years—and am not likely to ever be again. Elizabeth," he said, coming forward to take her hand. "The Wizarding Court battles against the deepest kinds of evil. I need not remind you of how dangerous it is; I believe you are well enough aware."

Elizabeth laughed. "Yes, indeed!"

"I do not approve of your involvement in any of this, or Jane's. Although I can understand your aunt and uncle's—as well as Mr Darcy's—desire for it."

Elizabeth's eyebrows rose.

"Your gift—while not magical—is powerful. Mr Darcy is aware of that power."

"Do you trust him?" Elizabeth asked.

Mr Bennet looked up, startled. "I knew his father much better, but after the events of yesterday—I have little choice in the matter. Lizzy"—he sighed—"I know what you desire; you have wished to use your gifts towards such ends since you were a little girl. You are angry with me for bringing you home."

"I understand your motivations, they are no different from everyone else's," Elizabeth replied. "But I do not understand why you have not told me of this before. If you are no longer a member of the Court, there could have been little danger in it."

"You would be surprised to learn how little I have heeded caution—and nearly suffered for it."

"What?"

"I should not have permitted you to go to Rosings. The connexion between our houses is too dangerous."

Elizabeth's eyes narrowed. "In what way? Beyond our connexion to Mr Collins?"

"Yes—my connexion to that family occurred before you were born." Mr Bennet shook his head, moving to sit in his chair across from her. "How much do you know of the Necromancer?"

"I know what most people know. That he was a dark wizard bent on power. That he learned the art of stealing other wizards' magic, and that he left his victims dead. I learned more recently that he was defeated by a member of the Wizarding Court called the Jester and—" She watched her father shift in his seat, her eyes widening with realisation. She took in a breath. "All of this time, the reluctance to pursue magic, to keep my ability to practice disenchantment a secret—your reluctance to go to town, to move in higher circles—it was all to keep you hidden away? Is that because it was you? You are the Jester?"

"I am. I was."

THE JEST

MR BENNET SMOKED HIS PIPE IN SILENCE FOR SEVERAL MINUTES. AT length, he set it aside and coughed.

"Shall I start from the beginning?" he said, waiting for Elizabeth's eager nod. He paused to clear his throat. "I knew Mr Darcy's father—George Darcy—at Oxford. We were idealists then; or rather, George was always the idealist, and I went along with him. He was the best man I ever knew, blessed with all of those qualities that made people love him."

"Such as?" Elizabeth raised a brow.

"Principles, good judgment, and determination," Mr Bennet said, returning her look. "The Court was his idea from the beginning, although its name was of my own creation. If it is possible"— he chuckled, running a hand through his white hair—"try to imagine me as I was in my youth. I thought entirely too much but was in possession of what were called 'lively spirits.' The combination of these two traits puzzles me even today, but there you have it. Now, my spirits are somewhat subdued," he said with a soft smile, "but my thoughts are perhaps more rambling than ever before.

"At any rate—" He cleared his throat again. "Imagine George, full of ideals and spouting grand notions about mankind and the greater good. I called him Arthur—our very own king of the round table—almost from the beginning of our acquaintance. Little did I know then how far my jest would take us.

"We were at the top of our class and fantastically good at enchantment. George was not as naturally gifted with magic, but he was the most dedicated. The Court began on a small scale, curtailing small mishaps that always occur at school—pranks and the like. But as we grew older, it seemed the world grew more dangerous…and so did our mission.

"George's Court was no longer a joke. Our numbers grew quickly—acceptance of its members was a far less complicated process, based upon good will and trust. As it remains today, we were never connected to the government, but they depended upon us. The Wizarding Court began near the end of our studies and continued successfully for some years afterwards." Mr Bennet stopped, a shadow passing over his face.

"Here we come to Lewis de Bourgh—brilliant, and far superior to any of us. George married some six years after the founding of the Court. His wife, Lady Anne, was an accomplished enchantress, and while not the sort who was willing to take up membership, supported him in all endeavours. Her sister was Lady Catherine, making Lewis brother-in-law to George. I do not remember the particular circumstances leading to his admittance, but we could not help but be grateful for the membership of such a wizard.

"There is no doubt that Lewis was good in the beginning. Cold, proud—but such were many of our numbers. His, shall we say, conversion was almost accidental. The Court operated on two different levels at the time, and still may to some extent: one was the guardianship of the nation against magical enemies, but the other was the betterment of its citizens through education. We wrote papers, published books, conducted experiments—"

"Experiments?" Elizabeth asked.

"You look rather alarmed. Most pertained to the four elements and were highly controlled. But Lewis often dallied on the dangerous side—there was an experiment, intended to test the truth behind a claim that wizards might exchange abilities at will through various and complicated enchantments. Lewis was one wizard, and I do not recall the name of the other. The experiment was half-successful. Lewis received the young man's ability, but his own did not transfer.

"I see your look, but believe me when I say that it was not intentional...not at the beginning. The young man's ability—strength with Fire, I believe, and one of Lewis's weak points—was transferred back immediately. He came to me later—Lewis, that is—I have no notion of why. We were not close. 'It was exhilarating,' he said, 'that rush of power.' I did not know then to what depths he would descend to achieve it again.

"When the attacks began, they were barely noticed. Lewis's earliest targets were those deemed inconsequential by most—a poor farmer here, a merchant there. We remained oblivious to the identity of the attacker for three years; it wasn't until his greed for power led him to thieve from one of our own. Even then, the evidence was lacking. George was the last to accept his treachery. Louis was a member of his family, their children were close in age. Lady Anne was close to her sister, and it was not until Anne herself convinced him of the truth that George was spurred to action. I was the reluctant spearhead of the operation."

"Reluctant?" Elizabeth rested her head on her hand.

Mr Bennet gave her a slight smile. "Reluctant, yes. I had met a young woman, an exceptional wizard, talented in the realm of fire. She was quite beautiful, Lizzy. She was well on her way to becoming a member of the Court, and we were recently married—"

Elizabeth's brows shot up in surprise.

"But it was my duty to fulfil George's request. He could not—would not—kill his brother-in-law. There was a fear that the Necromancer, as he was commonly called, would soon amass enough power as to make him invincible. Those were dark days." Mr Bennet sighed, passing a hand over his eyes. "Several of our number were murdered. After Lewis's eviction from the Court, we established what is now known as the code, offering some level of protection. But his power had become too great, and we had not discovered all of his allies.

"The plan was many-faceted, but none of it was ever carried to completion. We intended first to rescue his wife and daughter, who had not been allowed out of seclusion for two years. After which, we would launch the attack—intending to lay a trap of some kind. The Necromancer learned of our intention to capture his family before we were given the chance to act, and I, as head of the operation, was his first target for revenge.

"It was midnight on the day before we had intended to execute our plan when he descended upon us. I cannot—I will not detail the attack. It was only after he injured her—"

"Your wife?"

"Yes. Only then was I able to defeat him. I have told you before, Lizzy, that the rumours of the Necromancer's return are false. I killed him—and his dying curse blights us to this day."

"What?"

"You would not know of it—it is not any kind of ordinary enchantment, and one that you could never break, even if you wished to." Mr Bennet leaned forward, taking her hand. "It is a curse too powerful for ordinary enchantment—or disenchantment—to overcome."

"Your wife, she—she died?" Elizabeth asked.

Mr Bennet blinked. "No. No, she did not—she is very much alive."

Elizabeth gasped. "Mama? Mama was a wizard?"

"She is not now what she was—and has not been for twenty-two years. I do not know if the curse took my wife and left another in her form, or simply imprisoned her spirit. Perhaps it brought out all of her weaknesses, leaving little room for magic, or thought. The woman that I loved is gone, and yet not gone. She was not unlike you, Lizzy," he said, removing his hand to rub his eyes. "And I? Left as a mere shell—an ordinary man—without a jot of enchantment running through my veins."

"A dying curse," Elizabeth whispered almost to herself. She turned a reproachful gaze upon him. "Papa, how could you not tell me?"

"You forget, Lizzy, that you are still very young. How could I tell my daughters that their mother was left a fraction of herself because I could not defeat her attacker in time?"

"But we would have known who she was…once."

They sat in silence as Mr Bennet re-lit his pipe. "Do you see now what a fool I was to allow you to go to Rosings? I had grown careless—or perhaps, I might say uncaring."

"So you left the Court?" Elizabeth rose, moving to gaze out of the window.

"George would have allowed me to retain membership—but I was too deep in my own despair to accept his pity, or gratitude. I had triumphed, but at what cost! We wrote to each other, over the years, but I never saw him alive again."

"Is Mr Darcy—" Elizabeth's throat caught. "Much like him?"

"Very like in many ways," Mr Bennet replied. "His eyes…but George won friends wherever he was met; his son seems to only cause offence. On the other hand, he is far more talented than his father could have ever dreamed to be."

"Do you know of the circumstances surrounding his death?"

"George's? I know that they were suspicious—but there was little I might have done about it."

"Was there not?" Elizabeth turned to face him. "Forgive me, Papa, but—you have lived here all these years, secluded, in one turn not allowing those of us who are capable the opportunity to improve our talents, and at the other allowing me to visit the widow of the man you killed! All this time, you have been the one who saved our country from the greatest threat known to wizards in a hundred years! Why did you not tell me?"

His eyes glistened brightly in the firelight. "Can you forgive me, Lizzy? You and your sister Jane were what he never counted on—that we might still have children, and that they might retain the gifts their parents had lost. I could not bear to lose you, or any of your sisters. You are all that remain."

Elizabeth walked over to her father and placed a kiss upon his cheek. "May I tell Jane?" she asked.

With a sigh, Mr Bennet nodded. "You may tell her. But not tonight. You may tell her on the morrow. But by no means are you to mention any of it to your mother—is that understood? She remembers too much as it is. Bits and pieces. There is no need to cause her greater fear."

If Mrs Bennet was astonished by her second daughter's particular attention to her the next morning, she did not display it. She enquired after her brother and his wife, and whether there were any new fashions in town to report. She bemoaned that Jane had not had a chance to see Bingley—concluding that he was a very undeserving man after all. Turning then to Elizabeth, she asked whether the Collinses lived comfortably, and if they spoke of Longbourn often. But her inquiries did not extend much further; in fact, Mrs Bennet was much too distracted by the wailings of her two youngest daughters to pay her two eldest any undue attention. She had not been told of the attack on Rosings, and the affair had been well enough hushed up as to not reach Meryton's eager gossips. In any event, the populace was far too concerned with the imminent departure of the regiment to think of anything else.

Kitty and Lydia's behaviour had not improved in their absence, but Elizabeth was loath to approach her father again. She resolved to speak of it with him sometime during the next week, but in the meantime, she concentrated on speaking to Jane—with whom a talk was long overdue.

That evening, Elizabeth related the whole of their father's history with the Wizarding Court and the Necromancer. Jane was profoundly affected by the tale and made almost ill from tears at the news of their parents' curse. Elizabeth chose not to broach the subject of Darcy's proposal—or his letter—until a later date. The next morning, Elizabeth discovered Jane in the garden, weeping with their father. It would be a week before she was herself enough for Elizabeth to speak on any other subject.

~

It was not until the unexpected return of Mr Bingley to Netherfield that Elizabeth was provided the opportunity to approach matters of the heart.

"Affected by him?" Jane asked, incredulous. They sat together under the boughs of a large tree, the walls of Longbourn just within sight. "Why should you imagine it to be so?"

"Only because you cannot yet say his name without the hint of a blush." Elizabeth laughed. "According to Papa, Mr Bingley has come as lookout for my well-being, and to examine the safety of the area. But I do not believe a word of it. He has returned for you alone!"

"When we first met—that night, at Aunt and Uncle Gardiner's —I was most uneasy. But the next day, when we were able to speak again as friends, I saw that it was not impossible for us to meet and talk as we had before. Do not smile like that, Lizzy."

"Mama will be most pleased."

"I do not wish for Mama to feel happy at something that will never come to pass. He has not called on us—"

"Not yet."

"And there is no reason to believe he will," Jane said, folding her hands.

"You would have me believe that when Aunt Gardiner practically forced you alone into the garden, there was no indication—"

"None."

"I will believe you only because you insist," Elizabeth said with a mischievous smile. Her smile disappeared as she asked, "Have you any notion of his friend returning to visit him?"

"Mr Darcy? I know nothing more than you, Lizzy." Jane turned her eyes on her thoughtfully. "I am sure you would not wish him to, since you dislike him so much."

"And yet he saved my life."

"Of course!" Jane blushed. "How could I have forgotten? And you were together much at Kent. Has your opinion of him changed?"

"I do not know what to think of him—but yes, my opinion is very different from what it was then."

Elizabeth proceeded to relate the details of Mr Darcy's proposal, and what she could of the contents of his letter. It was a great relief for her to at last reveal what had been pressing upon her heart for so long —and there could have not been a more sympathetic listener than Jane.

"How painful for you to meet him again so soon after reading his letter!" Jane took her sister's hand. "And under such circumstances! You must forgive me—I was far too concerned with my own thoughts at that time to give consideration to yours. I assumed that your anxiety rested solely upon the attack."

"The attack was foremost in my thoughts. I could not think of his proposal at such a time, and yet I could not think of anything else!"

Jane nodded in understanding, turning her head against the breeze that threatened to undo her curls. "What a relief it must be for Aunt and Uncle Gardiner—for all of us—to have any doubts about his character laid to rest. But I cannot help but wonder whether there was some mistake on poor Mr Wickham's part. Perhaps he truly did not mean to—"

"No, Jane, they cannot both be in the right. Mr Darcy is the one to be trusted. He has proved his honesty to me on more than one occasion, and much weight now rests on his shoulders. If we cannot trust him, where would that leave us?"

"Yes, exactly," Jane said.

"We must be wary of Mr Wickham; it is fortunate that our aunt and uncle have not laid out details of their Court to Mama or Kitty and Lydia."

"You do not think him to still be a danger!" Jane's eyes widened. "I do not wish to destroy any hope on his part of re-establishing himself in the world."

"No, no," Elizabeth said, chewing her lip in earnest thought. "I will speak with Papa, but we need not expose him to the general public. Mr Darcy did not express any such desire. But as to your other question, I cannot help but be wary of almost everyone as a danger."

"Have you had a letter from Charlotte since you returned? How have they fared?"

"Charlotte writes that they are both in good health—although Lady Catherine was much affected by the attack, and has not admitted any company aside from her two nephews since that day. She indicated that Mr Collins seems to feel Mr Darcy and Colonel

Fitzwilliam's return eased her spirits, but I do not see that as anything other than speculation on his part."

"It is a wonder that so few were involved in the case—"

"But you must remember, Jane, the attack was most likely accidental, triggered by my lifting of the concealment spell. Even so, the Thief always attacks precisely; few have been involved beyond the selected victims and members of the Wizarding Court." Elizabeth frowned, her brow creasing in concentration.

"Are you all right, Lizzy?" Jane asked.

"Yes," she replied, shrugging. "I only—thought of something. But I must think on it a little longer before…"

"And will you be all right?" Jane rose. "What if you and Mr Darcy are thrown much in company?"

Elizabeth laughed, brushing dirt from her gown. "The same question might be applied to you, with Mr Bingley's presence in the neighbourhood. I am at an advantage, for I never liked Mr Darcy before. Unlike yours, my heart is in no danger."

Jane gave her a disapproving look but could not help laughing in return.

THE RUMOUR

PENDRAGON AND FORTINBRAS SAT AT A SMALL TABLE, THE
darkened room illuminated only by a flickering candle. They stared
intently at the object resting in the middle of the table—a small box,
shiny black as if carved from obsidian.

Fortinbras cleared his throat. "You have not touched it, have
you?"

"I could not have brought it here otherwise." Pendragon rolled
his eyes.

"But not with your bare hands?"

"You think me such a fool as that?"

Fortinbras sighed and rubbed his eyes. "We ought not to be
looking at it at all. It must have been left for a reason."

"Obviously."

"Then why, might I ask, have we been staring at it for the past
half an hour? As if staring will suddenly enable us to discover the
enchantment."

"There is an enchantment, I am sure of it." Pendragon ran a
hand through his hair in frustration, causing it to stand at odd ends.
"Have you opened it?"

177

"Once."

"And nothing?"

"Nothing." Pendragon rose, lifting the box with a gloved hand. "I had despaired of finding the hut, most especially after you left. But there it was, standing before me as if it had always been there. No enchantments surrounding it, and all of my precautionary spells for naught—I stepped through the doorway with ease. Clearly the hut had been abandoned, with not a trace of former power left. There was no way of discovering by what method it had remained hidden before, or to what purpose it had been used."

"But there is no doubt it belonged to our uncle," Fortinbras said, his expression grim.

"The coincidence of location is far too great…" Pendragon sighed, placing the box back onto the table and resuming his seat. "Our aunt was extremely upset over the course of events. She wept for days, even after you departed. But there was little to be done for her, and I could not remain any longer after the purpose of the visit had been completed."

"And this was the only thing remaining in the hut?"

"Aside from dust and cobwebs, yes."

"You found it sitting on the floor in the middle of the room?"

Pendragon threw his hands in the air. "Need I go over the details yet again?"

Fortinbras' eyes flashed. "If you do not want my help, you only need say the word—"

"Do not be a fool, Fortinbras."

Both fell silent and resumed their intense study of the box. Pendragon turned to Fortinbras with a raised brow. "Shall I?"

"Do you mean to say you haven't already?" Fortinbras laughed, pushing his chair back.

Pendragon stood. Flame burst from his fingertips with a flash, engulfing the entire table in blue fire. The table burned and crackled, melting into ash until all that remained was the black box, resting on the singed floor where the table once stood. "There, you see?" Pendragon said.

Fortinbras nodded. "It must be enchanted. But I have never encountered anything so undetectable."

"I have," Pendragon said. "And I believe there to be only one person who might uncover the spell."

Fortinbras shook his head. "Are you forgetting what happened the last time someone unravelled a spell for you?"

Pendragon's eyes glinted in the dark. "Aren't you?"

At first, Mr Bennet was set against the idea of Elizabeth moving from place to place. Hertfordshire had been safe for the past twenty-three years, and in his mind, there was no reason that it should suddenly not be. He felt that the attack at Rosings had been unplanned—a result of Elizabeth's unfortunate meddling with the concealment spell. Since there was no possibility of the Thief knowing her identity, she could not have been a target.

In truth, Elizabeth agreed with her father. Her reasons for wishing to leave Longbourn were entirely different than those set forth by her uncle—and thus, Mr Darcy—who continued to advocate in favour of moving as a precaution to any unforeseen events. Mr Bennet was, perhaps, the most aware of her desires, and that was his foremost reason for keeping her at Longbourn—he knew she could not put herself in any danger by doing something brave, thereby making herself into a real target.

Time moved slowly for Elizabeth. Their uncle did not write often with news; he and Mrs Gardiner were much occupied with business that took them all across the country. Very little of their business pertained to the Thief, as they were primarily occupied with the objectives of their own Court. By all appearances, the hunt for the Thief had come to a standstill. Elizabeth enquired of news from Bingley at every opportunity, always receiving the same answer: Darcy remained at Rosings with his aunt (who was very unwell) and had discovered nothing of importance.

The lack of news caused Elizabeth some consternation. She was certain that had she been permitted to return to Rosings and search for the hut, she would have discovered it, and perhaps the search for the Thief would be over. She tried by different methods to obtain permission from her father to leave Longbourn and perhaps return for a visit to Mrs Collins, but to no avail.

It would be by an unexpected turn of events that Mr Bennet's mind was changed.

On a Thursday afternoon, about a month after Jane and Elizabeth's return, the officers dined at Longbourn. Elizabeth had met with Mr Wickham only once since the occasion he had enquired after her visit to Rosings, and she had answered his questions coldly. He seemed in good looks, but Elizabeth could not help wondering what she had ever seen in him before. It came as no surprise when he approached as she sat with her father and struck up a conversation detailing all of the latest gossip from his most recent visit to town.

"Everything has quite died down, most people of importance now somewhere in the country," he said with a glance too eager. "But there is one point upon which everyone is talking. I understand you to have been a magical scholar in your day, Mr Bennet," he said, directing his smile at her father. "Perhaps you have heard of it?"

Mr Bennet seemed startled. "Of what?"

"Disenchantment."

Elizabeth nearly spilled her tea.

"Disenchantment?" Mr Bennet queried, settling back into his armchair as if he hadn't a care in the world. "It has been written of in some ancient texts, but none have ever been found to possess the talent."

"That is what was believed." Mr Wickham grinned. "But it seems someone has been found with the talent."

"Who, might I ask?" Mr Bennet said.

"That is the mystery—no one knows! Although I am sure it will be discovered at some point."

"Why must it be discovered? Is someone searching for such a person?" Elizabeth asked, barely a quiver in her voice.

"Searching?" Mr Wickham tilted his head. "Not officially. I am sure I do not know—I only thought the bit of information might please you," he said, glancing again at Elizabeth. She did not return his gaze, and he chose not to remain with them for much longer, turning to the rather warmer attentions of Elizabeth's younger sisters.

Mr Bennet sighed. "That young man is fond of spreading tales."

"If this is indeed the talk of London, then all of England must be whispering of disenchantment," Elizabeth said, her throat constricting. "Can it be a coincidence?"

"No." Mr Bennet frowned. "It cannot be. I was half right—you as Elizabeth Bennet are not a target, but only because the Thief does not know your name. But he is most certainly searching for the person who unravelled his spells."

"Perhaps it is to my advantage that I am not a him, but a her," Elizabeth said with a slight smile.

Mr Bennet did not smile in return.

∼

Two expresses—one from Mr Gardiner and one from Mr Darcy—arrived at Longbourn within a day after Mr Wickham's unfortunate gossip, both addressed to Mr Bennet.

Elizabeth was itching to discover the contents of both messages but was forced to wait two hours while Mr Bennet remained locked in his study under strict orders not to be disturbed. It was not until Mr Bingley arrived in the early evening that his door was opened, and he invited Mr Bingley, Jane, and Elizabeth to join him.

"Is Lizzy in grave danger?" Jane asked, gripping her sister's hand.

"Not immediately." Mr Bennet puffed on his pipe. "But something must be done. Mrs Bennet has learnt of the affair and is already expounding upon the possibility that one of our daughters might be capable of disenchantment. However reluctantly"—here he looked towards Elizabeth—"I must now concede that it would be best for Lizzy to travel to some place she is unknown."

Mr Bingley leaned forward. "There is only one location remaining where the Wizarding Court might provide real security—"

"I do not think I am comfortable with that scheme," Mr Bennet said. "Might I propose a happy medium?"

Mr Bingley looked disgruntled but raised his brows expectantly. Mr Bennet tossed a paper into Elizabeth's lap.

"This is the express from Uncle Gardiner," she said.

"The enchantment placed on it should be easy enough for you to unravel," Mr Bennet replied. "If you would read the third paragraph, please."

Elizabeth scanned the missive. "Lambton?"

"Mr Gardiner and his wife will be travelling there to visit their children in two weeks." Mr Bennet addressed Mr Bingley. "It is close to the portal, which I believe should satisfy Mr Darcy. Although how Elizabeth would enter, I cannot imagine."

Mr Bingley laughed. "I had not thought of that myself."

Elizabeth shook her head. "I do not like it when you talk in circles about me. How I might enter what, if you please?"

Mr Bingley looked at her, his expression serious. "I do beg your pardon, Miss Elizabeth, but that is something that can be explained only by Darcy."

"Do you see why I would rather you not be mixed up in all of this?" Mr Bennet said with some gruffness. "Secrets and portals and confusion—nothing but a nuisance. I had been quite comfortable without it for some time."

Elizabeth raised a brow. "Had you, Papa?"

"Shall I go with her?" Jane asked.

"Do you wish to?" Mr Bennet replied.

Jane paused, glancing at Mr Bingley. "I would wish only what is best for Lizzy."

"I believe Papa may need you more than I shall," Elizabeth said with a smile. "As well as Mama. She has not been herself, and Kitty and Lydia are more in need of guidance than ever now that the regiment is going away."

"So it is settled." Mr Bennet set aside his pipe. "Lizzy will go into the North, and Jane will keep up the appearance of normality at Longbourn. I suppose you will be leaving, Mr Bingley, now that your charge is departing."

"His charge?" Elizabeth frowned.

Mr Bingley had the grace to blush, stammering something unintelligible until Mr Bennet answered for him. "Mr Bingley was here to keep an eye on you, Lizzy, and to watch for any trouble. Do not be angry with me," he said, seeing her eyes flash. "Take your trouble to the Wizarding Court—it was their precaution."

"Miss Elizabeth will be safe under the care of her aunt and uncle," Mr Bingley said. "I will not return to the Court unless called."

All four rose, with Mr Bingley leaving first and Jane moving to see him to the front door.

"Will you stay a moment, Lizzy," Mr Bennet called, placing a hand on her shoulder. "If these rumours die down, as I am sure they will after no evidence of the anomaly is produced, you must return home."

Elizabeth took his hand. "You need not fear so for me, Papa."

"But indeed I must. I have told you before that I know what you desire. You feel that you alone might solve the mystery of the Thief through the uniqueness of your gift. No, no—" He waved away her protests. "I felt the same once, when I was young. But I would remind you of the outcome of my dalliance with glory."

Elizabeth sighed. "I know, Papa. I know. But think of what might have been, if you had not killed him."

Mr Bennet lowered himself into his armchair. "Few days pass when I do not think of it."

"Papa," Elizabeth said, kneeling beside him. "You forget that you still have us. Does that not count for anything?"

He did not reply, but Elizabeth saw the corners of his eyes soften. "Do not use your gift, Lizzy, under any circumstances. I will not have you risk yourself."

"I cannot obey you in that, Papa." Elizabeth squeezed his hand, her gaze unwavering. "You must trust that I will be safe—and that I will act according to my best judgment."

Mr Bennet frowned. "It is not enough."

"But it will have to be." Elizabeth rose.

"Promise me that you will return, Lizzy," he said, emotion colouring his voice.

Elizabeth smiled, bending to kiss him on the cheek. "That is a promise I can make, and will keep."

Her father's shoulders relaxed. "I suppose I must content myself with that."

THE PORTAL

To Elizabeth's mind, two weeks seemed to stretch on for an eternity. She was fortunate, therefore, that her aunt and uncle arrived at Longbourn's door-step an entire week early to collect her.

Mrs Gardiner kissed Elizabeth on both cheeks. "Things went far better than anticipated in Ireland and I am eager to see the children. We have been separated for too long."

"What is Uncle Gardiner doing with the horses?" Lydia called out from the doorway, seeing Mr Gardiner lead them away himself.

Elizabeth gasped, turning to her aunt with mouth agape. "Those are not?"

"Yes." Mrs Gardiner laughed, turning to gaze at the two silvery horses, their wings still beating gently at the air. "Rather unsubtle, but the concealment enchantment placed upon them is quite good— I performed it myself. The troublesome part is that they will not mind anyone but myself, or your Uncle Gardiner. That raises a few eyebrows, but not enough that it throws suspicion upon our identities."

"What kind of horses are they?" Lydia asked.

"Never mind, Lydia," Elizabeth said, watching until they were out of sight. "Beautiful," she whispered, before turning back to Mrs Gardiner. "I do not mean to be impertinent, but how could you ever afford them?"

Mrs Gardiner laughed again good-naturedly, a twinkle in her eye. "Afford them? Oh, we couldn't possibly! But we do have connexions in high places and have been given use of them for an indefinite amount of time."

Elizabeth's eyes narrowed at her aunt's smirk, but she did not enquire further.

"Will you reveal them to me, Lizzy, sometime before you leave?" Jane whispered as they walked back into the house. "I can only guess what might have caused such a reaction."

"Wings, Jane." Elizabeth smiled. "The horses are winged. Which is all the better for me, since they are magical creatures in their own right, I will be able to ride with them. I have never before been able to travel by enchantment."

The Gardiners stayed at Longbourn for the night, giving Elizabeth a proper amount of time to pack her things, and satisfying Mrs Bennet's hunger for town gossip. The regiment had relocated to Brighton four days before, leaving most Hertfordshire residents in despair at the loss of their company.

Lydia felt the loss most acutely; she had been invited by her particular friend, a Mrs Forster, to accompany them to Brighton along with the regiment, but Mr Bennet forbade it. The regiment had been moved, he said, because of the number of magical disturbances in Brighton. It was not a safe location. Under other circumstances, he assured her, she might have gone, but the state of things made it quite impossible. Lydia's disappointment was perhaps less acute than Kitty's triumph (who had been most put out by not being invited). As it was, nothing interesting remained for them in Meryton, and even their insufferably boring aunt and uncle were a welcome distraction for the evening.

Mrs Gardiner listened with a sympathetic ear to first her youngest niece's complaints, and then to Mrs Bennet, who, although grieved that anything should be disagreeable to Lydia, was very glad that she had not gone to Brighton.

"My nerves," she said, sighing rather shakily, "have not been the same since the attacks last winter. I do not like your gallivanting about the country at a time such as this; I would much rather you brought the children here and stayed with us. We are very comfortable in Meryton, even if it is not so fine as town."

Mrs Gardiner patted her sister-in-law's hand and assured her that they were grateful for the invitation, but of course found it impossible to accept.

"Lizzy has always been far too headstrong, you must watch out for her." Mrs Bennet looked over at her second daughter with disapproval. "And I am glad Jane is not going with you. Mr Bingley has come back to Netherfield, and I think that all will turn out very differently this time than last fall. He calls often. And you know he has five thousand a year?"

~

The next morning at breakfast, Elizabeth was struck by a thought which filled her with dismay. "Uncle Gardiner, how is it possible for us to travel during the day? You cannot conceal me—and people will talk when they see a young woman flying alone through the air."

Mr and Mrs Gardiner exchanged puzzled glances. "How is it that we did not remember such an important detail?" Mrs Gardiner queried.

Mr Gardiner shrugged. "There is nothing for it, then. We must travel under the cover of darkness."

"And you shall wear your black cloak, Lizzy," Mrs Gardiner said, and the matter was settled.

The company was forced to wait until an hour after midnight for a proper level of darkness. The night was clear, and the stars twinkled in the sky. Mr Bennet, accustomed to staying up well past two o'clock in the morning, saw them off. But Elizabeth was touched to see her mother and all four sisters descend in their nightcaps, yawning and rubbing their eyes.

"You will be careful, Lizzy." Mrs Bennet fussed as she tied the strings of Elizabeth's dark cloak. "None of your usual foolhardiness."

"Never, Mama."

"You must write if you meet any handsome officers," Lydia said, yawning again.

"I think that unlikely," Elizabeth replied.

"Or any handsome men of any kind," Kitty said, "as we shall not be seeing any."

With a tight hug from Jane and a kiss to her father's cheek, Elizabeth approached the carriage, expecting to be stowed inside.

"Would you like to ride with me, Lizzy?" Her uncle smiled. "There is room for two."

At Elizabeth's hesitant look, Mrs Gardiner nodded. "I will be sleeping in any case, Lizzy."

Her eyes shining, Elizabeth mounted the high black seat next to her uncle, who flicked the reins and started the horses with a softly-spoken word. Elizabeth turned, waving at her family until they were well out of sight.

"We will let the horses warm up a bit," Mr Gardiner explained, "and wait until we are a distance from Meryton before we begin our ascent."

Elizabeth nodded, the earlier sleepiness she felt disappearing. She watched the familiar road disinterestedly for some miles, her eyes adjusting to the darkness surrounding them until the light shining from the stars and crescent moon were bright enough to illuminate the woods on either side. After three miles, her uncle turned away from the road into a meadow. He uttered another word that she did not understand, and the silver horses unfolded their wings, rising through the air, the wind blowing back her hood. She laughed in delight, gripping her seat as the horses leapt forward, their hooves beating against nothing, and flew into the shining sky.

The earth fell away, the nearby farms looking like little doll-houses. Elizabeth turned to gaze back towards Longbourn where the house was no longer visible, but a single light shone out through the night. The carriage used no lanterns, and so they passed unseen over the heads of the people below.

"Pull your hood up, Lizzy," Mr Gardiner said after some moments. "I wish that I could block you from the wind."

Elizabeth smiled. "The air is warm, Uncle Gardiner," she said, but pulled up the hood all the same. She would not risk being told to sit inside the carriage.

Two hours after their departure, following a long struggle to keep her eyes from closing, Elizabeth finally succumbed to sleep. She awoke just as the sun broke on the horizon in flushed pink.

"There is Lambton"—Mr Gardiner pointed towards a small town, the lights still darkened—"and Margaret's great-aunt lives in that cottage below, just past the town."

Elizabeth glanced at it and then turned her eyes to the surrounding woods. "And Pemberley," she asked after a moment's hesitation. "Where is it located?"

Mr Gardiner pointed westward. "Just beyond those woods."

Elizabeth squinted, but saw nothing.

"If you should like to visit, we might arrange a tour tomorrow," Mr Gardiner added. "I understand the family to be away at present, but the house has always been open to visitors. It is a fine place, and full of magic. I imagine you would enjoy seeing it."

Elizabeth was glad that the sky was not light enough for him to see her blush. "Yes. I should like to see it."

~

In spite of the early hour, Mr and Mrs Gardiner were welcomed to the cottage by the sight of their four children, fairly leaping from excitement. They had many tales of adventure to relate to their parents and adored cousin; so many, in fact, that for several minutes all that could be heard was a loud clattering of high-pitched voices. Mrs Stone, Mrs Gardiner's great-aunt Betsy, was a tiny, wrinkled old woman who spoke very little, but served Elizabeth some of the most delicious tea she had ever taken. The cottage was small but cosy, and Elizabeth noticed with surprise that there were no concealment enchantments placed on it—or many spells at all.

"I had thought the children were here for protection," Elizabeth said to her aunt later that day, as they sat in the rose garden outside under the sun.

"The enchantment is not on the house." Mrs Gardiner smiled. "Otherwise your presence here would put us in some jeopardy. The spell connects the children to Aunt Betsy. As long as they are with her, they are in little danger."

Elizabeth looked at the ancient woman dozing in her seat next to them, her cap askew. "That is quite a burden of responsibility for Mrs Stone," she said hesitantly.

Mrs Gardiner laughed. "She is rather a fine wizard in her own right, and adept at keeping the children close within her sights."

"The boys, for example," Mrs Stone said, her eyes still closed, "are sneaking up behind you, Miss Elizabeth, in hopes of a surprise attack."

Elizabeth jumped at the two small wooden swords poking at her back.

"Great-Aunt Betsy!" the youngest (who was only just five) exclaimed in a whiny voice. "You always ruin our fun!"

But Mrs Stone had already returned to her sound sleep.

Elizabeth was restless. Mrs Gardiner had found the idea of leaving her children so soon after arriving, even for a few short hours, to be an impossible feat. The proposed journey to Pemberley was put off for another day.

"I am sure if Mr Darcy was in the neighbourhood, he would invite you himself," Mrs Gardiner said slyly. "But perhaps he has not received our missive notifying him of our early arrival. Unless it is an absolute emergency, letters always take some time to travel through due to the numerous tests for authenticity."

"I am sure he would not, Aunt," Elizabeth said, remembering his cold eyes at their last meeting.

"I know the Wizarding Court has long intended for you to join them at some point, but how you might enter through the portal remains a puzzlement to everyone."

"The portal?"

"I cannot explain. I have not been through it myself. I have only heard of it."

"Mr Bingley could not explain either," Elizabeth said with some annoyance.

"You will understand, I think, if you ever see it."

Four days after their arrival in Lambton, Mrs Gardiner at last found herself prepared to part from her children for a few short hours. The three set off in the carriage with the silver horses, who trotted at an eager pace in the direction of Pemberley, put out that Mr Gardiner would not allow them to fly. The woods on both sides of the road grew darker and more wild with each passing half mile, and the magic surrounding them vibrated with intensity.

Her excitement mounting, Elizabeth's first glimpse of the house was not at all what she expected. Pemberley stood on a hill; what Elizabeth had assumed would be a well-kept, fine old home was overgrown by thick vines, the lawn cluttered with brush and saplings that tore at her dress as they walked towards the entryway. Each window was darkened; the door creaked with age as it opened, and a tall, thin woman with a sharp nose moved out to greet them.

"This is not what I had thought it would be like," Elizabeth whispered to her aunt in dismay.

Mrs Gardiner gave her a bright smile. "It is beautiful, is it not?"

"Beautiful?" Elizabeth said in puzzlement, but her aunt and uncle had already stepped forward to meet the housekeeper.

Elizabeth hung back as they made their way through the halls with the housekeeper, a Mrs Reynolds. She could not fathom why her aunt had spoken of magic, for within the walls of Pemberley, none seemed to exist. The house was empty and hollow, the halls dark and damp with cobwebs clinging to empty candlesticks and mirrors. Elizabeth was so astonished that she could hardly speak a word. This was the magnificent Pemberley, the finest house in Derbyshire? The longer she observed, the more she became convinced that something was amiss.

Mrs Reynolds continued her tour of the house as if everything were in working order, describing modern furniture and a new pianoforte in the music room—which in fact contained old furniture covered in dust and no pianoforte. Elizabeth's one consolation was that the woman spoke very highly of Mr Darcy—something that should not have come as a surprise but did all the same. She thought it spoke well of him that his servants should hold him in such high esteem. She could not fathom why his ancestral home should be left in such a state.

It was not until they climbed up the ancient stairs, which groaned with age under Elizabeth's feet, causing her to cling nervously to the rail, that she suddenly felt a pull of magic. It grew stronger as they walked down the gallery, where portraits of generations of Darcys hung, until her eyes rested on a portrait of young Fitzwilliam Darcy himself.

"This was taken before his father's death," Mrs Reynolds said, smiling rather sadly.

The picture seemed out of place from the rest, the frame surprisingly new and the paint unfaded.

It arrested her—it beheld a striking resemblance to Mr Darcy, with such a smile over the face as she remembered to have sometimes seen when he looked at her. She gazed into the painted eyes, so like the real ones, and blinked. Suddenly, she located the spell. The house was a shell—everything that Pemberley was, or might have been, was gone. What Mrs Reynolds saw, and what her aunt and uncle admired, was a beauty enchantment to make the house seem to be what it might have been long ago.

An overwhelming feeling of sadness washed over her, and Elizabeth straightened. "May I walk in the gardens? I feel in need of fresh air."

While her aunt and uncle finished the last of the tour, Elizabeth was led down the stair by a non-existent footman, whom she could only follow by tracing the enchantment that made him exist in the eyes of everyone else. Once out of the house, the magic she had earlier felt from the woods pulled at her, leading her through the garden to a small door in the rock wall, three feet high and barely visible to an unobservant eye. She hesitated for a moment, then pushed it open.

Through the little door was a walled garden with another door, even smaller than the first, and then another so small that Elizabeth could not fit through without tearing her dress and abandoning her bonnet. Once through the last door, she straightened, blinking into harsh white sunlight. She stood in a large field, covered with blindingly white flowers. Fifty feet in front of her glittered an expansive lake, shining golden from the sunlight. Elizabeth moved towards it, putting her hand up to block the bright light of the sun. Standing at the edge of the lake, she saw the sky and sun above her reflected in the water, but strangely, when she looked down, expecting to see her own face, there was nothing.

Puzzled, Elizabeth looked from side to side. Looking down again, she saw the flowers mirrored in the water against the sky, but still no reflection. Elizabeth felt a jerk at her foot and she lost her balance, falling face forward into the water, but instead of being greeted by a splash, Elizabeth found herself standing at what seemed to be the opposite side of the lake, looking down into the water at her own expression. Her long hair was now undone and fell loosely on one side of her shoulder. Elizabeth moved to put her hair back up but dropped her hands when she saw that while her reflection was there, it was not moving with her.

"Who's there?"

Elizabeth jumped. A tall figure in black stood twenty feet from her, his eyes covered by a hood. "Nay, answer me," she said. "Stand and unfold yourself!"

"Long live the King." The man threw back his hood.

"The Poet?" Elizabeth asked, her throat tightening as she felt a flush creeping into her cheeks.

"He."

"You come most carefully upon your hour."

Mr Darcy's lips almost curved into a smile. "Rosalind?"

Elizabeth made an awkward curtsey in reply to his stiff bow. "Who else?"

"I was not expecting you until next week—and not expecting you here at all," he said, moving a little closer.

"Where is here, if I may ask?" Elizabeth said, taking a step towards him herself.

"Here," he said, stopping when they stood not four feet apart, "is Pemberley."

Elizabeth raised a brow. "I have just been to Pemberley."

"You have been to a husk of what Pemberley was, long ago, before it was here."

"Of course." Elizabeth laughed as she looked behind him across the field of white flowers to the wall with the tiny door, identical to the other she had come through before. "I should have known you would find a way to live here. I only ever got through once, when I was a little girl."

Mr Darcy looked puzzled. "I do not quite know how you could have—the Otherworld is entirely made up of magic."

"Yes," she said, her eyes twinkling. "But it is the sort of magic far older and deeper than any man can employ—and I cannot disrupt it, much like I cannot disrupt the silver winged horses."

"You liked them," he said, his voice betraying some eagerness, even as he avoided her gaze.

"Like them?" Elizabeth breathed. "How could you imagine I would not?"

He reached out and offered her his hand. "Will you join me?" he said. "We are just through the three doors."

Elizabeth hesitated, remembering her loose hair and ungloved hands. But then, she looked at his eyes, so hopeful, and put her warm hand in his cool one. "I would be honoured, Mr Darcy. Can you actually fit through that little door?"

He threw back his head and laughed. "I am the keeper of that door—it rarely gives me any trouble."

The Otherworld

Mr Darcy led Elizabeth across the field to the little door, which now appeared wide enough to allow both of them through, although Mr Darcy still had to duck his head under the top of the doorframe. The next door was even wider, and the third, while still identical to the first Elizabeth had found on the other side, was nearly ten feet tall.

"Wait." Elizabeth halted. He turned inquiringly and she blushed at the realisation that his hand still held hers. "My aunt and uncle… they will worry. I am supposed to be in the garden."

A look almost like relief passed across Mr Darcy's features before he smiled. "Of course, I will have someone sent to fetch them."

"Is it difficult to find your way back, once we have gone through?" Elizabeth asked, looking back at the door they had just come through—which had returned to appearing small and barely visible. "The last time I came through to the Otherworld, I was lost all night before finding my way back home."

"I am very familiar with the patterns—you need not fear being a prisoner here indefinitely," he said with a slight smile. "I had wondered whether Longbourn might have a portal."

"It is not located in Longbourn, but close to where our land borders Netherfield, in the woods where I walk. Near where you used to practise."

"And did you meet anyone there?"

"No, that is—" Elizabeth's brow furrowed. "I cannot remember. I was very small."

"Most people cannot get through without permission from a gatekeeper—unless fae blood runs through their veins."

"I could not tell you one way or the other—I used to think my father would have told me if he knew, but he is altogether full of secrets as I have discovered. And my mother is…not herself. Did you know that? About—my mother?"

Mr Darcy shook his head.

"And you? How came you to be keeper? You cannot be fae!"

"And why is that?" Mr Darcy said, now grinning. "Because I am far too disagreeable?"

"Fae are not purported to be agreeable," Elizabeth replied, smiling in return. "Rather the opposite."

"It comes from my mother's line. I do not know the name of a particular person, or whether the ancestor is from several generations ago. But someone must have been not quite…human."

"You must sing, then, Mr Darcy. Fae cannot help themselves."

"I do not sing for strangers," he replied, turning his face away and pulling her towards the gate.

But Elizabeth did not hear him. "That must be the reason for your peculiar code name," she said. "Do you still write poetry?"

"I am a wretched poet," he replied, frowning. "I have not written a verse in years. I have neither the time, nor the inclination."

"Perhaps you will again someday, when things are different." He stopped, turning to look into her eyes. Memories of another day, and words spoken in anger, crowded into her mind and she could not hold his gaze.

"No," he said, releasing her hand to push open the heavy door. "I do not think I will write again."

Pemberley was visible just a few steps beyond the gate. Elizabeth came to a full stop, gazing upon the building in wonderment. The house seemed illuminated even in broad daylight, the glass in the windows twinkling in the sun. It was the same structure as the first in the real world, but so different as to be incomparable. There was a wildness about it that could not be helped, as anything in the Otherworld always became a little wild over a period of time, but that made Elizabeth like it all the more. The gardens were colourful, and the roses which trailed along Pemberley's walls were blooming in pinks and whites. Everything about it was alive.

"It is beautiful," she said to Mr Darcy, who was looking at her in nervous expectation.

As they stepped toward the house, the sound of music reached Elizabeth's ears. She was startled to come through the gardens and see several children running about on the lawn, and she turned to Mr Darcy.

"Unlike the Pemberley in the real world"—he waved his hand towards the house—"this Pemberley is full to the brim with house guests. Due to recent events, many of our Court's members have found it necessary to house here temporarily, along with their families."

Elizabeth's eyebrows rose, but she was prevented from speaking when Mr Darcy's valet, Barnaby, ran to meet them.

"They are here, and no doubt wondering where their niece is," Mr Darcy said, his tone curt. "If you would be so kind."

Barnaby was gone after flashing a smile at Elizabeth, and she was pleased to think that her aunt and uncle would join them soon.

"Will Pemberley look much different to them?" she asked as they walked up the steps at the back entry. "I could not see the enchantment placed on it."

"Much different."

"The real Pemberley is very proper looking, although elegant," said a voice from the doorway, where Elizabeth saw Colonel Fitzwilliam leaning against the frame. "Pendragon prefers it here. And Pemberley is far more interesting now than it was before. There are secret passageways and walking suits of armour."

"You must see for yourself," Mr Darcy said with a half-smile towards his cousin. "I will introduce you to my sister—she can take you anywhere you would like to go."

They walked through the long halls into what Elizabeth remembered to be the music room. A young girl with dark hair sat at a pianoforte by the window, accompanying herself while she sang with words Elizabeth did not recognise. Hearing the door click behind them, the girl stopped, turning to her brother with a smile. Her eyes widened at the sight of Elizabeth.

"This is Miss Elizabeth Bennet," Mr Darcy said, moving to stand next to her as she rose. "Miss Bennet, allow me to introduce my sister to you, Georgiana Darcy."

Elizabeth came forward, smiling as she took the young girl's hands. "How beautifully you sing, Miss Darcy."

Georgiana's smile was timid. "You think so?"

"Georgiana does not sing for strangers," the colonel said.

"But Miss Bennet is not a stranger," Georgiana said, "for she is to be a member of the Court."

Elizabeth nodded at Georgiana but sent a questioning look to Mr Darcy. He shook his head, and she found herself breathing a sigh of relief. He had not told Georgiana of her talent.

Elizabeth's second tour of Pemberley was far more interesting than the first. Her aunt and uncle joined them when they were in the art gallery, their eyes wide in amazement.

"We never should have guessed the portal to be through the lake. As soon as I felt myself falling, I was sure I would drown, but then there we were on the other side, and not a bit wet!" Mrs Gardiner laughed.

"She laughs now, but you should have seen her expression before," Mr Gardiner said to Elizabeth.

"I could not see the door; Edward had to point it out to me. He walked through as easy as can be, but I had to crawl on my hands and knees!" Mrs Gardiner gazed in admiration at the high windows that allowed the light to dance across the walls.

Mr Darcy overheard this remark and looked at his feet. "I do apologise, Mrs Gardiner, I was not concentrating on the entrance at the moment you must have come through. I will ensure the doors to be a more comfortable size the next time."

Mrs Gardiner's eyes sparkled. "It is quite all right, I assure you."

"I must remind you both that the invitation to you and your children still stands," Mr Darcy continued.

"You would be in good company," Colonel Fitzwilliam said.

"We are indeed flattered by your kind invitation," Mr Gardiner said, with a smile towards his niece, who had wandered away from them to examine portraits and did not seem to notice. "But we should return to Lambton this evening. We had not realised you were returned, Mr Darcy, or we should have called sooner."

"I have been at Pemberley for some time, but according to most reports, I am not expected for at least another week."

"Is such precaution necessary?" Elizabeth was standing several feet away from them, in front of the painting of the young Mr Darcy.

"Naturally," he replied, coming to stand next to her. "Does something interest you?" he asked, looking uncomfortably at his own likeness.

"Of course. This painting"—Elizabeth indicated with a sweep of her hand—"is faded and cracked. The frame is crooked and cobwebs cover your eyes. Your portrait on the other side looked new."

"No one has ever noticed the enchantment before," he said. "I should have expected that you would. The painting is what connects the here and there. I am the keeper of the gate, and in my likeness the reality of here is reflected there—through my portrait. Do you understand?"

Elizabeth nodded. "Your portrait links the true estate with the Otherworld—the one on the other side is untarnished, just as this estate is, while the portrait here is in tatters, just as the Pemberley in the real world?"

"Do not try to understand." Georgiana smiled, joining them. "He has attempted to explain it to me countless times before, but since no one can see the spell except for him, it makes no sense."

Elizabeth and Mr Darcy exchanged glances but did not contradict her. Another hour at least was spent exploring the halls of Pemberley; it was with eagerness that Darcy led them through passages that took them instantly from the highest floor of the house into the dark storage room below. Some rooms were overtly magical, with talking mirrors and opinionated rugs, while others appeared ordinary. But more fascinating to Elizabeth was Mr Darcy's easy manner with her aunt and uncle—she had never seen him so agreeable, so engaging. It was difficult not to smile at him.

When the sun started to set in the west, Mrs Gardiner began to fatigue, and mentioned that the children might worry if they did not return home soon. But she regretted her complaint almost the moment it left her mouth, for the master of Pemberley and his sister looked crestfallen to think their guests were leaving without having dined there even once.

"It has been most inhospitable of us to force you up and down stairs without even the nourishment of tea!" Georgiana protested. "You must stay for dinner—do you not agree, Fitzwilliam?"

"If it is not too much of an inconvenience," he replied.

Elizabeth sent a pleading look at her aunt and uncle, and Mrs Gardiner conceded to staying for another two hours. Following Mr Darcy and the colonel as they walked briskly ahead, Elizabeth was surprised when they passed the large dining hall on the right to step into a torch-lit passageway leading down to the kitchens.

She did not mean to be inquisitive but could not help turning to Georgiana as they walked down the stairs. "You do not dine in the great hall upstairs?"

Georgiana gave her a mischievous smile. "Are you afraid we eat in the kitchens, Miss Bennet?" she said with a giggle.

"But we do eat in the kitchens, Georgie!" the colonel called over his shoulder.

"We certainly do not eat in the kitchens," Mr Darcy said, before his face also broke into a grin. "We eat in the great hall connected to them."

They led their amazed guests into a large room far beneath the estate, the walls lined with torches and a long table in the middle of it. Twenty additional guests, some of whom Elizabeth had seen earlier, were seated around it, with at least twenty-five children sitting, standing, or running about them.

"Here," Mr Darcy said, his voice full of pride, "is assembled nearly two-thirds of the Wizarding Court."

"We have never all been gathered so closely before," the colonel explained. "And likely won't be again for some time. But Pemberley is a haven—and our members and their children are safest here."

Elizabeth was introduced to more faces than she could remember. Most members were from England, but the Court was represented by wizards from several continents: a tall, dark-haired man from Egypt, a bearded Russian, a glossy-haired woman not much older than Elizabeth herself from the Americas, and a small couple, swords still hanging at their sides, from Japan. They made merry as they ate, with boisterous stories being told on all sides, and spontaneous bursts of song coming from the end of the table where there sat a group which looked rather too beautiful to be completely human.

Elizabeth ate in silence, aware of Mr Darcy's subtle glances towards her, and remembering that she might have been introduced to this company as his wife, rather than a guest. She wondered if had she met Mr Darcy here, seeing him with the laughter and ease he felt in his Court rather than in Hertfordshire, she would have felt differently.

Suddenly, a clear voice filled the hall with song. As all other voices fell silent. Elizabeth stared unashamedly at Mr Darcy, who was now in a world all his own as he sang with words of the faeries. At first she could not understand, and did not expect to; but slowly, as the song progressed and the music filled her mind, she understood him. The meaning was etched into her heart, of love and loss —and seeking. She understood, and it frightened her.

"A fae song," Mrs Gardiner whispered, "can be more powerful than any spell. Mr Darcy is full of surprises."

Elizabeth could not answer her.

~

An hour passed, an hour remained. It was then that Elizabeth remembered why she was in Derbyshire in the first place, and that Mr Darcy had told her nothing of the Thief, or the stone hut, or Rosings. Before she was given an opportunity to ask any questions, there was a great scraping noise as the wooden chairs were pushed back and the table moved to the side.

Georgiana leaned towards Elizabeth. "Now they will dance." She nodded at the couple Elizabeth had noticed earlier, whom she was now quite positive were not human at all, but fae. "Once they begin to dance," Georgiana continued, "everyone dances. It is too difficult to resist."

Sure enough, as the music swelled from nowhere and the couple began to spin about the room, her own aunt and uncle joined hands and threw themselves into the fray. Georgiana did not dance herself but made a pretty picture as she clapped her hands and laughed at the colonel, who was trying to out-jig everyone around him.

"Will you dance with me, Miss Bennet?" Mr Darcy asked, startling her.

"I do not know this dance," she replied, smiling coyly.

"It is not one that can be learned," he replied, and took her hands.

For some time, Elizabeth was lost to his gaze, his touch, and the music around them. Something tugged at her mind, distracting her until she came to a full stop.

"The Thief, Mr Darcy," she said in response to his troubled look. "You have not given me news of the Thief."

"The hour is late, and your aunt and uncle will soon wish to depart," he answered, now avoiding her eyes. "We had best speak on it tomorrow."

"Tomorrow is much too distant, and I have been kept in the dark for far too long."

Something flickered in his eyes that Elizabeth could not quite place—was it uncertainty?—before he nodded. Glancing at the oblivious crowd dancing about them, he led her out of the hall, through the passageway, and into a darkened room she had not seen before. There was a burst of blue light, illuminating a large desk covered with books and parchment, three maps hanging on one wall, and bookshelves lining the others. A solitary window rose from the floor to the ceiling, where the moon was visible in the darkness, shining brighter here than in the other world.

Mr Darcy moved to the desk and lifted a bundle wrapped in black cloth. "I found the hut, stripped of all enchantments. You were right; had it not been stripped, I would never have found it again without your help."

Elizabeth tried not to be too pleased. "But you did find it."

"And this"—he pulled the cloth away to reveal a shining black box—"was inside it."

"A box?" Elizabeth stepped forward and stretched out her hands.

Mr Darcy moved the box back. "Have you seen it before?"

"No."

"Can you sense anything about it that is magical?"

Elizabeth paused, searching. "I—I cannot tell. Will you let me hold it?"

"I should not have even let you see it." His eyes flickered with what she now recognised as anger—or perhaps guilt?

"But you must let me see it," she said, a smile spreading across her face. "Because you do not know what it is—and you cannot know without me." She reached out again, taking the box from him cautiously and moving to stand by the window. "Have you opened it?"

"Once. There was nothing."

She frowned. "I have not been able to practise much since— Rosings. Jane hates to perform harmful spells, and there is no point of me learning how to undo the good ones."

"If you had come here, you might have trained better," he said.

"But I was not permitted to come here," she said curtly, running her hands along the black edges of the box. "It is very…cold."

"Is it?"

She moved her hands to the clasp. "You had not noticed?"

"Do not open it, Eliz—" But it was too late. She had felt the enchantment under the lid and could not help opening it.

Immediately a burst of dark light streamed from the opening.

Elizabeth dropped the box with a cry of dismay, and Mr Darcy threw the cloth over it.

"I am sorry—" she gasped, her hands shaking. "I am sorry."

Mr Darcy slumped to the floor, leaning his back against the wall. He looked up at her, his eyes betraying defeat.

"The Thief knows where we are," he said, "and is coming."

The Request

"You must go. Immediately." Mr Darcy jumped to his feet and kicked the box, still covered, to the side.

Elizabeth blinked. "Go?"

"It was a trap—not for me, not even for the Court, but for you. And I"—he swallowed hard—"fool that I am, allowed you to fall into it." He paced, running his hand through his hair in frustration. "You will take the grey—the larger of the two winged horses—and ride through the Otherworld until you reach the portal at Longbourn."

"I will not go," Elizabeth said.

Unhearing, he continued to pace. "No doubt the gatekeeper will remember you—they do not forget much. And you must take this." He pulled a golden ring from the fourth finger of his right hand, sliding it onto her thumb. "You will not be stopped if you wear it," he said, stroking her hand.

Elizabeth met his eyes. "I will not go," she repeated.

Mr Darcy gripped her hand. "You will."

Elizabeth lifted her chin. "You cannot force me."

"It is not a question of forcing—there is no argument. You must go."

"You think that I will leave now—when the Thief is coming and will be caught? More than half of your Court is here!" she cried. "Think of it instead as a trap laid for the Thief, rather than the other way around!"

Mr Darcy did not answer.

"I left before, do you remember?" she said in a quieter voice. "I will not leave again."

There was the sound of rushing feet in the corridor just before Colonel Fitzwilliam burst into the room, followed by Georgiana and Mr and Mrs Gardiner. Mr Darcy turned, but did not release her hands.

"The alarm sounded at the south gate," the colonel shouted. "You let her see that box!" he raged, raising an arm to swing at his cousin. Mr and Mrs Gardiner sprang forward to hold him back.

"Calm yourself, Colonel," Mr Gardiner grunted. "Exchanging blows will solve nothing. Mr Darcy, what are we to do?"

"Is the portal breached?" Mrs Gardiner said, her voice trembling. "Can I go back to my children?"

"The Thief will come by a different way—never through my portal. But if you are to return to your children, you must go now." Mr Darcy paused, catching sight of Georgiana standing in the doorway, her face pale.

Mrs Gardiner nodded, her eyes shining with tears of worry, and then motioned to Elizabeth. "Come with me, Lizzy. Your uncle will stay here, but I must keep my promise to your father."

"I am not going," Elizabeth stated.

"Elizabeth will not go to Lambton," Mr Darcy said, with a glance in her direction, "but neither will she stay here. She must return to her father at Longbourn. The Thief still does not know her true identity—and we will keep it that way."

"I will not go back to Longbourn!" Elizabeth wrenched her hand from his in fury. "I left home upon your advice! Do you not remember?"

"I remember. But circumstances are different now."

"They are not different!"

"Lizzy," Mr Gardiner said, silencing her with a look before turning to Mr Darcy. "How do you propose she get to Longbourn, if not by way of Lambton."

"There is another portal. She will take the faster of my winged horses and be there by morning."

"I will not permit her to go alone," Mr Gardiner said, crossing his arms.

"She will not go alone," Mr Darcy replied, turning back to her. "Please, take my sister. She will be safe with you."

Elizabeth was caught by surprise and did not reply. Mr Gardiner's face darkened but he nodded in agreement, and Mrs Gardiner could not prevent the tears from rolling down her cheeks.

"You are an idiot, Darcy," Colonel Fitzwilliam growled. "I could kill you."

"You may not have to," Mr Darcy replied, his voice low. The colonel did not answer, but turned and stomped out of the room, taking Mrs Gardiner with him.

"He will see her safely to the portal," Mr Darcy said to Mr Gardiner.

"I will not go," Elizabeth cried again.

Mr Darcy spoke to his sister, whose eyes widened at his words, before turning to disappear down the passageway. With a nod to Mr Gardiner and Elizabeth indicating they should follow him, Mr Darcy also started down the passage. They returned to the hall where they had eaten before, where the adults were now assembled. It took only a few short directions from Mr Darcy to send them all in different directions. Mr Gardiner was sent, reluctantly, with another wizard, leaving Elizabeth alone with Mr Darcy. Without saying anything, he pulled her out of the hall and through a different passage, leading them into the cool night air. To her right, Elizabeth recognised what were undoubtedly the stables. She stiffened, halting her steps.

"I will not argue with you," he said.

Elizabeth crossed her arms.

"Please, let me undo my own mistake."

"Must you blame yourself for everything?" Elizabeth tapped her chest. "I am the one who undid the enchantment."

Mr Darcy whistled, and instantly a silver horse stood at his side. Elizabeth opened her mouth again to protest, but Mr Darcy gave her a gentle shake. "Stop it," he said. His shoulders slumped, but his grip remained firm. "I cannot force you, but I beg of you. Elizabeth, take my sister to safety."

She swallowed. "There is nothing, nothing that could have taken me from here, but for this request."

Mr Darcy laughed at this. "You are so certain?" Sobering, his hand moved to her hair. "It would kill me to know that either of you died because of me."

Her lips parted at his touch. She tilted her head up towards his and brushed back the hair that always seemed to fall into his eyes.

"Will you come for her?" she asked. "Will you come for me?"

"Did I not come before?"

"But then you left again."

"Elizabeth"—he closed his eyes as she leaned her head against his—"I cannot stay where I am not wanted."

"You will come," she insisted.

"I would come with you now, were I able."

"Promise me. Promise me that you will not die," she said.

He gave her a crooked smile. "My insufferable pride will—"

"No," she said. "Not because of your pride. Promise me."

His eyes searched hers. "God knows I have tried not to," he whispered, "but I cannot help loving you. I will always come for you."

There was a movement close by, and Elizabeth turned to see Colonel Fitzwilliam, still flushed with anger, with Georgiana behind him, cloaked in blue, holding onto a small satchel. Suddenly, Mr Darcy's arms were about her waist, and Elizabeth was lifted onto the horse's back. The colonel brought Georgiana forward. Mr Darcy said farewell to her and kissed her cheek before setting her behind Elizabeth.

"Hold onto me," she said to the trembling girl, who immediately circled her arms about her waist.

Mr Darcy spoke a word in the horse's ear and, with a jolt, it sprang forward. Clutching its mane, Elizabeth turned in her seat, just catching Mr Darcy's words as he ran behind them. "Do not dismount until you reach Longbourn's portal. The horse will guide you there!"

She reached back to touch his outstretched hand just before the horse lifted them into the darkened sky, and they were gone.

~

Georgiana cried for the first half an hour of their journey. Elizabeth would not have known of Georgiana's tears had she not felt them dampen the fabric of her cloak on her shoulder.

"I had never thought Pemberley would be attacked," Georgiana said at length, her voice shaking from the cold air.

Elizabeth felt her stomach twist when she thought of her mistake. "All will be well," she answered, hoping that her voice did not betray her own uncertainty.

"I have ridden this way often with my brother," Georgiana said some moments later, resting her head against Elizabeth's shoulder with a sigh. "But that was a long time ago, before all of this began."

"It must be beautiful," Elizabeth said, looking at the hills and trees rolling below them. The sky was black above them, the stars hidden behind clouds.

"Very beautiful," Georgiana said. "Everything here is beautiful. But the land on the other side is almost so."

"Yes." Elizabeth smiled to herself. "I remember. Try to sleep now."

"Will you sleep?"

"No."

"Then I will not, either," Georgiana said, but not another half an hour had passed before she slept soundly against Elizabeth's back.

THE BINDING CORD

ELIZABETH DID NOT SLEEP. THE DARKNESS SEEMED TO STRETCH OUT endlessly before them as she watched for the dawn. Georgiana awoke two hours before sunrise when it began to rain. Their teeth were still chattering when light broke through the clouds in the east, and the silver horse lowered its head as it began to descend. Even in the new light, Elizabeth did not recognise her surroundings.

The horse landed, but Elizabeth did not move to dismount. It was not long before a woman with a long white staff emerged from the shadows of the trees, extending her hand in warning.

"You may not pass through here." Her voice rang out clearly. "The way has been closed."

Georgiana shifted. Elizabeth appraised the woman. She was neither young nor old, her hair falling loose beneath a purple cloak. She seemed familiar to Elizabeth, yet unfamiliar.

"I have passed this way before," Elizabeth said. "I belong on the other side."

The woman's eyes narrowed, and then she laughed, the sound falling much like babbling water. "Elizabeth Bennet!" she cried. "How did I not see? Of course you may pass."

Elizabeth smiled and slid to the ground, holding her hands up to aid Georgiana.

"But"—the woman's laughter ceased—"your friend may not. She is not from Longbourn—she has not often been to the other side."

Georgiana's hand trembled. "I can go back," she whispered. "I'll take the grey. Go to your family."

"No." Elizabeth shook her head. "Your care has been entrusted to me." The thought that there may be nothing to return to pained her, but she did not say that to Georgiana. Turning back to the woman, Elizabeth held out her hand. "Does this ring mean anything to you?"

The woman reached out, feeling the gold for a moment. She pressed her lips together. "I will not be responsible if anything happens once she crosses over. I have strict orders."

"From whom?" Elizabeth challenged.

The woman laughed again. "Why, from your father!" Elizabeth was startled at this but the woman spoke again before she could ask another question. "It will cost you. I will not let the girl through freely."

Elizabeth crossed her arms. "And is that one of your orders as well?"

The guard's eyes grew cold and she took a step back.

"Wait," Georgiana said. "Will you take the horse?"

The woman's eyes flickered from them to the winged animal. "That will do," she said. Before Elizabeth could protest, the horse vanished with a snap of her fingers. She touched the top of her staff to their heads. "Through there," she said, pointing to an opening in a thicket barely large enough for a rabbit to go through. "And you must guide her through, Elizabeth; I cannot help you further."

Elizabeth was not sure how she would guide anyone when she herself did not remember the way back but felt that to be beside the point. Instead, she took Georgiana's arm with one hand and, gathering her skirts together with the other, led them into the thicket, the sound of the gatekeeper's laughter still ringing in her ears.

"Your brother's grey!" she mumbled, not exactly intending for Georgiana to hear. "A hair bauble might have done just as well!"

But the young girl did hear. With a slight tremble in her voice, she said, "But for a gatekeeper, that would not have been enough."

Elizabeth regretted her words. "He will not be angry. He wanted us to reach safety, no matter the cost."

The brush and thorns around them grew larger and denser, pricking at their cheeks and pulling at their thick cloaks. Elizabeth found herself surprised that the way to the other side was as clear as if she had a paved path to guide them. Georgiana followed trustfully, faltering once at a fork in the brambly tunnel.

"Are you sure it is through there?" She hesitated, looking from the wide, light-filled path on their right to the dark one on their left where Elizabeth was urging her to go forward.

Elizabeth laughed. "It is always the treacherous way, Georgiana." Sure enough, in the blink of an eye they stood together in the familiar field that separated Longbourn from Netherfield. The thicket was gone, and the only evidence of a gate was a small rabbit hole at their feet.

The sun was rising in a clear blue sky, and Elizabeth smiled when she saw her father emerging from the trees.

~

Darcy sat on the floor in his study, his cloak still smoking and the smell of ash burning in his nose. He was tired, but at the sound of the colonel's footsteps, he scrambled up to stand by the window.

"All is clear, all secure," Colonel Fitzwilliam said, triumph in his voice.

"But the Thief has eluded us again," Darcy replied wryly.

Colonel Fitzwilliam's face darkened. "Need I remind you, Pendragon, that we are lucky to be alive?"

"You needn't," he answered curtly, stepping forward. "I need you to take a message to Longbourn, and then to Rosings."

"You cannot take it yourself?"

"Obviously, the Thief is on the run. I will not sit idly by and wait for the next attack." He raked his fingers through his hair. "No, this time I will hunt the blackguard down personally."

The colonel's eyes flashed. "And you propose to go without me?"

"You will join me as soon as possible."

"I had much rather you go. It is your sister and your lov—"

"Elizabeth Bennet is not my lover."

"I did not mean it in that way," Colonel Fitzwilliam grumbled. "I suppose you will marry her, then?" He did not like the look that crossed over his face. "Really, Pendragon, anyone could see that she loves you."

"I would know if she did," Darcy answered.

The colonel sighed. "I will be your messenger—but only this once. And then I will meet you in…"

"Istanbul."

"Yes—what?"

The corners of Darcy's mouth twitched. "You heard correctly."

"He got from here to there in an hour? And you are already tracking him." He shook his head. "It is another trap."

Darcy shrugged. "Perhaps."

"I am beginning to think you are rather less clear-headed than I used to think."

"Think what you like. I prefer to think that we are setting a trap for the Thief, rather than the other way around."

Colonel Fitzwilliam's brows drew together. "By doing what he expects?"

"Which is what the Thief will not expect."

"But what if—"

Darcy waved his hand. "Must we argue? Two of our men are already there, hot on the trail. Pemberley is once again secure, and you have messages to relay."

Colonel Fitzwilliam paused at the door. "It will not be Istanbul where we meet—I am sure he is moving again already."

"The Thief?"

"Who else?" The colonel shrugged and stepped into the hall.

"Fortinbras," Darcy called, stopping him. "What makes you so certain it is a he we are after?"

When Colonel Fitzwilliam arrived at Longbourn's door-step to announce that Mr Darcy would not yet be able to retrieve his sister because he was travelling about the world on a wild chase after the Thief, Elizabeth was most displeased. When asked why Mr Darcy had chosen not to deliver his message in person, the colonel shrugged and replied with a smirk that he did not know. Elizabeth was beyond words. She felt very strongly, as she told Jane later that evening, that Mr Darcy had used her ill. Her one comfort was that Georgiana remained at Longbourn, which meant that he must necessarily come to them at some point.

"Although he might send for her by post after it is all over," Elizabeth added with some venom, "and not come to me at all."

She resolved not to think of him, and in the fortnight following Colonel Fitzwilliam's unwelcome message, she managed quite well. Leaving Longbourn again was out of the question; Mr Bennet now restricted them from walking to Meryton unless properly escorted. Elizabeth was not to even walk beyond the gardens alone. Mr Bingley and Jane, who was soon to be Mrs Bingley, were of great assistance to Elizabeth in that regard. Jane apologised for being of so little help to Elizabeth before she had gone into the North and offered her intended's services as a means for her to practice.

Mr Bingley was more than happy to comply with both of their wishes and found himself escorting Jane and Elizabeth every day out to the field where Mr Darcy had trained previously, to facilitate a different kind of training. Mr Bingley's former duty as watchman to Elizabeth had resumed, with the additional burden of Georgiana. He bore the task quite cheerfully, but then, Mr Bingley was always cheerful.

Georgiana adjusted well to Longbourn. She was quiet, and the boisterousness of Elizabeth's two youngest sisters caused her some alarm at the beginning. It was not long, however, before her nature had a calming effect upon Kitty and Lydia, and even Mrs Bennet. Georgiana preferred to stay with them in the house, correcting their poorly fashioned spells and teaching them newer and more practical ones. Still, on most mornings, she followed behind Elizabeth, Jane, and Mr Bingley to the field and observed Elizabeth's progress. Mr Bennet was her constant companion, and they took some pleasure in calling out corrections to both Mr Bingley and Elizabeth.

It was in this pleasant manner that a month swiftly passed by for most of the inhabitants at Longbourn. News of the Thief was no longer spoken of by the local gossips, and except for the missives they received from Colonel Fitzwilliam once a week, they might have forgotten the Thief existed at all. The first message was sent from Egypt, the second from Moscow. Most recently, Mr Darcy and Fitzwilliam were reported to be somewhere in Siberia, following another lead. Their messages were always the same: "No news; both safe. Will return as soon as possible."

Elizabeth liked to think that she no longer cared what happened to Mr Darcy (except for Georgiana's sake), and that the adventure was no longer her concern. After all, she had been forced out of it time and again. But while she was successful at not thinking of Mr Darcy, the effort made her irritable.

∾

"Elizabeth," Mr Bennet said, calling her into his study, "did you know that Colonel Fitzwilliam went to Rosings before he met up with Mr Darcy?"

"No, but I am not surprised," she answered, coming in and closing the door behind her. It was late morning, and the sunlight shone brightly through the windows. "He must have been reinvestigating the stone hut—and no doubt informing Lady Catherine of their impending departure. Neither she nor her daughter are ever very well, and her nephews are careful to not alarm her."

"Hmm." Mr Bennet shifted in his seat. "Well, what I had to convey is a trifling thing, something that might interest you."

Elizabeth's brows rose.

"It is a letter from Mr Collins." Her father looked up and was gratified to see Elizabeth's look of astonishment.

"While Mr Collins is undoubtedly an amusing man, I fail to see a connexion between him and Colonel Fitzwilliam."

"Mr Collins writes to congratulate me on the impending marriage of my eldest daughter, that is no surprise. But here"—Mr

Bennet opened the letter and pointed to a particular passage—"he goes on to congratulate me on what he understands to be the impending marriage of my second daughter as well—to Mr Darcy!"

Elizabeth sat for a moment in stunned silence.

"His source, he says, is none other than Colonel Fitzwilliam, who apparently dropped a hint."

"I cannot think why—" Elizabeth paused, remembering their embrace that night by the stables. "It must be a misunderstanding."

Mr Bennet coughed.

"In truth, Papa, I do not know why Colonel Fitzwilliam would hint anything to anyone," Elizabeth insisted, her voice raised.

"The speculations are harmless. But Mr Collins warns me that his aunt, Lady Catherine de Bourgh, does not look on the match with a friendly eye."

Elizabeth smiled at this. "Whatever his aunt's opinion, I am sure it would not influence Mr Darcy one way or the other."

Mr Bennet chuckled. "If he is anything like his father, I am sure you are right."

The very next morning, while Elizabeth was sitting outside reading a book, a chaise and four drove up the lawn. The carriage was unfamiliar to Elizabeth, and she was at a loss to understand who it might be until the tall figure of Lady Catherine de Bourgh stepped out. Elizabeth rose from her seat in astonishment; the lady, upon seeing her on the lawn, approached her immediately rather than going to the house.

"Lady Catherine," Elizabeth exclaimed, curtseying low. "To what do we owe the honour of your visit?"

Lady Catherine did not acknowledge her greeting, instead appraising her coldly. "I am here," she said at length, glancing at Longbourn's windows behind them, "to speak to you privately. There seemed to be a prettyish kind of little wilderness on one side of your lawn. I should be glad to take a turn in it, if you will favour me with your company."

Her curiosity piqued, Elizabeth agreed.

They walked for some minutes in silence as Lady Catherine seemed to collect herself. "You can be at no loss, Miss Bennet, to understand the reason of my journey hither."

Elizabeth almost smiled. She had guessed that Lady Catherine would speak about her nephew, and her angry posture now confirmed it. Elizabeth meant to speak—to say that there had been a misunderstanding, to inform Lady Catherine that she might rest easy with the knowledge that she had no intention of allying herself to Mr Fitzwilliam Darcy—but she found that the words caught in her throat.

Lady Catherine continued to speak in angry tones, but Elizabeth did not hear her. It was clear to her what had been there all along—that she loved him. She loved him more than anyone, and it hurt her to think that he was off fighting the Thief without her—not just because she wanted adventure, but because she wanted it with him. Elizabeth felt a sudden tremor from the tips of her toes to the hair on her head. She shuddered, tears unaccountably shining in her eyes, and then returned her attention to the woman standing before her.

"Let me be rightly understood," Lady Catherine was saying. "A match between yourself and my nephew, Darcy—to which you have the presumption to aspire!—can never take place."

Elizabeth nearly jumped in surprise at the sound of a voice next to her. "And why can it not, Aunt Catherine, if we should so wish it?" Mr Darcy said, turning to Elizabeth with a hesitant smile. Lady Catherine was forgotten.

"You!" Elizabeth cried in surprise, a tear now falling unbidden down her cheek. "I do not understand how you are here!"

He took her outstretched hand. "Are you displeased to see me?"

"I could not be happier to see you."

He smiled broadly. "I do not understand it any more than you. I was in Siberia, hacking my way through trees in the pouring rain"—Elizabeth now noticed that his hair and cloak were dripping wet—"when, suddenly, I knew that I had to come to you. I knew—"

"You knew that I love you," she answered for him.

He drew a breath. "Do you?" he whispered.

"Fitzwilliam Darcy," Lady Catherine bellowed. "I am ashamed of you!"

They both started and turned back to his aunt, her face pale with anger, and she opened her mouth to speak when her jaw dropped in astonishment. Mr Darcy and Elizabeth turned to follow her gaze and saw Mr Bennet standing a few feet away by the hedgerows.

"What are you doing here?" he demanded, coming forward.

Lady Catherine closed her mouth, a look crossing her face that neither Elizabeth nor Mr Darcy could interpret. "I might ask the same of you!"

There was a thunderous crash and in a split second, Elizabeth and Mr Darcy both hung upside down, suspended in mid-air, an invisible cord binding their ankles and hands. They both twisted to see what was happening beneath them. Lady Catherine had changed, her face covered in darkness, her features contorted in rage. A young man with black hair stood tall before her, his face hard, his eyes familiar to Elizabeth.

"Papa?" she cried, and the young man looked up at her, his eyes betraying hopelessness.

"You!" Mr Darcy spat out towards his aunt in the same moment. "It was you all along!"

Lady Catherine smiled. "Must you look so stupid?" she sneered. "Who else could it have been but me? No one else had the ability or power to do what I have done—but you were always rather stupid, Fitzwilliam. More than happy to believe my play of the grieving widow—the devastated, innocent widow whose husband was a murderer!"

She took a step closer to Mr Bennet, still imprisoned in the form of his younger self, his arms pinned to his sides.

"Fitzwilliam," Elizabeth whispered, "why am I trapped in this enchantment?"

"But in truth," Lady Catherine continued, inches away from Mr Bennet's face, "I was a bereaved widow. I loved my husband more than anything in this world. And you—" She suddenly screamed, spitting in his face. "You took him from me!"

Mr Bennet did not flinch, and Lady Catherine staggered back to pace before them, wringing her hands.

"All the years I have searched, tearing myself apart in thinking that perhaps I was wrong—that you were dead, as all the reports claimed you to be. But I knew—I knew you had to be alive. I would have justice. I have longed for this moment, when I could kill you myself for all that you did to me!"

"Fitzwilliam," Elizabeth whispered more urgently, "why am I trapped in this enchantment? Fitzwilliam!"

Darcy wrenched his gaze from the figures of his aunt and Mr Bennet below. He looked at Elizabeth in confusion, when suddenly a slow smile of understanding spread across his face.

"Elizabeth, you love me," he said happily.

"Of course I love you!" she exclaimed in exasperation. "But that has—"

"It has everything to do with it! I love you, Elizabeth, with all that I am. Your returned love has bound us together with a cord that can only be broken by death—and sometimes not even by that. You are vulnerable now to magic, as I am vulnerable to it."

Elizabeth's eyes widened. "But if we are now both vulnerable to magic, shouldn't we also be invulnerable to it?"

He threw back his head and laughed, catching the attention of Lady Catherine. "Will you quiet yourself, Fitzwilliam. You have caused me enough trouble—"

"Siberia, Aunt? You had me chasing your shadow in Siberia?"

Lady Catherine smiled. "Anne is remarkably talented at mimicking my movements. She is an obedient child; she does as she is ordered. And I am remarkably talented at hiding my magical abilities."

"But this—" Darcy nodded towards Mr Bennet, who was still frozen in place. "Rediscovering him was not part of the plan."

"On the contrary," Lady Catherine replied, "it was my intention to find him all along. But on an estate in the country, with so little to his name, and five stupid daughters? I had not thought even Thomas Swann would allow himself to sink so low."

Elizabeth gasped. "Thomas Swann? You changed your name?"

"For the protection of my family?" Elizabeth's father cried out. "I would do anything, give up everything!"

"And still it was not enough?" Lady Catherine sneered again.

"Perhaps I should kill your second daughter first—is she not the favourite? Then you will know what it is to lose what you love."

"No!" Darcy cried, and with a flash of blue light broke the spell holding them in place. He and Elizabeth were on the ground, standing on either side of Mr Bennet.

Lady Catherine was so surprised that she dropped the enchantment holding Mr Bennet. He now appeared as he was, white hair nearly standing on end in his rage.

He stepped forward, arms outstretched. "I will have nothing else taken from me that I love," he growled. "I have given enough."

Lady Catherine stepped back and erected a dark shield around her. "You cannot touch me! You cannot hold me!"

"On the contrary," Elizabeth said as she unravelled the shield, "I will disenchant your protection spell shortly, and Fitzwilliam has already pinned you to the spot. You cannot fight both enchantment and disenchantment in the same moment."

"It was you!" Lady Catherine gasped. "You were the one I was searching for—in my grasp, this entire time?"

Elizabeth laughed. "To think, Fitzwilliam, that she found us quite on accident, because of a rumour your cousin began about a non-existent engagement!"

Darcy frowned, tightening his spell on Lady Catherine as Elizabeth finished off the last of her shield. "I will have to speak with him about that. But Elizabeth—why do you say it is non-existent?"

Suddenly there was another black flash and Elizabeth and Darcy found themselves flung back. Lady Catherine stood with a knife in hand and plunged it into Mr Bennet's side. Her laughter was high and wild. "You cannot win! I cannot be defeated!" she screamed.

Elizabeth and Darcy leapt to their feet and rushed forward, but there was no need. A large vase came crashing down on Lady Catherine's head and she crumpled to the ground. A shaking Mrs Bennet stood behind her, tears streaming down her cheeks.

"I could not remember the spell to render a wizard unconscious. I could not remember it." She sobbed, pushing Lady Catherine aside as she reached for Mr Bennet. "But once her defences were down, a vase is as good as anything."

THE CONCLUSION OF THE MATTER

IT WAS IN THAT MOMENT OF UTMOST CONFUSION THAT COLONEL Fitzwilliam arrived with a bang and a puff of red smoke. Within two short strides, he stood next to Darcy, who was bent over Mr Bennet.

"First you disappear without notice," the colonel began heatedly, dangling a burning red pocket-watch from his hand. "And then you summon me, burning my fifth waistcoat pocket this year! If I have been called for some trivial—good heavens!" he exclaimed, leaping back. "Aunt Catherine!"

Darcy held up a calming hand. "Fitzwilliam…"

"Has she been injured? What I'll do to the blackguard!"

"Fitzwilliam!" Darcy said again, more sternly, but the colonel was already storming about in a circle, looking for potential assassins. He came to an abrupt stop.

"Not Mr Bennet? I would never have thought—"

Darcy took hold of his cousin's arm with some force. "The Thief, Fitzwilliam."

"Mr Bennet!"

"No," Darcy said, looking him in the eye, "the Thief was—is— Aunt Catherine."

Colonel Fitzwilliam's mouth fell open.

"And if you do not secure her soon," Mr Bennet gasped from his position on the ground, "she will come to, and undo everything."

"Oh! My poor Mr Bennet," Mrs Bennet wailed, taking out a handkerchief and mopping his brow.

Fortunately, Mr Bingley appeared with Jane in the nick of time, along with three other members of the Wizarding Court (who popped up at various places on the lawn). Securing the Thief—or rather, Lady Catherine—from that point on was short work. Elizabeth was distracted from the action for a few moments as she and Jane tended their father, but Darcy's hand at her sleeve quickly caught all of her attention.

"I must ask you to help me with something entirely unpleasant," he said with a grimace.

Elizabeth nodded. "Something to do with Lady Catherine?"

Darcy sighed. "We must strip her of all magical powers—and not just her own abilities, but those of her husband as well."

"The Necromancer?" Elizabeth's eyes widened in understanding. "Ours is not a unique bond?"

"No," he replied, meeting her eyes. "It is now apparent that they also shared a magical bond. However evil the Necromancer, whatever wrongs my aunt has done, they did love each other."

"Love enough to last beyond the grave?"

Darcy nodded. "It is possible. Particularly if the one left behind is unwilling to relinquish her hold. And why would she have, with such power remaining at her disposal? What misery she has caused through her grief! When I think of her raging at your father—who lost much more—"

"Let us not think on it, and do what needs to be done," Elizabeth replied, placing a hand on his arm.

He ran a hand through his hair. "And we will be breaking the only good thing she has left of him. What an unhappy wretch!"

Elizabeth shook her head. "The magical bond may be broken, but we cannot break the memory of their love; that will always remain, if it was true."

Stripping the Thief's powers took up the rest of the morning and well into the afternoon. Lady Catherine remained incapacitated throughout the entire process, lying where she had fallen on the lawn with Darcy holding one hand and Elizabeth the other, the three other Court members stationed about them on alert. It required all of Elizabeth's strength to unravel at a constant, quick pace, while Darcy, the more practised wizard, and therefore the more flexible, moved back and forth between both enchantments and disenchantments to draw out all hidden magic.

They did not notice the activity going on about them in the meantime. Mr and Mrs Gardiner arrived, having been called to Longbourn, and quickly set the entire household to rights. Mr Bennet was taken to his room to rest, although he refused to be put in bed and sat up in his armchair with a rug thrown across his knees. Mrs Bennet, whose nerves were quite shattered, was placed in her own room where Jane and Mr Gardiner attended her. Mrs Gardiner was then obliged to find Georgiana, Kitty, and Lydia, who had been cutting roses together on the other side of the house and were completely oblivious to the morning's events. Gathering all of the girls in the sitting room, where Mary had been reading a book, Mrs Gardiner laid out the whole of the story. Kitty and Lydia joined their mother in her room, while Mary selected a different book and went to her father with the intention of reading aloud to him. It took the combined efforts of Colonel Fitzwilliam and Mrs Gardiner to convince Georgiana that her brother was much occupied and could not pause in his work, even to see her.

In the moment that Elizabeth and Darcy broke the last strands of Lady Catherine's power, several things happened at once. There was a large burst of purple smoke on Longbourn's door-step. Anne de Bourgh was soon rapping at the door, demanding to see her mother. Mr Bennet, who had nodded off to sleep while listening to the sound of Mary's voice, awoke with a shout; Mary dropped her book in alarm at the sight of her father leaping about the room, bright white sparks shooting from the roots of his hair and his fingertips. "It is back!" he shouted to no one and began levitating various objects in the room.

His bedroom door was thrown open with a bang and Mrs Bennet—who had only seconds before been lying on her bed in a state of fragility—stood in the doorway, her hair wild about her and her eyes shining with tears.

"Thomas!" she cried, her voice trembling.

Mr Bennet halted. Several books and a pitcher, which he had been levitating, crashed to the floor. Mary, rather frightened by this time, inched her way to a corner.

Mr Bennet turned and looked into his wife's eyes with disbelief. He moved his lips to shape a word, but no sound was produced.

Mrs Bennet understood him. She did not move forward, but her face broke into a soft smile—a kind of smile that Mary had never seen her mother wear before. "Yes," she said, her voice now barely a whisper. "It is Elinor. Truly Elinor."

With a low cry, Mr Bennet swept her into his arms, and they covered each other's faces with kisses and tears. Mary, too astonished for words, left the room as quickly as possible and, thinking of what might be best for all those concerned, shut the door behind her.

She was then startled by the presence of Mr Gardiner, Jane, Kitty, and Lydia, who had all followed Mrs Bennet from her room.

"They are—together—and—ought not be disturbed," Mary managed to stammer out.

Mr Gardiner grinned. "Well, then!" he said, laughing. "All is well in the world, is it not?"

"I do not understand!" Lydia stomped her foot.

"Come with me," Jane said, tears in her eyes, "and I will explain everything."

Jane's explanation, however, was put on hold as soon as they descended into the sitting room. There sat a wailing Anne de Bourgh, with Colonel Fitzwilliam on one side, Georgiana on the other, and Mrs Gardiner offering her a handkerchief.

"It is all completely and utterly my doing!" Anne let out a shuddering sob. "I should have told you everything I knew as soon as—"

"But, Anne, you were under the control of your mother by enchantment. There was very little you could have done," the colonel shushed. "Do you think she would have permitted you to reveal a word of it to anyone?"

Anne's lip trembled. "Whatever punishment you may devise, I will bear it all."

"There will be no need—" Colonel Fitzwilliam's attention was interrupted by Darcy's voice sounding at the door.

"There may be a punishment, Anne," he said, coming forward with Elizabeth, "but not until after a full investigation. At worst, you may be stripped of your abilities."

"You may take them all, I quite despise magic!" Anne burst into a fresh wave of tears.

"How is Papa?" Elizabeth asked Mr Gardiner.

"You will not believe it, Lizzy," he answered in a scratchy voice, blinking his eyes rapidly. "His magic has been restored—and Elinor—" Mr Gardiner was obliged to sit down and his wife came to place her hands upon his shoulders. "My sister is returned to him! To us—to all of us!"

Elizabeth gasped. "But the dying curse! It cannot be possible. They were under an unbreakable curse!"

"No, Elizabeth," Darcy said. "It might have been a dying curse, but it could not have been unbreakable. What was left of the Necromancer's magic is now gone from the earth forever—and any spells he cast with it. His curse held only because Lady Catherine held it there through their bond. Had we known of it—had we realised at the time—"

"You were a child, Mr Darcy," Mr Gardiner said, wiping tears from his eyes. "There was nothing you could have done."

"But my father—" Darcy stepped back and reached out a hand to steady himself against the wall. "He did know of it…he must have discovered her secret, but did not understand it. Not until later. And Lady Catherine killed him because of it."

Elizabeth took his hand. "All is well now."

"What has been done with Lady Catherine?" Mrs Gardiner enquired, and all the others in the room hushed to hear the answer.

"Her powers are irrevocably destroyed. There is no need to fear her, or the power of her husband, ever again."

"What will happen to her?" Anne said, her eyes still filled with tears.

"Permanent exile and seclusion," Darcy replied.

"Then I will go with her—"

"Anne, we would have to strip you of your abilities. If there is a trial and you are not guilty, there will be no need—"

Anne shook her head. "I will stay with her. Where is she now, so that I might go to her?"

"Still unconscious. She is being guarded by Bingley, along with several other members of our Court. They are awaiting transport, and then she will be taken away from here."

Anne rose to move outside, with Colonel Fitzwilliam and Jane following behind her.

Darcy turned to Elizabeth. "After I have seen my aunt turned over to the appropriate authorities, there is something else I must attend to at Rosings."

"The stone hut," Elizabeth said.

"Yes, that exactly. We cannot allow any magic to remain within its walls. I will destroy it and then return as quickly—"

Elizabeth laughed. "Oh, no, indeed! You do not think that I will allow you to go anywhere without me?"

He smiled. "Perhaps I was not thinking."

"Obviously not. Do you know, if you had not forced me—twice —to run away when the Thief was drawing near, I would have discovered at once that it was Lady Catherine, and all of this might have been resolved much sooner."

Caring not for the other people around them, Darcy laughed and pulled her into his arms. "Then I shan't make that mistake again. How many I have made since we first met!"

"We both have," Elizabeth said, standing on her toes to put her arms about his neck.

"You?" he exclaimed. "Where did you ever go wrong?"

"By rejecting you."

He sobered. "No, Elizabeth. By you, I was properly humbled. You showed me how insufficient were all my pretensions to please a woman worthy of being pleased."

"And until you, I did not know myself."

They did not notice that the rest of the company had slipped from the room.

"Accept my hand, Elizabeth," he said, drawing her closer.

Elizabeth laughed, turning her face up to meet his. "On one condition," she said, drawing a start from Darcy.

"And that is?"

"That you will never again leave me behind—or force me to go ahead," she replied, moving her hand to brush aside the familiar lock of hair from his eyes.

"Never?"

"Only under extenuating circumstances—which I myself will determine!" Elizabeth replied.

"Done."

"Will you promise?" she said with a twinkle in her eye.

"A promise easily kept," he answered, leaning forward.

"You must also promise that you will write me poetry." She halted him. "I want to know why you earned your name."

"Shall I compare thee to a summer's day?"

"Your own words! Unless you still feel that you have no reason for it."

"I warn you that I am a very sorry poet," he replied. "Fitzwilliam found four ridiculous lines one afternoon and now I much prefer Pendragon."

"But perhaps now a new name is in order."

Darcy's brows rose.

"Something to match my own," she insisted.

He laughed. "For you, my own Rosalind, anything." And with that, he claimed her lips with his.

EPILOGUE

A BOY, ABOUT SIX YEARS OF AGE, SAT IN A CHAIR ACROSS FROM HIS father, squirming. The sunlight streamed through the study windows, falling across the young boy's face and causing him to look with longing outside at the green grass.

"Now, William," his father began, "tell me why you threw the book at your sister."

"Because she is a horrid sister, and I can't stand her—or Edmund—or Godfrey! I hate them all!"

His father leaned back and waited for him to continue.

The boy took a deep breath. "Ella said she would take my puppy and turn him into a frog—all because I pulled her hair. But she is wretched to me, always making me fetch things for her, and all because I cannot do magic and they can! Even Godfrey can do magic and he is the smallest—" He broke off, wrinkling his nose in an effort to check the tears threatening to spill down his cheeks. "I wouldn't know how to change Troy back if she turned him into a frog. He would be like that forever!"

"Elinor will not be turning Troy into a frog—or anything else, for that matter." His father frowned. "And you know that your mother or I could remedy such a trifling spell in no time. That is not a reason for you to throw spell books at people."

William sniffed, still glowering.

"It would be better," his father continued, "if you would say what is on your mind, rather than beating about the bush."

"It is all completely unfair!" William burst out after a short silence. "They can do everything and I can't do anything!"

"You can work disenchantment, and it is a power in many ways greater than all others."

"That is not true," William ventured, his voice trembling.

"Your mother is a disenchantress."

"But Mama can work magic as well, I know she can! Everyone can, except me—even Grandmother and Grandfather Bennet, and they are exceptionally old."

His father's mouth twitched at this. "Your mother can only work magic because I can."

"Then can you make it so that I can as well?" William asked, forgetting that his father was displeased with him as he moved to stand next to him.

"You know I cannot. We have discussed this before."

William hung his head, a tear slipping down his nose. "I suppose I am doomed to never do anything important. Ella says only wizards can battle other wizards."

"And you want to battle wizards?"

"The evil sort."

"Disenchanters are very good at doing battle against evil wizards," his father said as he pulled the boy onto his lap. "Perhaps better than anyone else. I have told you before that your ability is very powerful."

William looked up at him, brows raised.

"But the most powerful is the combination of the two—enchantment and disenchantment."

William thought about this for several moments. "Am I to be punished?"

At this, William thought he heard his father chuckle, but was not certain. "You and Ella will both be punished. For the next week, your lessons will be conducted together"—the boy opened his mouth as if to protest, and then thought better of it—"and I will oversee them personally."

William leaned his head against his father's waistcoat, somewhat comforted. If their father was present, Ella would not be able to get away with the secret spells she usually managed underneath the governess's nose.

"You know, William," his father said at length, "I defeated a fearsome wizard once, long before you were born."

The boy's eyes grew wide. "Of course, I knew that! Edmund told me a long time ago!"

"Did he tell you that I could not have done it without your mother? Or without the aid of disenchantment?"

"I don't remember," William said, cocking his head to one side. "Well, then, perhaps it is now time that you should hear how your mother and I met. But it is a long story"—he paused—"if you would rather return to the outdoors?"

"No," William answered. "I would like to hear your story."

His father laughed. "Back in those days, I was called by the name of Pendragon, although your beastly Uncle Fitzwilliam had given me the name the Poet long before—"

"But I thought Mama calls you something else now?"

"She does."

"What is it?"

"It is a great secret."

"A secret?"

"Someday, when you are old enough, you will know."

"I like secrets."

"Then you will like this story."

William settled back down against his father's shoulder. "Will you start again? I have already forgotten the beginning."

This time, he was sure he felt his father chuckle. "Back in those days, when I was known by the name of Pendragon, and the truth about your mother's ability was still a secret—no, no. It goes back further than that. A very, very long time ago, your Grandfather Darcy and Grandfather Bennet were together at school…"

Finis

AFTERWORD

Many of the code names in the novel are allusions to several famous characters in British literature, especially Shakespeare. The first, Fortinbras, is a character from *Hamlet*; it means "strong in arm" in French, and in the play, he is a man of action, in contrast to Hamlet, who is not. Pendragon is the name associated with mythical King Arthur's father, who was traditionally (or according to legend) Uther of Pendragon. The opening of the code is also from *Hamlet, Act 1, Scene 1, lines 1-4*. Benedick is a character from the Shakespearean comedy *Much Ado About Nothing*. Rosalind and Orlando are the main characters (and lovers) in Shakespeare's comedy *As You Like It*. I supposed I liked to imagine that Darcy and other members of the Wizarding Court would have been as much of a Shakespeare nerd as I am.

ACKNOWLEDGMENTS

This book has had a long journey. I wrote it back in 2007 when I was a senior student at the University of Maryland, finishing up a degree in Russian language and literature with a minor in English. At the time, I noted that the spark of the idea for this novel came to me after the publication of the final installments of the Harry Potter series—a huge event in our household. (which involved a midnight purchase and an 11-hour reading marathon).

I love a good fantasy—my first love being JRR Tolkien, whom my father introduced me to at the ripe old age of six. *The Lord of the Rings* was such a big deal for my family that we read it in its entirety every year for seven years in a row. As a young adult, my fantasy tastes expanded to include Diana Wynne Jones, Patricia Wrede and Caroline Stevermer, C.S. Lewis, Neil Gaiman, and my younger brother Zeb (who started but never finished many nspiring pieces). At the time of writing this story, I was also in the thick of an English course on Arthurian legend and a Shakespeare course devoted to Hamlet. While I didn't seem to see the influence at the time, reworking my material brought forth for me the influences of Shakespeare, Chretien de Troyes, and Thomas Morley.

But of course, the Ur text here is Jane Austen's *Pride & Preju-*

dice. I cannot overstate this author's influence on my life—as a missionary child from America living in Siberia during the late 1990s, the world of Jane Austen fanfiction was a link to a life we had left behind. I was introduced to the 1995 miniseries adaption of *Pride and Prejudice* in 1998 when it arrived in a care package; we must have watched the miniseries every weekend for a year. Not long after this, I devoured all of Austen's novels and couldn't get enough. My mother discovered a fanfiction website called *The Derbyshire Writer's Guild*, and it was there that I would spend nearly 10 years both as a reader and a (terrible-at-first) writer. I owe a great debt to this online community (and later *A Happy Assembly*) where I was able to share my work and receive feedback on it.

I also owe a great debt to my literary family who fostered and instilled a love of stories and words in me from a young age. Thank you to my parents, who read aloud to us as children and into our teens. My father probably has read well over 10,000 hours' worth of stories aloud over the course of 30 years. My mother was an unswerving advocate and critic at the same moment—with a keen eye and an honesty that is both challenging and refreshing. Mom and Dad: you are the reason we are all such nerds. Thank you to my three brothers, Zeb, Zach and Zephan, who all read my work, critique my work, and even occasionally write with me. Thank you to my Grandma Sharon, who taught me to love poetry, and taught me that I am a poet. Thank you to Grandma Ann and Poppa Dick, in whose basement I began writing this story, and who both supported me (and later my husband and children) immeasurably with love and generosity. To my other family and friends who are buying and reading this book, I'm thinking fondly of you (yes, *you*) too.

For many years I didn't count myself as a real writer, and I stopped writing fiction when I embarked upon a career teaching it—first to high schoolers, then college students, then middle schoolers, and now high schoolers again. I wrote when I was 15 that I wanted to publish a novel by 25, but I didn't consider my fanfiction as a novel that counted. I dreamed, of course, as all writers do that my work would be discovered—and am indebted to the unknown-to-me fans of this work, shared over a decade ago, who brought it to the attention of Amy D'Orazio and Jan Ashton. Thank you both for taking a chance on this tale of wizardry and magic, which was written (really) to have a bit of fun, and thank you for making a dream of mine come true. Lastly, my gratitude to my editors, Marcelle Wong and Lisa Sieck, and to designer Amanda Matthews.

ABOUT THE AUTHOR

Kara Pleasants lives in a lovely hamlet called Darlington in Maryland, where she and her husband are restoring an 18th century farm in Susquehanna State Park. They have two beautiful and vivacious daughters, Nora and Lina. A Maryland native, Kara spent a great deal of her childhood travelling with her parents and younger brothers (who were missionaries); she spent six years living in two different Siberian cities: Barnaul and Irkutsk, as well as five years living in Kalispell, Montana, before finally making her way back home to go to college at the University of Maryland. Kara had intended to pursue vocal education at UMD (but was denied twice) and settled for a Russian Language and Literature Bachelors, a Curriculum and Instruction Masters of Education, and Masters of Arts in English instead.

Kara is currently a high school English teacher at Parkville High School. In past jobs, she taught for Aberdeen Middle School, the University of Maryland Professional Writing Program, Anne Arundel and Prince George's Community Colleges, Bowie High School, and Oxon Hill High School. She has had two students win writing awards at the University of Maryland and was once awarded a teaching excellence award by the City of Bowie. She will never forget, in particular, the first 9th grade English class she ever taught at Oxon Hill, whose courage and artistry might just be the reason she still teaches today. Her hobbies include: making scones to sell at the farmer's market, writing poetry, watching fantasy television shows, making quilts, directing an Episcopal church renaissance choir, and dreaming about writing an epic three-party fantasy series for her daughters.

Disenchanted is Kara's first book.

For more information about Kara and other great authors, please visit her publisher at QuillsAndQuartos.com

facebook.com/pleasantauthor